ALICE

ALICE

a novel by

JOHN BAYLEY

Duckworth

First published in 1994 by
Gerald Duckworth & Co. Ltd.
The Old Piano Factory
48 Hoxton Square, London N1 6PB
Tel: 071 729 5986
Fax: 071 729 0015

A catalogue record for this book is available
from the British Library

ISBN 0 7156 2618 3

Typeset by Ray Davies
Printed in Great Britain by
Redwood Books, Trowbridge

Contents

I refuse to believe that there is a thing called life, that one can be in or out of touch with.

Philip Larkin, *Letters*

For

I.M.A. & B.

Part One

The White Woman of Sorrento

THE BALCONY was only just big enough for two white-painted metal chairs, with crimson plastic seats. A hotel guest might well feel safer sitting down, for the rail at the edge of this projecting porch was flimsy and barely waist high. Below the balcony a hairy cliff, mottled with eruptions of old brick and crumbling stonework, dropped fifty feet or so to the bathing station, where wooden catwalks led over piers and bridges to the outer breakwater. Its dark jumbled rocks strewed the passage from the blue sea outside into the bathing lagoon. In the sunrise stillness they glowed beneath the surface a livid green, like giant sweets in a bottle.

Ginnie sucked in her lips automatically as she looked at them.

She had woken up early on this first morning of her holiday. Not exactly out of excitement but because the room and the bed were unfamiliar, and she had mild symptoms of indigestion from the hotel dinner the night before. While she lay considering them, and wondering whether to get up for a tablet or some bicarb, she remembered that Vesuvius was supposed to be visible across the bay from the window. There was something slightly comic about remembering Vesuvius with her own inside a trifle out of order, and she giggled internally as she turned over, and must have dozed; for the next moment there was much more light outside the window, and she got up at once.

Although the bed was more or less double-size the room was small, and the bed itself in a kind of tomb alcove, from which a few steep steps led down to the narrow area round the window and balcony. As with most up-to-date effects at a hotel the idea was to save space; but Ginnie had rather enjoyed sampling the split-level the night before, and retiring to bed on her little platform. The hotel had no single rooms – she knew that from the booking agent and the brochure – but these doubles were certainly smaller than single bedrooms in houses at home.

Reluctant to go near the window in her nightdress, Ginnie put on yesterday's clothes and ventured down to the balcony. She could change and have a shower later. She liked the idea of a shower. At home she only had the bath, and an Italian shower seemed dashing: she had enjoyed one already the night before. Going to the window she saw Vesuvius first thing, misty and unmistakable across the already blue water, but decided she would not look at him properly yet. Like a work of art he could wait.

Instead she looked gingerly over the edge, sitting down to do so, and becoming at once aware that the plastic seat was sticky with the dew. After a few seconds the damp sensation was not unpleasant, setting off the already warm sun. Barely up as it was, it already had an air of reliability, quite unlike its precarious morning shine back home. Shirt-sleeved beneath it, a fisherman propelled his tub-like boat a little way out from the bathing place, standing up to do so with short reversed strokes, and then remaining motionless in a meditation which seemed to result in a small orange ball drifting away from the stern. Seeing from her watch it was not yet half-past six, Ginnie leaned out a little further to look down the row of neighbourhood balconies, but there was nobody on them. Holidaymaking required a late rise of its workforce.

The morning stillness of the bathing area now revealed a pattern of shadowy rectangles on the bottom, traced in ink green. They might be the remains of a Roman nymphaeum, but Ginnie had not yet read in her guidebook about this interesting possibility. It looked to her more like some peculiar holiday-making activity, perhaps a sort of underwater ping-pong, which the hotel authorities had long since given up. It seemed to confirm, in a reassuring way, what she had begun to feel the evening before: that Sorrento, famous for its song and seagulls and general aura of romance, was in reality a mildly dowdy oldfashioned place, not so very unlike the Folkestone she had visited in her childhood.

Most of the guests were a good deal older than she was, and so were the other tourists she had seen when the bus arrived from the airport. At dinner she had been put at a table with two elderly ladies. The head waiter had dumped her on them without apology, and flashed her a tremendous, meaningless smile before hurrying away to sort out a group of Swedes. They had made her welcome, the old dears, in a remote way; but soon their humped shoulders and frizzy white heads had turned together again, softly gossiping about some acquaintance.

Already that seemed a long time ago. Looking down at the bathing-place, Ginnie found herself picturing the scene as it had been when she arrived the previous evening. The mild haze over the silky sea had been so inclusive that no one would have guessed that Naples and Vesuvius lay just opposite across the bay. Indeed Ginnie had no idea it was a bay: it might as well have been the English Channel. The early September twilight, looking like the north though much warmer, had done nothing to dampen the animation of the scene below her window. It was alive with bathers, old and young, all doing their thing with joyful and frenetic abandon. Children rocketed off the staging and hurled themselves up and down in the water, throwing balls to each other. Their elders stood up to their necks and conversed with animation, or gathered in semi-circles of beach chairs. Shrieking and talking came up alike to the balcony as a shrill continuous murmur.

Shrinking a little, Ginnie had watched it, her fatigue subsiding into despondent shyness. How could she possibly fit in down there? It was not like a conventional beach as portrayed in the travel agent's window, with a few bronzed and sunlit figures. The bathers down below were bronzed all right, men and women, but not exactly with brown and golden suntans. They were dark, like animals, especially some of the women: positively swarthy. And their movements and gestures possessed not grace, nor any sort of poise, but a vigorous animal spontaneity.

Ginnie realised that if she watched them any more she would get depressed. She was about to go in and get herself ready to go down to dinner when her eye had been caught by an unusual figure, just emerging from some subterranean changing-place at the foot of the cliff. It was a tall woman in an aubergine coloured bikini, a woman with dark hair, and – wonder of wonders in that

11

setting – a very white skin. She stood for a moment on the concrete apron, as if considering whether or not to join the bathers. She seemed quite at her ease. After a few moments she wandered slowly down to one of the wooden piers, took a step or two down the ladder, methodically folded her white towel and laid it on the edge, and entered the water. She swam slowly away, seeming to create an area of calm around her amid the agitated frequentation of the pool, her long white legs bending and straightening quietly behind her in the green depth.

Ginnie watched her with admiration: and also, as she slowly and amazedly recognised, something like desire. Was it a weird kind of fellow-feeling for a person who, although she was beautiful, seemed more like herself than any of the others down there? But a person, also, who seemed to belong to another world: a world not like her own, but certainly not like that of the Italian tourists and bathers.

The girl in the purple bikini was not at all provocative: indeed her costume had an old-fashioned look about it, and in consequence an air of almost staid respectability. Not that the swarthy girls around her in the water were in any sense less respectable. Their swimsuits might be up-to-the-minute in terms of cut and style, but they were all decently clad. Nothing topless about the beach at Sorrento. Perhaps Italians were instinctively decorous? And the men she could see appeared more interested in each other, in some intricate pattern of male badinage, than in eyeing the women.

The girl swam back to the landing-stage, climbed out with the same unhurried movements, took her towel. No one else bothered with towels, Ginnie noticed, although the September evening was by now only comfortably tepid, no longer hot. Strolling back towards the cliff's foot she wrapped herself in its folds, and disappeared in the same way she had come.

Ginnie continued to stare downwards, tingling with curiosity. Not for the first time she felt herself beginning to take part in some old-fashioned novel, which, in chapters as leisurely and methodical as the movements of the girl in the water, would waft its readers through scenes and confrontations in romantic places … Until the hero, who had been secretly hoping all the time, while concealing his true feelings under a masque of sardonic indifference, at last popped... The hero? What was she thinking of? The apparition below should have been her first sight of the hero, down to the sexual frisson which had undoubtedly passed through the centre of her body, and which now felt connected to the beginnings of vertigo as she continued to peer over the edge.

But instead it was something quite different: a glimpse of a woman who must be not far off her own age, as Ginnie had been quite sharp enough to register: who might indeed be the sort of woman who would bear off the hero under her nose. Even as he popped, or was about to pop, the question.

In the dining-room a little later Ginnie had scarcely bothered to wonder or to look around. The woman, she knew, would not be there; or if she had been it was by no means sure that Ginnie, a trifle short-sighted as she was, would recognise the other, featured and fully-clothed. In any case the woman might not be staying in the hotel. Though doubtless affiliated in some way to this and other hotels on the front, the bathing-place obviously catered for all, the locals as well as the now late-season tourists.

As Ginnie ploughed her way – the verb seemed apposite – through limp fluted columns of *cannelloni*, lying massively in tomato sauce, she had hardly thought of the woman by the bathing-place; she had been too occupied with the paradoxical business of satisfying somehow her considerable hunger while not becoming uncomfortably bloated. A little cannelloni went a long way. Her elderly companions obviously grasped the problem, having experienced it themselves on a possibly diminished scale. They encouraged her by stating that the sweet was excellent, a cream sweet, similar to what one had in a hotel at home: and indeed it was.

Ginnie had caught up with them when she finished the sweet, and the three had gone together into the lounge for coffee, conversing more easily after their convergence on the food question. She had excused herself early, and collecting her key had gone to the entrance and hesitated over a possible short walk. In the end she had gone no further than the grounds of the hotel, laid out like a municipal garden but well supplied with dusty palm-trees. How one got down to the beach was not apparent, and she was not inclined to venture. Thankfully tired she found her way

13

back to the little split-level room and mounted to the platform bed, and to sleep.

Gazing down now she wondered who would be the first to appear on the deserted scene – children, hotel staff, beach attendants? The morning calm was suddenly struck by a deep and low reverberation, as if Vesuvius over there had decided, and in imperious fashion, to call Ginnie's attention to his presence. She was startled to see that a large liner with two blue funnels had soundlessly entered the bay, and was gliding with what seemed implacable intent towards the sand and the ornate cliffs. It stopped quite smoothly, swinging round; and Ginnie could easily make out the two words on the bow in neat block capitals. ACHILLE LAURO. However pronounced, they sounded delicate and pretty, reminding her of things to wear. There had once been a dry cleaner's, she remembered, with that name 'Achille'.

And at that moment the figure in the dark purple costume appeared. The white towel was wrapped round her, but enough of the bikini and the white flesh showed for there to be no doubt about it. As on the previous evening she walked unhurriedly down the wooden pier, folded her towel, and slipped into the sea. So calm was it now that every detail of her arm movements, and the batrachian grace of her lazily kicking legs, looked up through the green water.

Ginnie never hesitated. Leaving her room unlocked she ran out and down the stairs. At the reception desk she collected herself, and asked how to get down to the beach. They showed her, with that paternal but impersonal courtesy of the Italian senior staff which made her feel suddenly happy. Seconds later, as it seemed, she was coming out of a passage-way on to the sloping concrete apron. The ship, *Achille Lauro*, looked even bigger now, closer, and almost up in the sky: the sky itself a settled blue, with no more dawn look. But Ginnie had eyes only for the green water near at hand, and for the woman now swimming back towards the landing-stage. She climbed out in an inelegant movement, as was natural in tackling the short vertical wooden ladder, and then came towards the entrance, towelling herself casually as she had done the evening before.

Ginnie found herself saying: 'Is it nice in?'

The girl walked past not looking at her as she dried her neck and shoulders, and remarked 'Not bad', as if the question had come anonymously from the void. Then she stopped, still rubbing, and looked at Ginnie. 'Going in?'

'Not now.'

'The sun gets bad later. At least it does for me. The water and the sun give me a rash. I only swim early morning and evening.'

'Yes. I think I saw you last night.'

The other looked at her more closely after Ginnie had said this. She *was* tall – an inch or less under six feet Ginnie reckoned – but at close range there was nothing strange or exotic about her.

'You English then? Holidaymaking?'

The word sounded funny, as it always did, evoking between the two women as they stood there some swaying country ritual, half laborious, half erotic, being conscientiously but rather absently performed.

'Yes. Are you too?'

'No. I work here.'

'Oh.'

Ginnie could think of nothing else to say. Both girls looked out towards the ship.

'That's the one they killed the man on. You know, those terrorists in the Med. Pushed him over the side in a wheel-chair.'

'Oh.'

Ginnie gazed beseechingly at the tall girl – woman? – as if begging her not to go on like this; to be again the pure white figure striped with dark purple she had seen last night, making her leisurely way among the Italian crowd. The morning seemed dark; any holiday feel gone: and the feel of desire.

'What age are you then?'

Ginnie felt herself recoil under the query. But she said at once in a small meek voice 'Thirty-three'. She was actually rather more than a year older than that.

'Don't mind me asking,' went on the woman with a laugh. 'I grew up in Aussieland you know. They like to knock you down there. Never lost the habit. On your own here I suppose?'

'Yes. Do you live here all the time then?' It was Ginnie's feeble effort at a comeback; and contradicted on her part as she realised,

15

by another beseeching look. She was beginning to feel pleasure in her subordination.

'God no – just the summer. Live in London.'

To Ginnie's disappointment this was a flat statement, not another of the queries which came like a playful punch. The woman seemed not to care where Ginnie herself lived, nor what she did. And now she turned away, towelling her hair, which had been freely exposed to the not specially clean water of the bathing place. That wavery green, as Ginnie now saw, took on a soiled look at close quarters. The place might be empty now, and the blue sea wash in over the dark boulders; but it had not been empty for long, and even its greenness embraced the fact. A few cigarette ends and a piece of something limp and pouchy, near the ladder where her friend had gone in, seemed perfectly at home there.

Her friend? Yes she did feel like that, rather surprisingly. The encounter had been too bracing to be a disillusionment. Those questions had simply taken intimacy for granted, with none of the English mode of politeness which Ginnie knew to be just a way of keeping people at a distance.

The girl turned now towards the dark entrance, rubbing vigorously, and disappeared without further remark. That seemed a sort of comradeship, without dismissal, implying they might see one another around. The mystery of another world, which had seemed so potent when glimpsed among the bathers the night before – that was gone, or at least in abeyance, but it had been replaced by something raw and stimulating, rather thrilling in fact.

'Rather thrilling,' said Ginnie satirically to herself, as she climbed the stairs back to reception, and then up to her room. If it was a story in a woman's magazine, and Ginnie not infrequently saw herself taking part in one, her holiday might be said to have begun well.

At breakfast-time she was on her own. She sat in a little alcove in the smaller room next to the big dining area, and a waiter brought her coffee and squashy buns with yellow jam in them – an Italian form of lemon curd she thought it might be. She had eaten her breakfast with appetite. The mild indigestion, traceable probably to those great limp drainpipes she had had to get down at dinner, was gone. Even her bowels, Ginnie felt, had responded nobly to the holiday challenge, and demonstrated a new and vigorous personality quite unlike their stolid daily selves. Then she had looked at the postcards near the reception desk. She would send one today to her mother and perhaps to Susan at the office; she would decide later about other suitable recipients.

Having selected the cards, and had them gravely counted by the polite young desk clerk, she paid with the Italian change she had been careful to bring, and wandered through an indeterminate area of the ground floor where she had already noticed a glass-fronted bookcase whose comfortably shabby contents had English titles. Now she paused to read them more attentively. They certainly were shabby; the paperbacks practically coming to pieces. Freeman Wills Crofts, Hammond Innes – she thought she had read that one – a couple of Agatha Christies and a Barbara Pym. A dim-looking much older book in grubby orange-brown cloth, the title ornate in curly black. *Ramazan the Rajah*, by Ruby Tredgold. Self-indulgently – but she was on holiday – Ginnie opened the glass door and took it out. It fell open on an already shattered spine, and Ginnie read a few words on the brownish paper in an unexpectedly clear and decisive print. *His dark face, so dignified under the big turban, now had anguish in every line as he gazed compellingly upon her. 'My Virginia!' he uttered at length in imploring tones* ... Ginnie could not help smiling. What a coincidence that the name should be the same as hers! She put the book back and turned, still smiling to herself, to see a man sitting in an armchair quite close to her.

She had not noticed him before, and indeed he was not very noticeable, but she had a feeling he might have seen her smiling; and she quickly turned back to the bookcase when she saw him. He was forty plus, she supposed; going rather bald but not aggressively so. What did strike her was his total non-commitment to holiday apparel: to those shorts and fat-looking Hawaiian shirts that were now the usual uniform. He wore a dark suit – possibly tweed, certainly shabby – and a sleeveless pullover. Seated low in the small chair, his book on his knee, he seemed quite relaxed; as if prepared to spend all day there, mildly indifferent to the attractions of sun and sea, and outings to picturesque places.

And he had seen her? She certainly felt that, and it cast rather a gloom over holiday freedoms and irresponsibilities. The figure in the armchair somehow represented not just work – work back home in the office – but the threat of having to take action in terms of the immediate future. Here, and away from it all, she feared the very thing which should be the main point of these holidays on her own: the idea of meeting new people. The white girl seen in the evening and this morning was the opposite. She represented no anxieties. At the thought of her Ginnie quickly turned away from the bookcase.

But she was too late. Looking round, but not at her, the man said, 'Not much there, I'm afraid.'

His voice was so unemphatic, not more than a murmur, that she hardly heard him; but of course she could not just drift away now – upbringing and habit were too strong. She made noises of agreement, and he said 'Have you just arrived?' After that it was quite easy, although she felt her spirits drooping further as they talked. Not that he seemed to want to talk. He showed no eagerness to know her, let alone 'pick her up': like all her sex Ginnie knew by instinct when this was in the wind. In fact she couldn't make him out at all. His nature, whatever it was, seemed as out of place as the clothes he was wearing.

At the end of ten minutes they had got nowhere. Holiday sensations had gone – she might as well have been at home, chatting to one of the office group, or a friend of her mother's. He came here every year, she found that out; and with a sort of civil reluctance – Ginnie knew that quiet male self-deprecation of old, and she knew how little it usually signified – he spoke of things to be seen and enjoyed in the neighbourhood. The impression he gave was that he had not visited them himself; or if he had, that single original visit had merely been the prelude to the serious business of coming back each year, as a settled thing. 'Sorrento is a nice place to relax in,' he informed her, in tones that were low rather than quiet, and in what Ginnie vaguely thought of as a genteel voice, but with a London accent. He did not seem in the least lonely; and when she managed to withdraw slowly like the Cheshire cat, with some murmur about meeting again, he looked as if satisfied to have done his own duty, and turned back to his book.

Ginnie strove to recapture some of this morning's happy and irresponsible feeling by going back to the reception desk and asking about coach outings. The young clerk was helpful, and after some explanation he left her with two or three brochures as his attention was claimed by a guided tour party. For a few seconds Ginnie felt at a loss, as she had done in the past on the first day of her one-woman holidays: a vertigo of pointlessness seemed to descend on her, and she wanted to sit down. But something in her knew how to deal with that; and she marched resolutely to the main entrance.

The streets of the town were just ahead and she set off towards them, beginning to enjoy again the sense of novelty, the friendly sun, the loud harmonious Italian chatter from a café and from dark cool shop-doorways. These things had a permanence, not like shops and fashions at home. And people too, Ginnie thought, looking at the solid women, many in black, all full of an animation that seemed independent of today's trends, and the behaviour that news or TV projected.

What about the man by the bookcase? Ginnie's spirits drooped again as she remembered him, for in a rather ghastly way he represented just the sort of man she might have supposed that she might like to meet. No one could have looked less as if he moved with the times. Would he be gay perhaps? That was the thing to declare yourself now, if you felt that way presumably. Gaiety, in any sense, had seemed noticeably lacking; but Ginnie was aware that you never could tell. She had quite happy memories of a single man she had once met in Venice, a cosy undemanding sort of fellow, who seemed to like walking about with her and going on the *vaporetto*, and who vanished every evening on some evidently purposeful jaunt of his own.

But then, she thought, thinking of herself, sex was not something you necessarily had in any easily assignable form. If indeed you had it at all. Maybe there were lots like that, but there weren't supposed to be, at least not now. Did one have 'normal feelings', and if not why not? – or rather, what form might normal feelings be supposed to take? Ginnie's own feelings, insofar as they existed, never seemed to have got her very far.

There shot into her mind the unexpected vision of last night – the Pure White Woman of Sorrento, as Ginnie now decided she thought of her – and the unmistakably positive feelings the sight of her at the bathing-place had bestowed. Ginnie was not 'les', so far as she knew – the term had been fairly common when she was a teenager, and now, like so much else of that time, had a slightly old-fashioned air – but she had never seemed to herself to be anything else particularly either. She was waiting for Love no doubt; because she felt, partly from observation though mostly from what she read, that one wanted that rather than sex, or at least the two together, or something. Ginnie had sometimes felt slightly appalled at her own inner scepticism about either of these things, though scepticism was rather too strong a word for something so indeterminate.

But it certainly made Ginnie feel happy, as she strolled along, to remember the Pure White Woman; a happiness she had experienced for a day or two from various minor crushes at various ages. As with those flutters and excitements in the past the great thing was that there was nothing to be done about it. Romance was an end in itself. She looked forward to seeing the woman again of course, down at the bathing-place or elsewhere; and perhaps they would exchange a few words. About what? Ginnie had to admit, in retrospect, that she just wanted to enjoy again the swoony feel of being addressed by the imperious Loved One, and finding a few words to say in reply. Would they swim together? Ginnie was not even sure she wanted to. Imagining possibilities like that became as unsettling as the depressing feel of 'duty' she had experienced for a moment when in contact with the man by the bookcase. She knew she ought to try to follow that up, but she had not the slightest wish to. Nor, it seemed, had the man himself. And that was a relief.

Feeling gay again – though not in the modern sense – she looked at some more and better postcards outside a small tourist shop. Visible inside were shelves of ceramics: bijou plates, coloured and decorated; carts, donkeys, ashtrays, far more than could ever be bought surely; they must survive from year to year. A small animal, a lamb perhaps, patterned with green leaves, was rather appealing. She might get it for her mother. It would be a ritual post-holiday moment; and her mother would be pleased at the thought, although Ginnie had the feeling that, as with several other little holiday offerings in the past, it would probably disappear into some limbo and not be seen again. She postponed decision.

Back at the hotel she went up to her room and looked out from the balcony. The swimming-place was filling up, mostly with children, who were yelled at from time to time by minders and mothers. A few sleek dark-haired men, getting browner by the minute, lay on their chests or backs, detached and immobile. It was comparatively a peaceful scene, and Ginnie wondered if she might not nerve herself to go down and have a swim before lunch. The *Achille Lauro* lay now as indolently as the Italian men by the pool, a very slight haze of smoke going up from one of the two blue funnels. Vesuvius, behind, gave the illusion of having produced the slight fume himself; but in the mid-day blue the volcano's bulk looked unimpressive, and equally peaceful.

Getting into her costume, a standard one-piece affair in mocha brown which was not difficult to put on, Ginnie shuddered slightly; partly at the prospect of venturing to the bathing-place, and partly at the recollection of what the White Woman had said about the terrorists on the ship, and how they had treated the poor old man in the wheelchair. Time had effaced these things in its usual way; and the ship now, like a huge cat, looked as if butter wouldn't melt in its mouth.

Though Ginnie had brought no dressing-gown she had a short bathing-wrap, and wearing this she presently emerged through the doorway at the foot of the cliff. Her legs at any rate were nice enough, she felt, and well cared for; and she had hoped when she bought the brown swim-suit that its colour would communicate itself to the rest of her, confusing the fact that she was not sleek and bronzed, nor white either, but merely an indeterminate shade. The inoffensively grubby look of ordinary flesh would have to do: and so it did when Ginnie got promptly in – it was nice to know in advance there would be no shock as the warm water closed over her – and swam quickly out to where she had seen the fisherman's boat that morning. Nobody paid her the faintest attention, as she could feel, and that was reassuring. If male heads had risen to eye her momentarily with lazy indifference she would have felt rejected.

Out again she walked briskly to the doorway, as the White Woman herself had done. Knowing she wouldn't be there at mid-day had been a reason why Ginnie had decided to have her swim, and now she thought only of getting back to her room and ready for lunch. So it seemed part of the natural cussedness of things that she promptly ran into the woman in the subterranean changing area, before the stairs going up. Wearing a whitish overall, a bit like a nurse, she was stacking piles of towels and linen in a side area, working with calm unhurried movements and humming to herself. She saw Ginnie at once.

'Been in have you?'

'Yes. It's nice isn't it?'

The woman folded her arms on the top of the pile and contemplated Ginnie peacefully. Everything seemed peaceful today. Feeling like a nervous horse surveyed over a stable door, Ginnie shifted her legs and began to murmur something about getting dry and changed for lunch.

'So you don't sunbathe either?' The sound, Ginnie noticed, was 'bithe'. The long languid Antipodean vowel seemed to include all beaches and their activities in the same mildly contemptuous amusement. Ginnie liked the sound.

The woman seemed not to listen to her reply, dismissing her in a good-natured way as if Ginnie were a little girl who had to hurry off to the next school activity. As she turned to go the other said 'I live in the hotel too.' The sound was definitely 'tew'. 'Have to work though – worse luck.' Murmuring some vague commiseration as she went, Ginnie felt warmed by the encounter, and by the words the lazy voice had uttered.

She was almost on the steps when it spoke again.

'I'm Alice by the wy.'

*

It was siesta time. Coming into her room, Ginnie had a brief fantasy that someone else was already there. She investigated with caution. The whoever it was must be asleep. She imagined herself tip-toeing back, so as not to awaken the unknown sleeper, down the steep steps to the rest of her little room. She would look out into the afternoon glare. Her slippers were on

22

the floor, and visible through the open door of the minute wardrobe her two dresses waited for her, hung up tidily.

But which sex was the person on the bed? Ginnie couldn't decide. Could it be the chambermaid, who had supposed the occupant was out for the day, and had made up her mind to use the room for a nap? That was plausible. But why not an Australian voice, drowsy but commanding, from the bed alcove?

'Come on up. What are you witeing for?'

Like a sleep-walker Ginnie would turn, and start to remount the steps. As if by magic her clothes seemed to fall off. She was drawn under the sheet. A cool firm body, big and strong, seemed to envelope her. Lips were on hers; a dark torrent of hair flowed over them. '*Alice, she whispered to herself, lost in submission. Alyssia, White Queen of Sorrento ...*'

That was all very well, mused Ginnie indulgently, turning over on her back. She stretched herself under the sheet – she had nothing on and to that extent she corresponded to the state in which she and the White Queen had been abandoning themselves – and meditated in comfort on the real pleasures of a holiday. To go frankly to bed in the afternoon and have a sleep, instead of feeling drowsy at work; to feel the blessed heat and yet not have to lie in the sun; to look forward to her dinner, and before that a drink in a café. It was for such pleasures that she had come to Sorrento, and gone to similar places before.

Now she was half asleep. White limbs wavered in her mind's eye. White Queen? No, that sounded too like Alice in Wonderland, not the Alice of the bathing pool, the Alice she had met that morning. White Woman was better ... Or should she prefer Ramazan the Rajah, with his strong brown limbs no doubt ... not bronzed, just naturally brown. She thought not. But there might be time for Ramazan before dinner ...

The light snore which heralded unconsciousness became a snort. Ginnie sat up abruptly. Dinner! My God, she had completely forgotten! The man by the bookcase. Happily immersed in her fantasy about the White Woman she had forgotten all about her lunchtime encounter with him.

In fact it had been after lunch. Coming out of the restaurant with a banana in her handbag which she thought she might eat upstairs in her room, she had run slap into him in the corridor.

The banana had never got eaten, partly because she had felt in quite a flap about the meeting with him; partly the result of the day-dream that had begun when she opened her door and looked up the steps towards her bed. She must remember to remove it from her bag.

The bookcase man, as she still thought of him though she now knew his name, had obviously recognised her. But he had given no sign of it, so Ginnie too had walked on without stopping. Lunch had been pleasant enough – a sort of buffet selection – and she had got herself a tuna-fish salad: actually much the same sort of thing she ate when at work, in the pub round the corner from the office. As she went on down the passage she had heard the bookcase man stop and turn round. A voice said 'Oh sorry' as he approached her from behind, and she too had stopped and turned. She smiled dutifully, though unable to think of anything to start off with. There was no need to, however. He said at once, not quite looking at her, 'What about having dinner tonight. There's a place I go to. Much better than the hotel I think you'll find it.' He had the air of having relieved himself by having got this out. His face and eyes now looked at her with the relaxation of a man who has finished a job.

Ginnie was genuinely amazed. The overture was in a sense so obvious – it had happened to her reasonably often before on holiday – but she couldn't help feeling surprised this particular person had made it. He hadn't seemed that sort of man at all. Now he looked at her in a peaceable way – Ginnie couldn't help being reminded of the also peaceful stare of Alice, the White Woman – as if he had nothing further to do with the matter. It didn't bother him either way. It was because she felt this that she found herself saying without any trouble, 'Well, that's very kind of you. I should like to very much.'

She had felt she now joined him in his state of satisfaction, and they looked at one another without difficulty. He was wearing his tweed suit, she saw, just as in the morning, and a stripy shirt with a dark tie. The air of faint grubbiness was somehow rather distinguished, more so than the correspondingly hot and har- assed kind of grubbiness seen at times with men at meetings in the office. He smiled quite formally, as if he had only done the polite thing, and could now go about his business. 'Suppose we

24

meet at the bookcase, like this morning. About half-past seven?' This time he did manage a note of interrogation, and she tried to please him by sounding in her agreement as pleased as could be.

There was plenty of time anyway. Probably he was not the sort of person who liked to sit drinking in cafés, and so had named a moderately late hour for their meeting. The comical thing was that in a way there had been no need to meet him at all. As she went past reception the polite young clerk, perhaps a different one by now, went and got her key for her, and with it a note from the little pigeon-hole where it hung. This duplicated what the bookcase man had just asked; he was clearly the type who left nothing to chance. Would she care to dine with him; suggesting where and when to meet; and signed 'Mark Brassey'. The young clerk gave her a faintly knowing, perhaps congratulatory, look; as if he were quite familiar with the message on the half sheet of folded hotel writing paper; and it occurred to her that Mr Brassey, who might be a well-known figure at the hotel despite his apparent low profile, had sent such notes before – perhaps a good many of them.

It seemed more than likely. The folded paper was neatly addressed to Miss Thornton. He had clearly made some enquiries, perhaps routine ones. She wondered whether to reply to the note, but decided there was no need. Two queries from his side were best answered by a single acquiescence from hers.

It was a little odd he hadn't mentioned the note when he spoke to her, but he seemed not to be a talkative man. And yet he might be, thought Ginnie rather despondently, imagining a scenario this evening in which all sorts of things came tumbling out of him because it was such a relief to have somebody to talk to; and then perhaps taking her hand across the table. She contemplated the possibility with distaste. It had all the banality of a contemporary moment. She hoped he might be, as it were, an older model than that: more buttoned-up, more instinctively polite. How old? Ten or a dozen years more than her she supposed. Well, cheer up, it would be some sort of evening; and if he was a bore she would just have to try to keep away from him for the rest of her holiday.

Ginnie stretched again, looked at her watch – the only thing she was wearing – and decided she had better get up. No longer feeling the modesty of this morning, when room and hotel had been unfamiliar, she amused herself by walking down the steps to the shower – Nude Descending a Staircase, she thought – taking her watch off as she went. Self-pampered, she put on powder and a dress. With bag and cardigan over her arm she exchanged what seemed by now a routine smile with the desk clerk – another and older one – and strolled down the familiar road to a café quite close, which she had noticed that morning. There was an hour or more before her appointment with the bookcase man.

*

If only she could change position and stretch out a bit more, as she had in her bed that afternoon. Ginnie crouched on her side, ruefully reflecting how much more at home she had felt in bed then. Behind her, on the other side, there was deep and regular breathing, with just a faint hint of a snore at the end of each exhalation. Nothing obtrusive about it: it was not the sound itself which was keeping Ginnie awake. It was her thoughts – naturally enough in the circumstances – which went galloping on. And the discomfort of being in bed with someone else of course, even though the bed was nominally a double one.

She thought now almost with nostalgia of the little café, where she had sat outside the night before. When she had first come abroad Ginnie had been wary of cafés and had felt rather painfully self-conscious sitting alone in one. But she had soon realised nobody looked at her much, or found it odd; there were usually plenty of other single persons sitting about waiting for someone, or just on their own. Last night she had ordered tea, taking care to have it with lemon instead of the hot substance that was provided if you asked for milk. She had sipped it with pleasure, feeling quite experienced and at home. Later she had drunk a vermouth before paying and strolling back to the hotel for her appointment.

It was like the end of innocence, really. And yet the dinner had been a happy prolongation of it; almost an exaggerated form of those mild predictable pleasures Ginnie always welcomed on her holiday. As the pair of them had gone off purposefully

26

together into the dusky streets, with the bookcase man, Mark Brassey, murmuring softly but not shyly about how he had found the little place they were going to, she had begun to feel happy; and even confident that the evening would become a success. And so it had. The 'little place', though situated in a dark narrow street some distance from the hotel, turned out to be not little at all, but a capacious and solid bourgeois restaurant, with mahogany fittings and white table-cloths, and the waiters in long white aprons. It was fairly full but there seemed to be no tourists; just big and rather distinguished-looking Italian business men, in what Ginnie thought of as city suits. Her host was known, was welcomed, ushered to a table: it seemed he had booked beforehand. Ginnie sat down and looked about her almost with abandon. Nobody bothered to look at them. Animated but deep-toned talk, like the male chorus of an opera, continued all round.

Mark Brassey (she thought of him as Mark now) had smiled equally on Ginnie's obvious pleasure. Clearly he was gratified the place pleased her, and she felt she had passed a kind of test. He seemed relaxed, very much on top of things; and when she pretended not to know much about the dishes on the menu, though in fact she probably knew as much as he, or more, he explained them with a nice kind of courteous diffidence – no sign of showing off. In fact courtesy was what he had; and Ginnie began thoroughly to enjoy giving herself up to it as the elderly waiter conferred with her host. His Italian she noticed, though subdued and flat-sounding, was highly competent. Harmony was achieved; the waiter went off with satisfied gestures; and soon the mixed hors d'oeuvres arrived – bits of squid and fried little fishes, slices of oily pepper, aubergines and artichoke.

They talked about food, quite effortlessly, and Ginnie took mouthfuls of cold delicious white wine between her nibbles of salami and fresh sardine. Heaven! It was natural not to ask questions; she did it without having to take care. She had perceived, of course, that he wasn't married; that, not unlike herself, he was settled fairly comfortably in a groove of his own. He held strong views on *antipasto*. He then said quite abruptly, but it seemed to flow naturally from the harmony they had already established: 'Not many people like us left nowadays. At least if we're to believe the papers and the television, and all that.'

Ginnie was not bothered by this remark. She went on with her discreetly greedy eating, and smiled at him. It was a thought she had often had herself; yet she was also inclined to think there were really many more people like them than the papers and the television cared to know, or to pretend. At any rate the numerous books and manuscripts she read for her publisher employers invariably gave the impression of a modern world quite unlike the one she knew. The stuff in them gave her the horrors sometimes. Not because of its nastiness, though there was usually plenty of that; but through its lack of attention to – or understanding of – what for her constituted normality. When much younger she had thought of books as being true, somehow; as well as exciting and colourful and full of possibilities and profundities. They held – quite properly it seemed – allurements lacking in ordinary life. But now it seemed to her just the opposite. She was frequently staggered, after wading through something she had to read, to find herself back in the nice staid old world which she knew, and which the author had seemed determined didn't exist. That was a bit naive she realised; and she was careful not to make a point of it, certainly not in public; but it seemed to her to be the case none the less.

Mark Brassey evidently felt much the same, though he might have put it differently. She hadn't replied, and hadn't seemed to be required to do so. He was studying the label on a dark bottle the waiter had put on the table; and she looked over his shoulder at a smartly dressed middle-aged woman, who was talking with a kind of furious jollity at her two male companions. The woman, her mouth going like a bellows, was gazing at Ginnie but didn't apparently see her; and that was so agreeable, just as it was agreeable to stare dreamily over Mark's shoulder. Ginnie always liked being taken no notice of. The old waiter was putting dishes down on their table with his rapid deft movements. They had both ordered brains with black butter, and fried tomato and zucchini, which came strewn with white and green slivers of fennel. The chaste look of the raw vegetable suddenly reminded Ginnie of the previous evening – it seemed already

28

long ago – and Alice's white back as it swayed indolently down to the water.

'What's amused you?' asked Mark in a tolerant way. Concerned only, she comfortably felt, to have an unassertive dinner companion, he seemed quite free of any male possessiveness over her responses. She indicated the woman behind him as the most convenient reference for his question. He did not turn his head but nodded with a smile himself.

'I think I know who you mean.'

'Do you come here often then?' They both smiled at this time-honoured banality which had slipped so naturally from Ginnie.

'Quite a lot when I'm down here. She's a friend of the proprietor.' Ginnie liked the idea of all this vigorous life going on, which she would never know anything about. Mark was filling her glass with dark red wine. 'Grown near Vesuvius, I believe,' he observed neutrally, as if he didn't expect her to be interested, and was barely interested himself. His lack of emphasis was more soothing every moment. They sipped, and smiled at each other again, and turned back to their *cervelli fritti*. It was a dish that Ginnie had never ventured on before, in spite of her fairly wide Italian experience, but Mark had recommended it as a thing the restaurant went in for, and she agreed to please him. Now she was glad she had – it was so beautifully light and tasty she felt she could live on it the rest of her days. What a change from those drain-pipes at the hotel the night before!

'Could you make it then?' he wondered, as she exclaimed how good the dish was.

This, his first unguarded comment, seemed to pull them both up short. The answer was, of course, no. She couldn't; but this point, which seemed obvious to both of them, was not the thing in question. His query had shot an accidental probe – or was it so accidental? – into the potentialities of her own domestic being. For a moment they had stared at one another in something like consternation, but, thankfully, the moment was gone at once. Ginnie realised that it had bothered him a bit too, and this reassured her. Both seemed to sit back and draw a thankful breath. Both reached instinctively for their glasses of wine.

'Good heavens, no,' she laughed cheerfully. 'Think what you

must have to do to prepare it.' And then they had laughed together, secure in the repossession of their previous relationship.

Ginnie went on to speculate about the offal itself (what a word! – she didn't use it aloud) which would surely not be available in London, unless you went to Harrods or somewhere.

Chatting about things one could or could not buy, and where, got them nicely to the sweet stage, as Ginnie thought of it. She remembered the sickliness of the one last night, and the old ladies benevolently telling her to look forward to it. Now Mark ordered cheese, and encouraged her to try a cassata. 'You could have some of the cheese too,' he told her, as if conspiratorially, and this sort of familiarity over the food exactly suited them, she thought. He looked happy as he said it, too, giving her a jovial glance, almost a wink.

Now they knew where they were with each other, after that tiny suggestion of a crisis, and an escape. And this made it all the more remarkable when he leaned back with an air of placid repletion – coffee had just been ordered – and seemed to ruminate. Finally he said contentedly: 'Have you ever'? – and stopped.

Or rather he had not so much stopped as seemed to complete his sentence. It was as if he had said: 'That was good.' And Ginnie found herself uttering, 'Well, no, actually,' as if she were saying, 'Oh, yes, and thank you so much.'

Their eyes met harmoniously, seeming to know that a matter of passing interest was closed, or had never been opened. He poured out coffee, stirred it. She resumed her ice, which was perfect. So, she found, was the black espresso coffee.

It seemed the last of her happy holiday moments, thought Ginnie ruefully. Predictable moments, suitable for an ordinary person. Although the 'ordinary people', beloved by the media, were probably entitled by its attentions to a much more exotic time when they were on holiday than she required.

She cautiously turned her stiff legs into a different position. The bed might be double but it was small – no doubt of that. In some curious way Mark's unexpected query had been the perfect sign of the equilibrium which their relationship had so tranquilly achieved. And so indeed it had been. They had made their way back to the hotel, chatting of this and that. He had not suggested brandy in a bar, or anything of that sort; and there was no attempt to take her arm or apply pressure to an elbow. They had said goodnight in the reception area, with words of satisfaction on his part, and of gratitude on hers; and they had uttered a polite sentence or two about a further meeting.

So it was not Mark Brassey who was at that moment in the bed beside her.

Did she wish it were? No – certainly not. After their dinner together such an idea seemed not only absurd but improper. To herself Ginnie did not use the word; but it was what she had in mind, none the less. The word and the idea were both equally unfashionable in today's media: what the media would, on the other hand, approve, was what was now taking place – or had been taking place – in her room.

Indeed Ginnie at the moment was, morally and socially speaking, in the height of fashion. The thought gave her an amusement that was not pleasurable. For she felt no satisfaction at all: only a forlornness that went with sleeplessness.

Cautiously, and by stages, she turned over again, towards the centre of the bed. It was just light enough to make out the mass of dark hair on the other side. Not so different from the hair Ginnie had imagined on the pillow that afternoon, in her little daydream.

The White Woman of Sorrento was a good sleeper. Except for the hair, there was nothing visible of her. She was turned towards the wall, which was natural enough, as Ginnie had a wall on her side too. The bed, snug in its alcove, had also just room each side for small plastic shelves, with bedside lights over them.

It had all taken place with absurd and almost nightmare naturalness. Having said a contented goodnight to Mark, Ginnie had mounted the stairs, deciding not to bother with the lift, and walked along the corridor to her room. A woman in a dark cotton dress was walking in front of her; and as Ginnie turned the key in the door the woman stopped and turned too. 'Oh hullo,' she said, 'I was looking for you.'

It was Alice.

Helplessly Ginnie unlocked her door, and they entered the room together like a married couple. Thereupon Alice had

31

pulled the dark purple dress over her head. She stood contemplating Ginnie in her knickers, and a bra which looked dingy against her skin.

Ginnie had felt not so much embarrassed as simply blank. Her first thought was that everything happened at the wrong time; this was no moment for the pursuit of daydreams. The spirited thing, no doubt, would have been at once and with a welcoming smile to remove her own clothes, but this did not occur to her.

'This was what you wanted, wasn't it?'

Alice sounded a little brisk, like a salesgirl who has no time to stand around while the customer goes on dithering. I've got a job to do – don't keep me waiting. Like the shy and harassed shopper Ginnie had to make her mind up. No, it was not what she wanted; or not now, not in this way. Like the customer who buys to avoid offending the seller she found herself muttering 'Well, yes, – thank you,' even as she cast a despairing thought at her comfortable fatigue and bed. Agreeable recollections of the evening, in the glow of a mild alcoholic wooziness ... Now all that was not to be.

'Well, yes – thank you' – what a lamentable response to an offer of love, even in this form! And an offer of love from *the very person who had fascinated her*; who had made her feel slightly weak in the middle; who had walked to the water like a god or a goddess, it hardly mattered which.

But everything was abruptly too much – far too much. Ginnie found herself wondering if a real couple, or the wife at least, ever felt the same when home from a pleasant dinner-party. To find that partner, so far from being ready for repose, and a snug desultory chat about their fellow-guests, had distinctly amorous intentions. Or suppose each thought the other had them: and both were wrong? Possibly a couple came to foretell each other's responses, or intuit them? Ginnie honestly had no idea.

And what on earth could she have done? Should she have attempted to turn the White Woman out? Then she would have felt miserable, really miserable. Despairingly, she knew she had no choice. In her daydream had begun the responsibility for the event. She must see the thing through now. She was in the woman's hands.

However, after she had recovered a bit, and smiled, and still looked bothered no doubt, the whole thing had turned out easier than might have been expected. She had to admit that. Alice had stood implacably, looking amused, her arms folded. But then she had laughed right out and seized Ginnie in a little dance. After that it was easy. Ginnie was thankful that her period was over, although only just, as it happened. To have had to remove the apparatus would have been too shaming.

And Alice, she supposed, had done her best. Her instinct, no doubt, had been to proselytise Ginnie, to turn the clueless one who had to be shown the ropes into an enthusiastic performer. In the course of vigorous massage she had kept up a running commentary which reminded her involuntary client of sports commentators heard on the radio, in what now seemed another world.

The thought of all the business of it opened her mouth in a great yawn, but without bringing sleep any closer. Alice's bossiness had been predictable, she now saw, and a relief in its way. At least it was better than anything in the romantic line. A little like having to submit to a medical examination: more like being roped in for a weekend sport for which another player was needed.

And this was the woman who had looked so wonderful and mysterious, down by the bathing place the previous evening! A woman who had stepped in from another world, and had vanished into it again, wrapped in her white towel, among all the gaudy trappings of the beach. Where was that otherness now? It looked as foolish as the romances of Ramazan the Rajah. So much for Alyssia, the White Queen.

Commonsense, as well as what she had read, made Ginnie well aware that the rewards and satisfactions of life must be looked for and worked for in the real world. And so on and so forth. She had often been inclined to wonder about this, all the same. And she had never done so more sharply than when Alice's not entirely gentle hand was doing these intimate things: and her own mind, instead of being filled with happy swoonings and fantasies, was full of nothing at all. Stuffed yet blank.

Alice had blown into her ear, muttering in her gritty patronising voice not to worry: that she knew Ginnie didn't know the first thing about it. In the throes of the encounter Ginnie quite forgot the first giddy pleasure of being taken up, and taken over, by Alice – her first true romantic enslavement. The woman's assumption of superiority had been so irritating that she had felt inclined to stop the hand in its tracks.

It would not have been polite of course, apart from anything else; but as for not knowing the first thing, she felt she knew quite as much as anyone needed, *and* could act on it. She lay under the white girl's fingers smouldering with a resentment she knew to be comic, and hoping it wasn't palpable to her partner (that had to be the word she supposed). It was equally comical, and no doubt ungrateful, to be longing for her own true country, where she could give herself the thrills she liked. The whole thing was pretty comic really; but, as she realised with sudden panic, getting there was going to be no joke when someone else was bossily doing it for you. It was not going to be at all easy to pretend to a climax, a convincing, even if subdued and genteel, convulsion, under the searching eye and in the grasp of this white-handed imperious queen. She believed wives managed it; but men, being absorbed in their own thing, were probably more easily deceived. Oh dear: intimate social anxieties could be quite as pressing as more public ones, if not more so.

Fortunately she need not have worried. Either Alice was really the expert that her general demeanour so confidently proclaimed her to be, or Ginnie's own body was more seduced by the situation than her mind realised. Whichever it was, some moments of intense satisfaction had presently arrived, in which Ginnie had clung to the big body beside her, careless whether it was man or woman, dog or dolphin. Imagination was in abeyance: she wasn't in her own country, but for a few seconds it hadn't mattered where she was.

Alice stirred. A hand reached out and gave Ginnie a pat. Suddenly touched, almost overcome, Ginnie seized the hand and kissed it. In the grey light growing inside the room she saw Alice's face had turned on the pillow, a faint smile on it but her eyes still closed. Impulsively Ginnie snuggled up beside the big woman, kissing her bare shoulder. The other paid no attention and that was nice. Indeed the best part of the thing, Ginnie thought later, was that twenty minutes or half an hour as it was getting lighter. She had even slept, she thought.

*

Seeing Mark Brassey after breakfast was a trial. Not that Ginnie was embarrassed exactly. What had happened was clearly too fantastic for it to show. And Mark was just the same as he had been before their dinner, giving her a smile and a word or two: the equivalent of a dismissal satisfactory to both. Yet Ginnie suddenly decided she would not be dismissed. Smiling at him quite boldly in return, as if she had become indifferent or daring as a result of her nocturnal experiences, she asked him whether he might like to go with her into town, or even walk to one of the places he had told her about. That too he didn't seem to mind: on the contrary. Ginnie realised he was one of those people who seem dismissive because it was the easiest way of showing a distinguished independence, a not caring one way or the other. Nail him down as if he were known to be always unwilling but to be coaxed, and he was gratified.

So off they set for the shops, and for a viewpoint beyond which the Victorian guidebooks especially recommended, so Mark said. Ginnie vaguely wondered if other girls had nailed him similarly; and, if so, how he was still walking about tranquilly on his own, returning here unscathed and unbothered, year after year. That interesting question might solve itself later, she felt quite happily: feeling, too, almost inclined to take his arm and see what on earth would happen as a result. She forbore though, and gazed out over the sparkling blue sea towards the anaemic outline of Vesuvius, nearly lost in the haze. That liner, the *Achille Lauro*, lay motionless near the land, looking as if it would never move, or was intended to move, again. She seemed deserted too. No doubt all the passengers were enjoying themselves on a holiday excursion ashore.

The sight of her gave Ginnie a sudden drop in spirits. The ship had been visible out of the window after Alice had departed and Ginnie in a rather benumbed way was showering and powdering and getting out a fresh dress to wear. After her blissful snooze beside the woman, when the night and its events had suddenly seemed worth-while, things had deteriorated again. Very much so. She could hardly bear to be reminded of it,

35

although she realised it was unfair of her to blame Alice, who had simply given the dozing Ginnie a jog with her elbow and said, 'Got to go soon – want another go?'

Roused from that heavenly late doze Ginnie tried to show affection, even passion. But it was no use, or no go, as the other might have phrased it, her friendly drawl elongating the word into 'gow'. After the first encounter in the bed the night before Ginnie had been more than a trifle appalled by Alice saying, 'Mind if I stay? The cubby-hole they've given me downstairs gets so filthy hot, and the bed's not as good as this one.' The thought of that other body in the bed all night had at once deprived Ginnie of the prospect of sleep; which indeed had not come. The thought of solitude and her own smug unconscious-ness seemed so desirable at that moment she could hardly bear it, and yet – irony of ironies! – it turned out that the best part of the night had been those few moments in the early morning when she lay cuddled up to the other, and dozed off.

It jolted her now, an almost sickening sense of love, so that she looked wildly up at the sun and down the street to escape it, hearing Mark's level tones beside her. That Alice had wanted, or at least asked, to stay with her, had not struck her in the night as anything but a bore, an awful and unexpected sequel to the amazing and unexpected goings-on. To be left alone then was all she thought she wanted: to meditate before sleep in the pleas-ures of a private amazement.

But Alice had wanted to stay – or at least had asked to stay. She might have felt lonely; and, being the sort of person she was, have welcomed even Ginnie beside her, as an aid to sound repose. She might have understood and been amused by Gin-nie's romantic silliness, however unlikely that seemed; and so have taken pity on it. Or she might have come to Ginnie for Love?

That was an awe-inspiring thought, and the street itself looked quite sunstruck by it. But no, hang on, it couldn't be true. Even if she herself had found a moment of love, could Alice have come to her for the same reason? The word itself, in this context, was a bit of a joke. When Ginnie had demurred, as civilly as she could, at the offer of another 'go', Alice had leapt out of bed with some flippant remark, and with no sign of petulance.

36

She stood by the steps for a moment, looking magnificent, and went down as she had gone down for her swim, only without the purple bikini. Because the room was so small Ginnie thought it easier to stay where she was. For some reason she had felt close to tears. She'd heard Alice break wind with a long comfortable sound; the toilet flushed, and the shower began to run. Ginnie had lain paralysed until the voice said, 'S'long – be seeing you.' She had jumped up crying 'Wait a moment!' and had just caught a wave of Alice's hand as she shut the door. With nothing on, Ginnie could not pursue her.

Distractedly she turned to Mark, and tried to concentrate on what he was saying. His face was a comfort anyway, with nothing in it for her except his own calm interior satisfaction. But suddenly his expression altered, and his eyes widened as he looked away from her. Ginnie looked too; and there, confronting them on the pavement, was Alice.

She was surveying them as she had surveyed Ginnie at the bathing-place the previous morning, but with a wide smile. Then she opened fire.

'Er, darling, did er leave mer bangle in yer room? Waren't it luvly by the wy? Come agine, as they sy.'

Why was she so grossly overdoing the Aussie line? Almost sinking through the pavement with embarrassment, Ginnie hardly dared look at her companion as she murmured no – she didn't think a bangle had been left. Was it when she looked in for a moment about the towels? Perhaps she'd dropped it somewhere else?

Ignoring Mark, the White Woman went on talking to her with exaggerated animation, until suddenly patting Ginnie's cheek, and then giving it a resounding peck, she appeared to vanish as suddenly as she had manifested herself in their path.

Ginnie could hardly bring herself to look at her companion. What must he be thinking. But she saw, to her relief, that he seemed to be thinking nothing at all. If he had noticed the phenomenon of Alice, her special awfulness – as Ginnie could not help but think of it – seemed to have passed him by. It occurred to her that Mark, if he came here every holiday time, must surely have seen Alice too; but then she remembered that this was the Australian girl's first season as holiday help, and that Mark was

37

not the kind of man who would visit the bathing-place, or notice the staff around the hotel.

What did he notice? She looked at his indeterminate but reliable features with new curiosity, realising how little a person like herself knew of other people. She knew from last night's conversation that he was a solicitor, but without seeming at all secretive he had not revealed anything else. She might find out more if she was part of a couple, so to speak: presumably living with someone else made the difference. Or did it? Married couples might have lost interest in people – each other included. A girl whom Ginnie had once known had told her that marriage was like a slow process of becoming strangers. Whatever intimacy you achieved at first came by degrees to be tacitly, almost voluntarily, given up.

Instead, the girl had said with an air of solemnity – she was an earnest little creature who had worked in the office for a short period, and Ginnie had liked her – you made a world of your own, which you didn't allow your husband or children to enter. Not that they knew about it, or would have been in the least interested if they had.

Ginnie had been rather fascinated by this, while realising that it could hardly be general in marriage, or even common. The girl was only in her late twenties, she remembered, but seemed already quite ancient, as if husband and family had come upon her prematurely, and trapped her in the form of a now wizened little girl.

Ginnie had little to go by – her parents had always seemed to get along pretty well – but this view of the married state struck her none the less as more convincing than the stylised rubbish in Sunday-paper feature articles, or on TV, rubbish that seemed as unreal, in its bright emancipated way, as Victorian morals must have seemed to the women who lived in those days. These things were all part of a universe of power, which, if it had not been entirely dreamed up by the media, as she sometimes found herself suspecting, must presumably exist somewhere. But real power was a mystery to her, and one that failed to attract. She had once been teased by her colleagues for reporting on a novel script she had been reading that it was 'good but powerful'. She suffered some confusion when she realised from their reactions how odd that must sound.

Did this man Mark have a world of his own, which he allowed no one else into? It seemed more than likely, considering the sort of person he seemed to be. She remembered the way he had said in the restaurant the night before 'Have you ever – ?' and then stopped in the most natural way in the world, as if the words were not even a query, let alone a sign of real curiosity. It had been a peaceful moment. She recalled the delicate taste of the dish, and the full cool freshness of the wine. Would he ask her again? She hoped so, for she was confident there would be nothing to it but the dinner, and the pleasure it gave them both. Should she offer to pay her share if he asked her again? Possibly. There was time to decide that if asked.

Did Alice have her own world? That somehow seemed improbable, and yet, why not? In her dark cotton dress and sandals, in the full glare of the sun, the Australian girl had looked nothing special, nothing like the apparition who had come to the bathing place that evening, an evening that already seemed long ago. For a few seconds Ginnie tried to imagine Alice's life, and failed totally.

'Let's sit down and have a coffee, shall we?' said Mark, subsiding rather heavily into a café chair which stood in the deep shade at the side of the pavement.

When the cappuccini had arrived, and been drunk with the calm appreciation each seemed to extend to the other over food and drink, Ginnie began to feel none the less that something unwelcome had jarred the promise of their morning walk. As if wishing to disguise the fact, Mark got to his feet again and went purposefully over to a newspaper kiosk on the other side of the road, returning with a serious looking pinkish paper, and a continental *Guardian*. He offered the latter to Ginnie, who had no intention of looking at it, although she did not wish to appear an indifferent or unserious person. She was addicted to newspapers at home; but on holiday their world did not seem appropriate. Since she did not open it Mark courteously took it back and unfolded it himself, seeming to become involved at once in what Ginnie, glancing over his shoulder, could see was an article on drug abuse among the young of the inner cities.

Was he tired of her company, and using this as a polite method of suspending it? But only a few seconds later he looked up at her again.

'When did you meet her?' he enquired.

Ginnie was by now accustomed to him enough to know that he wanted to hear about Alice. Feeling gratified by his interest rather than otherwise – it gave them something to gossip about together, and might give them more – Ginnie told him about her encounter with the Australian girl, omitting of course, as was only natural, the visit to her room after she and Mark had said good-night.

'She'd heard there weren't enough clean towels on our floor,' she lied easily in conclusion, 'and was just checking. I suppose she thought she'd dropped her bangle, as she called it. I didn't know people still used the word. My mother talked about bangles, I remember.'

'And is your mother still alive?' he asked with his usual friendliness, but beginning to unfold the pages of the *Financial Times*.

'Oh yes.' And Ginnie told him about that. It was hard to know whether he was interested or polite, and she didn't much care either way. She liked talking to Mark, she realised, but would rather he speculated about Alice than asked after her mother.

It was all the more disconcerting that he got abruptly now to his feet. 'Do keep this one,' he said, giving her back the *Guardian*, which she did not want. What had gone wrong?

Nothing apparently. 'Something in the *FT*,' he told her. 'Got to ring my broker. Better go and do that now. I'll pay for the coffees.' He plunged into the dark interior of the café, emerging to say, 'You'll excuse me, won't you?' And with that he left her.

Standing awkwardly at the café table Ginnie gazed after his departing back. She was wretched. No doubt people like Mark, just because they were so politely self-contained, so friendly and settling, could with equal ease be abrupt and dismissive, almost rude: but as if their two modes of behaviour were essentially the same. Which no doubt they were. Ginnie subsided again on to her chair. But feeling demoralised and unnerved – she saw the waiter looking at her from the dark doorway – and in no mood

40

at the moment to sit and appreciate the Italian scene, she got up, smiled timidly at the waiter, and wandered off into the town.

*

'Oh fuck,' said Alice.

She was standing beside the bed, her hands fumbling behind her with the fastening of her bra. Gazing at her beautiful back Ginnie felt neither excitement nor admiration; only a dull sense of non-existence. The life of her holiday seemed to have given up. When she had been roused by a tap on the door, in the drowsy middle of the afternoon, she had been genuinely surprised to see the Australian woman standing there, not as she had looked on the pavement that morning but wearing her white overall. It had occurred to Ginnie that a chambermaid, even an auxiliary English-speaking holiday season one like Alice, had unique op-portunities for making love to hotel guests if the parties were willing. What could be more natural than that she should knock and enter, as she had done now?

But there had been little time for reflection. 'Oh come on, Honey,' said Alice, fastening her mouth to Ginnie's, and propel-ling her backwards up the steps, as if she were Tarzan sweeping Jane up into the treehouse.

Unresisting, Ginnie had allowed herself to subside onto the bed. She had put on her dress to go to the door, and now it was taken off her. Presumably, if Alice had been a man, this approach would either have been more terrifying or more exciting. But in the featureless desert of misunderstanding she now seemed to find herself, she could hardly make even a show of response.

And for the first time she was struck by the fact that Alice's talk and behaviour seemed false and overdone, as if she were putting on a performance of desire. Or did the falsity of the performance indicate in some contradictory way a real need, a real feeling?

Ginnie felt there was no reason to find out. For the moment she had ceased to feel much interest in Alice, let alone admira-tion for her. Accidentally, as it seemed, she had involved herself in a parody of misconceptions, a pantomime of the sex necessity,

41

and the sex difficulty. And of the difficulties the sexes notori-
ously had with each other.

But she and Alice were the same sex. This undeniable fact
none the less seemed at the moment perfectly deniable to Ginnie,
as she realised with a slight shock that she had never thought of
Alice being a woman like herself at all.

That was after Alice had gone. She had of course rumbled
Ginnie's absence of enthusiasm, or even of desire, although she
had not seemed in the least put out by it. But what were her
motives, Ginnie now wondered pedantically. Was it the pleasure of giving a shock, or a thrill, or the simple exercise of power?
Once again she had a pang as she remembered how Alice in bed
that morning had lifted herself on one elbow and given her a
long stare: not lover-like, not tender exactly, but thoughtful and
searching. It was far more flattering than a sexy look, and more
of a compliment; for why should the woman take this amount of
interest in her?

Was it just a kindly impulse? Such things no doubt did happen. A woman holidaying on her own must be bound to seem
lonely, and in need of something or other.

But not necessarily of this, for goodness sake. Had Alice 'read'
Ginnie's fantasy somehow, like Robinson Crusoe reading the
footprint, and acted as swiftly as a savage? And as shamelessly
as the tart of a modern Aussie girl she certainly was, Ginnie
could not help reflecting sourly. For after Alice had put her
clothes on she had plumped down on the side of the bed,
grinned at Ginnie and said, 'Right, you owe me thirty quid. OK?'

Her client, or beneficiary, had smiled nervously, her hands
clasped in front of her. Was it a joke, or was it a real if jokey way
of requiring payment? 'Well, of course, yes. Can I give you a
cheque?' Ginnie got out, trying to make it sound both like a
serious offer and a suitably facetious response. Sitting up in bed
as she was she felt supremely foolish, but Alice had just given a
hoot of laughter.

'Only kidding. You're a simple soul, Ginnie. I like you. But
you don't think I always do it for free, do you? This sheila's got
her living to earn.'

'I thought you worked in the hotel.'

'So I do. And I work with the tourists – the older ones sometimes get a bit fussed, you know, and need a bit of sympathy. The old dears like to be cooed over. I get tips that way. Often on the buses for that. But then I go down to the beach when a boat comes in, like you saw me. Chaps on the bateau see me and think about a bonk. Girls too sometimes.'

Ginnie thought of Alice strolling out, inviolate, unnoticed, in her purple bikini. Others seemed to have had the same vision as herself. For a moment her inside felt ripped out of her.

'Course the wops don't go for it so much. Their women see to that. Not that I don't get one or two on the side sometimes. But it's mostly tourists, or off the cruise ships. Saudis and Japs are the big spenders, believe you me – Scands too sometimes.'

She jumped up and then flopped down again, and looked at Ginnie as she had looked that morning in bed. She reached out and stroked Ginnie's leg, as if shyly.

'You're sure you like me, Gin?'

'Oh, Alice.'

'I only ask because I'm not queer, you know.'

'I didn't think you were,' said Ginnie, in some confusion.

'You're not either. I can tell you that for sure. You're just very sweet and innocent.'

Ginnie was not sure she liked this description. 'But people aren't necessarily one thing or another, are they?' she began pedantically.

Alice exploded in a laugh that shook the bed to its flimsy foundations. 'Oh Gin, you are a one! Don't know your arse from your elbow, do you, as we used to say down under.'

'Well, aren't I right?'

'No doubt you are, my sweetie,' said Alice absently. 'But I've met some real butches in my time, believe you me.'

There was the sort of companionable silence which Ginnie had begun to enjoy in the big girl's company. It was far from being the delphic speechlessness of her fantasy White Woman, as Alice proved the next moment by beginning again.

'Y'know, Gin, I like you 'cos you never seem to want to do anything. God, I get tired of those female shits always making a fuss about being a woman; or wanting to be caring, or do a job, or have children, or get a husband, or something. My Auntie was like that – always striving away – drove me Dad crazy. Men are damn good at just hanging about. Women always feel they've got to be strong characters – that kind of balls. Why shouldn't we just do fuck-all, same as them – same as you too? I admire you for it ever so – do, reely.'

So formulated, Alice's view of herself did seem an agreeable one; but Ginnie no longer felt greatly complimented by her praise. She would like to have asked more about Auntie, and how she drove Dad crazy; but Alice's provenance, however full and fascinating, seemed somehow too fabulous, and even unbelievable, for any standard query to penetrate it. Besides, she was already starting off again, in her rambling reassuring monologue.

'S'fact though, Gin. We Aussie girls been known to get a bad press sometimes, even down under. Why, I met a New Zealander once told me that we know nothing about sex – more like kangaroos, the bastard said. Sounds bad, don't it? – coming from a Kiwi like that? But, you won't believe this, I knew another guy – Pom, bloody handsome feller, and real virile with it y'know – no poofter. He told me that when he saw Aussie girls round a pool, nearly nothing on, he thought there must be something wrong with him. None of the usual reactions. That's funny too, because I had a girlfriend – stunning girl – we called Try Again Susan. That was because she used to tell us how she was having a go with this hell of a guy in bed once; and he couldn't get himself anywhere, or her either. In the end she had to tell him, "Come on, try again." We all laughed like drains of course. She thought it was funny too. But I've never seen a girl with more of what it takes, you'd think.'

Alice broke off and appeared to muse on the bizarre frailties to which the sexual instinct was prone. Ginnie only hoped she was not going to be required to 'try again' herself, like the eponymous Susan.

But the other seemed to have lost interest even in the ever-interesting topic. She got up and strolled about in the very limited space, fiddling with the back of her coarse dark hair and humming a little song. 'Who was that feller I saw you with this morning?' she asked. 'Staying here, isn't he?'

Ginnie was tempted to say 'Why don't you ask him if he wants a bonk,' but she forbore. 'He's called Mark Brassey,' she stated instead. 'He asked me out to dinner last night.'

'Did he now? Anything going to come of that?'

The nice thing for Ginnie had been their comfortable knowledge that nothing was going to come of it. But she could not help being a little pleased by what appearances might have suggested to Alice.

'He comes here on holiday he told me.'

'I got a lovebird from him this morning. Didn't tell you that, did he?'

So Mark was smitten too. Remembering his precipitate departure, Ginnie thought it likely that she might not be dining with him again. Everyone but her seemed to be hurrying to join the real world, or to be there already. But, come to think of it, perhaps she had now joined it herself?

'What is he then? Some sort of lawyer?'

'A solicitor I think he said.'

Mark Brassey had, she remembered, mentioned this during their comfortable evening together. She had not enquired further, nor had he asked her about her job and daily life. That had been restful.

Alice seemed to lose interest. Flopping back on the bed, which now seemed more hers than Ginnie's, she put her long legs up and did the splits. Ginnie too was dressed by now; in an odd way she had begun to find the other's company soothing, erratic as it certainly was. Fatalistically, she contemplated losing both her new friends almost simultaneously, and to each other. Well, there was nothing she could do about it. There would probably be other acquaintances to be made in the hotel.

Alice sat up and began to scratch one of her toes. 'Growing crook, this bugger,' she remarked. 'Got any good scissors, Gin? Be an angel if you have and cut the nile for me. I can never reach the bastards properly.'

While she knelt and attended to the proffered toes Ginnie forgot all about Alice's vulgarity, even the little joke about the thirty quid. Besides, she thought, whatever appearances might suggest, her friend was *not* vulgar: indeed there was an awkward sort of refinement about her, comic but beguiling. What she said, and what she apparently did, made no difference. She

45

felt now at last quite familiar with Alice: just girls together, gossiping idly in the bedroom.

Alice thanked her, flexed her toes and yawned and started to go down the steps, swinging her sandals. She stuck one foot in Ginnie's basin and ran the water. Ginnie followed, and saw, suddenly visible above Alice, the dark bulk of the *Achille Lauro*. She shuddered, and clutched Alice round the waist, her face against the other's shoulderblade. Alice stood like a stork, with a foot cocked up in the basin, and made comforting noises. 'Never say die, kid,' she said, contriving to reach Ginnie a kiss over her shoulder. 'You've got me behind you.'

The comforting sounds began to hum themselves as the little song she had sung earlier. 'I had my baby on the kitchen table,' hummed Alice in a husky contralto. 'That's a song we used to sing when I was little, Gin. Made us laugh no end.'

They looked out on the liner together, dark in the afternoon glare, with smokeless funnels. 'The song's clever, you see, Gin,' explained Alice with quaint laboriousness, 'because you can tike it different wies.' Ginnie saw, after a moment or two, that this could indeed be the case.

*

And it might be the case that she had Alice behind her; but for the rest of the day Ginnie felt very forlorn. There was no sign of Mark downstairs, and she had her dinner in the hotel, almost glad of the two old ladies, to whose table she was again allotted. They made her welcome with soft incurious serenity. Yet she suspected they had noticed her absence the night before. They probably noticed everything, at least everything native to their outlook and their way of life. That would not include Alice, and her activities; but no doubt they had seen Mark Brassey around, and had placed him with unspoken accuracy.

Ginnie hadn't the heart to go out after dinner. She wandered into the small sitting-room, and on an impulse took out *Ramazan the Rajah* from the bookcase. *It is many moons, oh my beloved, since you came to me, said Ramazan, his great dark eyes burning into Virginia's, so that she felt herself swooning as she sat in the gharry.*

How could she escape this man, whose spell over her was as potent as ever?

How indeed. Ginnie smiled to herself, but not happily. She supposed Ramazan and his Virginia lived in the same world as she did, or had come to do. She could certainly recognise their feelings. Only they seemed confident of the nature of their world – confident or oblivious, it hardly mattered which – while her own world seemed now to have got so mixed up as to become demoralising and incomprehensible. She wondered if other people had this sense of living in an ordinary timeless state, much like her own; while they were vaguely bothered, if not positively badgered, by a consciousness of the whole apparatus of contemporary life. Aids and crime, single mothers and what she thought of as libs of various kinds, the papers and the TV and sex and violence and racism – all seemed to loom up and come upon her, and yet pass by.

She supposed the place where she lived must be already in the past, even though it was an intermediate past, not as far back as where her mother lived. The mixture of comforting predictability and mild excitement which she had hoped of her holiday, as of previous ones, had exploded into an unstable compound, in which other sorts of consciousness had invaded hers. About Alice she couldn't think at the moment. The simple romantic privacies, familiar to her own life and person, seemed to have run into Alice with stunning force, like a quiet pedestrian into a speeding yuppie. She was left sitting dazed on the kerb, with her mental possessions strewed about her. She would recover in time no doubt.

Was the Alice of the bonks and the libidinous tourists – the Saudis and the Japs – the same girl whose toenails she had been cutting? Of course. Why not? As she sat with *Ramazan the Rajah* in her lap Ginnie found herself shrugging her shoulders, like a Frenchman or an Italian. She realised she was sitting in the same uncomfortable little armchair in which Mark had sat when she first saw him. And about Mark there *was* a pang. He had seemed predictable: on their brief acquaintance the word had seemed exactly to suit him. Unusual as it had been, their evening together had reassured her, like the restaurant with its avuncular waiters in their long white aprons.

47

She had known where she stood with Mark. But now he was gone; for Ginnie was in no doubt about that. Something in the way he had apologised and left her that morning had been positive, terminal. Her version of him was evidently not his own, closely as the two had seemed to correspond when they were together. For all she knew he often behaved like that: leaving one woman he had acquired, for the use he had made of her, for another who offered something much more stimulating.

And yet Ginnie didn't really think so. Left her he may have done – insofar as he had ever got hold of her – and yet such behaviour did not seem characteristic. Something had happened to Mark. In fact Alice had happened. And quite suddenly, as she thought of Alice, Ginnie could not hold back the tears. Averting her face from the people there she went quickly through the main lounge and took to the stairs. With the tears still streaming she looked for the handkerchief in her bag, and found there the banana left over from yesterday's lunch. Once safe in her room she ate it. That restored her; and she began the still more restorative process of washing her things.

If she had indeed 'lost' Mark he seemed ready to remain unaware of it. As she came down for breakfast, the thought of which had cheered her when she woke, as it always did on holiday, she found him sitting in the lounge as if waiting for her to appear. He looked like a man carrying an awkward burden, of considerable weight, who was looking for somewhere to put it down. The sight of him filled Ginnie with foreboding. He was going to spoil her breakfast.

And she already knew all, she felt. Just as he had spotted her as the person to take out to dinner, a person who would cause him no trouble, so he might now wish to confide in her about Alice.

But here it seemed she misjudged him. Clenching her teeth in anticipation she approached him to say good-morning. He replied, but only just, and with an absent-minded and dismissive smile. Coming out of breakfast she found him still there, seated in the uncomfortable easy chair, his fingertips lightly touched together. More chagrined than relieved, she saw he had no intention of having a word; and she went on upstairs.

Standing at the window, and looking down unhopefully at

the beach for a sign of Alice, she saw that the *Achille Lauro* was almost imperceptibly on the move. The big oldfashioned-looking ship receded backward into the bay, as if on a voyage to a still more distant past. She must in her time have carried so many cruise passengers, one or two of whom could now be seen waving a scarf or a handkerchief from the deck. The sight of the ship gave Ginnie the shudders as usual; less from a sense of the horror that had once been on board her, first heard of from Alice's throwaway mouth, than from the knowledge of the disappearance of that horror into an indifferent present.

Who on board at this moment cared, or even knew, about it? Helpless in the equal disappearance of her modest holiday hopes, she felt herself drowned in different lives and beings, all linked in obscure but impenetrable fellowship. She would rather they were not. Mark had a purpose now; and so had the terrorists and the surgeons, the politicians, poets and TV performers. In her black abandoned after breakfast mood, she had a vision of the insane world ending as one vast National Health hospital, with patients kept unendingly alive on pigs' livers and the kidneys of chimpanzees, while they listened on the radio to 'serious' discussions, and to ever more 'exciting' new developments in the arts. Perhaps the poor old man in the wheelchair had been lucky to have been pushed overboard when he had been.

Come come – this was no mood to be in on her holiday. But she still felt linked, in that horrifying fellowship, to what was really going on in the world. It was going on with Alice, somewhere down in the unknown bowels of the building: in the *Achille Lauro*, now sidling inexplicably sideways, as if in sly retreat from something on the shore; in the tips of Mark Brassey's fingers, poised together down in the empty lounge. And she had hoped to come on holiday, to Sorrento, for what was *not* really going on.

A large party of holidaymakers – what a demanding occupation it could seem to be – came bustling and exclaiming past down below, skirting the blue water as they strove towards some bus or boat stop where an outing was to be assembled. A beautiful Norwegian courier with a little national flag counted them purposefully as she strode along behind: like a shepherdess, Ginnie thought, who only lacked a dog, a crook, and a sunbonnet to be painted beside her chattering flock by a modern Watteau.

Wearily she considered that she had better fix up something of the kind for herself. She could not face it today: she wanted time to recover, to see what was going to happen, or not happen. But tomorrow it had better be Ravello, or Amalfi, or Positano. Experience told her there would probably be someone on boat or bus with whom a temporary relation could be established. One that would fend off demoralisation, and yet be swiftly and painlessly relinquishable.

Below her the dark uncertain outlines of the nymphaeum underlay the clear green water. Ginnie knew now what it was, or at least what it was conjectured to be; for even in the midst of the day's events she had found time to glance through the guide the hotel had given her.

Normally she would have been really quite interested; but today it failed altogether to cheer her, any more than did yesterday's fisherman, who might have been an old friend by now. He stood there meditatively in his little boat, further offshore this morning, running a dark loose material – too fine to be a net it looked – through his hands. Out of it leapt something that wriggled and flashed in the sun for a moment, and then vanished in the bottom of the boat. The fisherman paid it no heed, neither did he seem preoccupied. He stood there peaceably; and Ginnie envied him for a moment, feeling that he must be as outside things as she was, but unaware of the whole business, and therefore unbothered by it. Ginnie automatically gathered her things together and left the room.

*

Mark Brassey's room was in the older part of the hotel. It had a high ceiling, discoloured in places, a bed that creaked deferentially as he got into it, and a cavernous little bathroom with a mottled floor in imitation marble. It faced right away from the sea; and outside the window, from which could be seen the top of a dusty palm-tree, were old wooden shutters which worked, and which he often closed in the afternoon.

It was afternoon now. The shutters were closed, with the glare

50

coming through the cracks between them into the cool darkness of the room, as he sat meditating in the armchair.

That morning Alice had proposed to him.

Like most selfish and self-contained men he was interested in other people without really believing they existed. The first sight of Alice had indeed had a strong effect on him – the effect Ginnie had noted. The effect was what he cared about, and was now thinking about. Alice's existence had in a second become his own. Her own life must for that reason be utterly non-existent.

So much he took for granted. The point was that she had fallen for him: of that he was certain. He had been seen as he was, in all his perfection, for the first time. Someone, he was now convinced, had at last realised that the wonderful and indeed the essential thing, the only thing in the universe that mattered at all, was Mark Brassey.

Of course he did not actually feel like that. Mark was a shrewd man, who in his own way had made a success of his life. Only for a very few seconds did he experience the revelation that he was the person, the only one in the world, who mattered to Alice: but they were important seconds none the less. Later on, by the time she popped the question as he put it to himself, tasting the phrase with relish, he had reached a much more settled view of things.

He had realised, for example, that marriage must have become for Alice a question of self-respect. An aunt of his, for whom he had once had some liking, exhibited the same characteristic. So at least it now occurred to him. She had been married three times, since it was clearly the appropriate setting for her lifestyle. Mark could remember almost nothing of her husbands, one of whom was still around.

And, strangely enough, he did not find it at all difficult to reconcile his first conviction that Alice was the only woman to have experienced this total recognition of him, with a realisation that for some reason of her own she wanted to get married: more specifically, to marry him. On the contrary, the two notions seemed made for each other. Alice should be married, as a bird must fly. And as he was – well – the only real person in the world, naturally she would fly to him.

Mark Brassey did not put it to himself in quite that way.

51

Instead he was ruminating about the other women in his life. None of them, of course, had displayed Alice's astonishing characteristics, her absolute and impeccable response. On the contrary, they had all been feeble in various ways: feebly preoccupied with their own tedious activities: quite unable to conceal how little they were really aware of him. One or two of them had even amused him by this trait. He had fended off their intentions absent-mindedly, while continuing to make whatever use of them seemed suitable.

Lately he could hardly be bothered with them at all. He had got into the regular habit of this Italian holiday because it suited what he sometimes thought of as his new model sex life; one more satisfactory, by and large, than that of the bedsits and sofas he had once been made free of. When enquiring, or rather not enquiring, the previous night about Miss Thornton's sex life, he had not been dishonest in suggesting that he, no less than her, belonged to a category who had become displaced in the world of today.

A felicitous displacement. In his own case at least. Women had now come to occupy an unusual but satisfying role in his life, even if a marginal one. There were always women about here, lured by the romantic associations of Sorrento. Getting on for middle-age as a general thing, and in couples. It amused him to take one of them out to dinner, generally the most promising of a pair; and the initial pleasure lay in seeing how readily the one he chose accepted his invitation without reference to her companion.

But the real fun, the prelude to a solitary climax when back in his own room, lay in the puzzlement of the women themselves. What was he after? Their uncertainty on this point, their growing doubt about its being the usual pass they might expect, and were in consequence prepared for, was for Mark a bizarre but reliable aphrodisiac.

It had been particularly successful the previous night, after he had taken out Miss Thornton. Surprising in a way; because it had been clear to him early on that she had dropped her guard, if indeed it had ever been up, and was happily enjoying the evening on her own terms. Which, up to a point, were his too.

It had been an engaging experience, and one he had especially enjoyed. For there was no doubt that she was unusually – if quite accidentally – out of the ordinary. He had enjoyed popping, or almost popping, that question, on the spur of the moment. Although he had already intuited, and anticipated, her reply, he had been entertained by the form in which she had made it.

He had been further amused by the way in which she had previously been bothered by that other harmless and more domestic question: the question of whether she could or could not have made the *cervelli fritti*. For a second or two then she clearly *had* wondered if he were investigating her capabilities as a partner. It had amused him then, and subsequently, that she thought he too was flummoxed by the tiny misunderstanding. She had felt for him as well as for herself. A woman of sympathy: definitely an amiable woman. It pleased him that she had soon realised her mistake.

Their unexpected *rapport* had not only excited him at a later stage of the evening, when after padding about on the cool floor of the bathroom he had turned expectantly into his solitary bed, but had even made him feel friendly to her morning suggestion of a walk. And, by George, it was just as well he had! Alice had risen out of the pavement before him.

In the cool dark room he contemplated that new phenomenon for a minute or two, with a smile of which he was barely conscious creasing his eyes and face. But then, not altogether expectedly, his thoughts returned to that Miss Thornton. How well they had seemed to understand each other, yet how little she knew what he had been up to, later on last night! That thought made him smile faintly, as he imagined her going up to her room on the seaward, the tourist side, all contented within after the dinner and the wine, and cleaning her teeth. Thinking about him a bit, Mark flattered himself, before a night of chaste and sound repose. Oddly enough, he recalled, he had never found out her first name. With most of his dinner ladies it was Penny or Jill right from the start. They proffered their names with eagerness, and used his own at once with equal facility. It gave them an option on future intimacy and the security of an immediate chumminess. But the Thornton had never addressed him by name, nor he her.

Time to stop further reflection about her. Of course he had

53

behaved in a cavalier manner (but weren't cavaliers much politer than roundheads?) by leaving her like that, on their morning walk. The fact was, the sight of Alice had staggered him.

Just to remember it made him get up, and gaze unseeingly, through the gap in the shutters, at the motionless and dusty leaves of the old palm-tree. He had been seized on the spot with a curiosity so intense that he could do nothing else.

He must see her, talk to her. A man with a weakness for measured self-congratulation, Mark was filled with insensate pride as he recalled the helplessness of that moment.

Back at the hotel he lost no time in directing his enquiries through reception, where they were familiar with his methods. This time it was not a fellow-guest he wished to get in touch with, but a girl, an Australian girl (Mark could hardly have failed to notice that accent) who worked in the hotel. Yes, there was such a girl: and the young hotel clerk, his olive features quite expressionless, dipped down a moment behind the desk and came up with a bit of paper in his hand.

'*Per lei*, Signor,' he said, with the authority of his own tongue; they all knew Mark spoke passable Italian.

On the paper were a few words scrawled in pencil. 'I must see you at once.'

No signature. No signature was needed. He saw that.

It was he, Mark, who had to see this girl at once. And now it seemed she must do the same. The coincidence was colossal: it was awe-inspiring. He remained standing motionless by the desk. He had felt giddy. Taking no further notice of him, the hotel clerk was turning over papers as if nothing had happened.

Mark was methodical, not romantic. At school a report on him, which he still remembered his father reading out, had said, 'Brassey is the most capable and reliable boy in the sixth this year.' His father, a self-made man, had been pleased.

That capability remained; had been enhanced no doubt; and also the power of consideration that went with it. Brassey, the 'cold-hearted bastard', as a friend had once admiringly described him, would have wasted no time if this girl had remained indifferent; or even if she had made it clear, at their meeting, that a one-night stand might not be unacceptable to her.

54

That was all old familiar stuff. He no longer bothered with it. But here was the real thing. He had suffered a *coup de foudre* (though Mark did not use the expression to himself, his Italian being more workable than his French) and this girl – amazingly – had suffered one too.

She must see him.

She must see him, certainly. For what did not strike him, then or later, as being in the least relevant. It turned out she wanted to marry him, and for Mark that made perfect sense. There was an absolute oldfashioned rightness about it. She wanted to get married – a perfectly sensible thing for a girl in her position and with her background to do – and here, in the street, she meets what is obviously the perfect husband. Mark was a man of figures, of calculations and probabilities. To him it all made sense.

And no doubt to Alice too. She had made that clear when she met him, later on that morning. Mark was struck by her repose. A man of no excitability himself, he had viewed with awed relish her own complete lack of fuss and bother.

Alice, indeed, had made a second conquest. Given the difference of sex and temperament, as it had been with Ginnie, so with Mark. In both cases, their private selves, the sturdy comfortable little illusions that normally kept them going, had been abruptly invaded by an unforeseen reality.

The consequences for Ginnie had been that short sleep in the early morning; and the look that Alice had given her when, propped on a big white arm, she had gazed meditatively into Ginnie's face in the half-light of the little alcove. Mark did not know it, but Ginnie, unobserved in her room, was uttering a sob – a wail more than a sob – as she thought of that moment.

Mark uttered no sobs. On the contrary. His features, habitually unexpressive, now relaxed into a dreamy smile. Alice had looked at him in much the same way she had looked at Ginnie. But she had said: 'I'd love to marry you, you know.'

*

It was, as usual, a fine evening. Touched by the last rays of sun Vesuvius glowed a delicate pink, making a belated concession

55

to all those vanished Victorian water-colourists. The outline of the nymphaeum darkened and disappeared under the water.

Ginnie still sat on in her bathing-dress, her towel beneath her. She had determined, perversely, to sunbathe; even though she didn't like it, and was pretty sure, like Alice, that it wasn't good for her skin. But because Alice had said that, she would do it none the less: she would try to exorcise the memory of the face that had leaned over her in the morning. But now the sun was going down, and the strand was deserted. A fisherman was still there, far out, but the *Achille Lauro* was long gone. The slaty waters of the roadstead were empty.

It was at this moment that Alice appeared with Mark. They drifted gently along the edge by the nymphaeum, deep in talk. So deep, in fact, that Alice stopped at one moment, and emphasised a proposition by putting one large forefinger into the hollow of her other hand. Mark inclined his head towards her; and then they strolled on, reached the steps at the end, went slowly up them and disappeared into the hotel gardens.

Ginnie was sure they had not seen her. They bothered to see nothing but each other – so much was clear. During the next few days she saw them again at odd moments, between her own excursion visits to Ravello, and Amalfi, and Positano. She saw them in the town together, and once sitting equally deep in conversation, in deckchairs in the garden. Alice seemed to have abandoned altogether whatever work she was supposed to be doing at the hotel.

Ginnie continued to wonder; but now only rather numbly. She had got over Alice, she felt; and she felt it as strongly and as conscientiously as she could. She had teamed up with quite a nice woman whose friend was laid low with sunburn, after incautious exposure at the bathing place.

'... *And* everywhere else we've been to. She *will* go in; and then lie about, making such hard work of it, you know – sort of really concentrating on it.'

'*What* bad luck for her – and on holiday. I *am* sorry.'

The holidaymaking woman had welcomed Ginnie's sympathy, making her a substitute for the invalid friend. 'An Australian girl who works here,' she went on, 'such a lovely person – she offered to get the doctor of the hotel you know – but my friend didn't want that.'

Ginnie had been taken up to see the friend, who lay prostrate under a sheet in an odour of calamine and witchhazel. 'I can't *bear* anything over me,' the friend said plaintively. 'But I'm not going to let this spoil it.' Sunglasses – she couldn't bear the light in her eyes – made her cramped little face expressionless, but Ginnie had warmed to her resolve, and was touched by their pleasure at the visit. She could, at least, it seemed, be a bit of comfort to others.

But what about her own holiday – had that been spoilt? She had looked forward to predictable pleasures, and some very unpredictable things had turned up instead. Remembering, as she sat at meals, the food and drink at Mark's restaurant, she found herself regretting him, in a way, more than she did Alice. She forced her thoughts to shy off Alice as resolutely as the friend upstairs had resolved not to let her holiday be ruined. Just how this was to be done, in either case, was not entirely clear; but Ginnie felt that at least she must make a good try.

She was all the more unprepared, therefore, for what took place one morning. Concentrating on small routines, she was just setting out for her morning stroll in the town when she saw Alice running towards her, and shrieking out her name with her old Aussie joyousness. 'Now where you bin, you bad girl?' she yelled, jogging on the spot and seizing Ginnie by both arms above the elbow. 'Markie and I bin looking for you all over.'

Reminded by the cheerful grin of the way Alice had plumped down on the bed and demanded thirty quid, Ginnie said something about having been on excursions. She was determined not to seem to have hung around, hoping to see them.

But Alice was taking no notice. 'You've hidden yourself away,' she cried, in mock accusation, 'and just when we wanted to tell you our news. Oh, Gin darling, it's good to see you! And of course we wanted you to be the first to hear.'

As if on cue, Mark Brassey came strolling down the hotel steps, not precipitately like Alice, but none the less he was obviously as excited as she was. Both seemed to fizz with a complacency they had been bottling up for days. Abandoning

57

Ginnie's arms Alice now seized one of Mark's, and affected to swing up and down on its unagitated length.

'Let's tell her the news, Markie,' she shrilled. 'We want her to be the first, don't we? Gin's got to be a real pal, haven't you Gin?'

Relinquishing Mark she seized her pal again, round the waist this time, and executed a few dance steps.

'You'll never guess, Ginnie darling.'

Funnily enough, Ginnie had guessed several days before. There was really nothing to guess about. 'No I can't guess,' she said, obliging with a mystifiedness which was partly self-respect. She was not going to let on that either of them had been in her head at all.

Releasing her again, Alice capered about solo.

'Shall we tell her now, Markie?'

Mark gazed benevolently on both of them: clearly the man who is above such things but is pleasurably amused by the antics of women. He easily tolerated Alice in this tempestuous vein, but he preferred the way she had been with him during recent days. Alice had charmed him not only by her modesty but by her good sense, her business sense, even. For the first time, when talking to a woman, Mark found himself actually becoming absorbed in the topic under discussion: and some not at all uninteresting things had been discussed.

But now he was content to let his fiancée play at being a girl, as he thought of it. Nothing of the sort went on when they were alone together. And nothing else went on either. That was profoundly, if rather mysteriously, gratifying to him. Having decided he was the only man in the world for her, Alice had seemed to sink into a deep bliss of conviction, a nirvana in which nothing more needed to be done.

After dining together their first day at his restaurant they had strolled back to the hotel, and, putting on a show of gallantry, he had invited her up to his room. Alice had actually blushed. She had squeezed his hand and thanked him with what seemed artless warmth, as if her fiancé had paid her the supreme compliment. But would he mind? – would he mind very much? – if all such joys were kept for their close and shining future?

Mark didn't mind at all. He was enchanted by the intimacy she reposed in him. A lesser girl might have sought to be eager about sex, or at least nervous of hurting his feelings by any appearance of hesitation. Alice seemed to display the kind of sense which showed how much she wanted him.

She wanted him as a husband. Anything else would have been the merest irrelevance. But for the next few days, none the less, he continued to be fascinated by her demeanour about sex. Former diversions with the tourist ladies he had taken out to supper were nothing to it. She asked him to take her to Capri – a little engagement outing – and so they went on the *aliscafo* (Ginnie, as it happened, was on her bus-trip to Positano that day) and stayed the night at a pension in the most picturesque part of the island, run by a German couple. In the years he had been coming to Italy Mark had never been to Capri, and never had the smallest intention of going.

But now the idea seemed delightful. As soon as they got off the boat Alice took his hand, and they walked together like two children, with Alice the taller and elder sister. That amused him greatly – it was so novel an experience – and still hand in hand they had gone into the German pension, where she instructed him in a whisper both soft and loud to ask for two single rooms. The proprietress had been surprised, but eyed them none the less with respect. Obviously a *hochanständige Paar*. While necessarily familiar with modern lifestyles the two middle-aged Germans could recall the more discreet days of bourgeois tourism. Alice was clearly a good girl, and they smiled on her with almost parental fondness. And was the gentleman her intended? Alice blushed prettily and said he was. Mark seemed to them the timeless Englishman: decorous, neuter, obscurely but never offensively condescending. He too enjoyed and was amused by their approval.

In the evening they had sat with everyone else in the little main square. Alice was all aflutter with interest in the haggard men in immaculate blazers who strolled about the square on the lookout. Since it was so obvious who they were looking out for, and why, she felt quite ready to be voluble in her queries. If those middle-aged men had been chasing up the girls she would have made no comment; but gay men seemed a fair target for premarital vivacity. Naturally she wanted to talk about everything,

59

without reserve, to the dear bloke who would soon be her spouse.

Mark had not been deceived by her for a moment. But nothing gave him more pleasure than Alice's attempts to deceive him. It was so warm a compliment: and it showed the yet more gratifying motive behind the compliment. She deceived him because she must marry him; and the age-old manoeuvre had become transfigured for Mark into something like the moment when Adam had first reached out and touched the white hand of Eve.

After their dinner there was a thunderstorm. The Italian tourists in their multi-coloured shorts put on transparent mackintoshes, or got soaked in their singlets with great good-nature, chattering and laughing together like toucans in a tropical forest. Alice and Mark got wet too, had a *grappa* in a bar, and arrived back at the pension among the pinetrees running and laughing, with their coats over their heads, and a scream or two from Alice as her feet went into a puddle.

'*Casa Wagner*,' Mark had read solemnly, as they stood waiting to be let in, arm in arm in the downpour. '*Ein friedliches Eckchen in herrlichen Natur* ... I fancy that should mean a peaceful little corner in upper-class nature.'

'How sweet,' said Alice, as their host came to the door, with profuse apologies for his delay and for the bad weather. And as they went up to their rooms she had squeezed his hand and given him a chaste kiss on the mouth with her wet lips.

*

'We're going to get marri-ed,' chanted Alice, seizing Ginnie for the third time and doing a little ring o' roses with her.

Ginnie did what she could, and felt she had acquitted herself respectably. Mark still gazed benevolently on them both, and Ginnie was aware that he was watching her performance with pleasurable expectation. He would want to know how she really felt. Alice poured out their plans. How they had clicked at once; how they had decided to get married as soon as they were back in London. 'Oh, I just love all that old stuff,' she enthused. 'They say folks don't get married now, but I don't go for that. I've just been waiting for Mr Right to come along and here he is – eh,

Markie?' She dug her intended in the ribs with a big elbow, as if demonstrating that he was as solid as he looked, and as full of marriageable matter.

'You darling!' she screamed at Ginnie, 'I knew you'd be so wonderful!' Then suddenly breaking off she fled away, shouting something they couldn't catch.

Mark and Ginnie confronted one another. 'Well, what do you think?' he said, in such reasonable accents that he might have really wanted to know. How unlike the old Mark of peaceful smiles and tranquil non-queries! Unnerved by the difference, Ginnie found herself replying in similar vein, with a question that sounded absurd to herself as she spoke it.

'Will she look after you all right?'

Mark seemed less amused by this than amazed; and she felt as surprised as he was. But at least her question effectively startled him out of any appearance of gloating over how she, Ginnie, would respond to their news.

Further communication was interrupted by the return of Alice, who now tore down the steps of the hotel waving a bottle of what turned out to be *Asti Spumanti*, while a waiter hurried after her carrying glasses. He opened the bottle with a flourish, but, as he prepared to bow out, Alice seized hold of him too. 'Have one for us now – come on Marco!' she cried. 'Markie – this is Marco – an old friend of mine. Ginnie, Marco's a real sport. He got this booze out of the bar for us. He'll do you a good turn any time, won't you, Marco?'

Marco supposedly assented, with an embarrassed grin, seeming from the native angle to feel an element of impropriety in Alice's inclusion of himself in the celebration. His English namesake appeared to feel the same. But Alice raised her glass, and they all had to follow suit.

'Brought me kodak too,' she told them, producing a small camera. 'Just press this little tit here, Marco.' She took hold of Ginnie with one arm and Mark with the other.

'Mark sweetie, I know you're the condemned man, but try to look happy this once. OK. Now you press the tit, and Marco, come here. We'll have one with you and my pal Ginnie; and I won't be the gooseberry – I'll just be hanging around the edges.'

She peered over their shoulders, with an arm around each,

and Mark impassively recorded the moment. Then he handed the camera to Ginnie and took his betrothed's arm with an oddly dignified gesture. Marco scurried away to his duties in the hotel.

*

It was Ginnie's last day. After Mark and Alice had given her their 'news' time had seemed to pass quite easily and more quickly, although she had hardly seen them again. She had been to Capri on a day outing with the two friends. It had not been a great success, because the sufferer was still weak from the effects of sunburn. And by the time they had got up to the square, and failed for what seemed a long time to find chairs at a café (they had not noticed the men in blazers, who were perhaps not around at that hour) it seemed almost time to begin the arduous journey back to the quayside. They were all nervous – the invalid friend especially so – in case they should miss the ancient steamer and be left for the night on the island.

Ginnie would have liked to see San Michele, which she had read about; but the bus advertisements for it were confusing, and her companions not interested. Quite accustomed by her travels to outings which consisted of going somewhere and coming back, she was not really disappointed. It satisfied all of them to feel they had been to Capri; and a pleasant relief to get back on the steamer again, with the jolly incurious Italian crowd all around them, and see for the second time the famous 'Leap of Tiberius', as they slowly rounded the steep cliff at the tail of the island.

For the second time the boat's loudspeaker told them how the wicked emperor had ordered those who offended him to be flung from its summit; and Ginnie was again asked by her friends to explain: they had not quite got there the first time. The loudspeaker's version in English was not easy to comprehend, but fortunately Ginnie was already familiar with the legend from the same guide which had told her about the nymphaeum at Sorrento.

Her new friends now listened avidly to Ginnie's rather sketchy account of the monster of vice, and his imperial depravities. At dinner-time in the hotel, where they by now formed a

62

regular table for three, renewed chat on the topic produced an unwonted degree of animation, making up for the insipid meal and the unexciting visit. But in the dark of the early morning Ginnie had her first nightmare at Sorrento. She dreamed a tall nude shadow had come up the steps to her bed, and carried her down to the balcony where both had been sucked over the edge, Ginnie helpless in the arms of the phantom. She was weightless in the dream as well as powerless, and the white ghost seemed to blow her like a leaf. The drop was as high in her dream as the cliff on Capri; and though she weighed nothing she fell like a stone.

She woke up writhing and mewing; and yet instinctively clutching for comfort at the place in the bed where Alice had been.

But breakfast saw the dream almost gone; and so strange are the uses of night fear that she enjoyed her coffee and bun all the more for it. Holiday compensations: always as homely as they were unexpected. And what was she going to do on her last day?

That question was soon solved for her. Mark and Alice, glimpsed only once or twice since they had told her the great news, bore down on her as she stood with her new friends by the reception desk, making a final selection of post-cards. The friends still had a few days of holiday left, and no excursion plans had been made at breakfast time: now they watched this new development in curiosity and with mute reproach. It was clear they felt a little abandoned in favour of the more exotic pair, whom they eyed with the stoic resignation those haphazardly connected on holiday feel for what seems a closer and more intimate bond. As she was borne off, Ginnie made a faint attempt to introduce her new friends; but Alice was burbling at high pitch and took absolutely no notice. Mark only spared them the brief leisurely glance of a man who, in his previous incarnation, might have detached one from the other as an evening's dinner partner.

'Gin! – you absolutely *must* come and see what I've been kitting meself out with! Now you're not going to believe this, but I've got me wedding-dress already. Isn't that a scream? Y'know, all that big-time church stuff. Veil and head-dress and all – satin shoes – lime-green satin – that's the colour of the dress did I tell you? And this silk taffeta ruching all over – it's a dream! And all so cheap! Kind of second-hand, but who cares?'

She paused, not so much for breath as to give Ginnie a boisterous kiss on the top of the head. Involuntarily Ginnie remembered how tall the phantom in her dream had been.

'It just struck me you know,' Alice burbled on, 'what a place to get it! 'Course the Eyties are mad over anything like that – do it all in style – all just wonderful and old. You know, like a costume drama on the box. You see there's a guy here told me all about this little place – a little sort of shop way down town where they do all sorts of things like that. I'm going to take you there, I promise. Oh, what a shime you're off tomorrow, Gin! We could have got *you* something, for when it's your turn! But wait till I show you now. I'll pick it all up from recep. It'll be there. The shop promised to send it!'

She belted on with Mark standing contentedly by, surveying her less with admiration now than with total confidence, as if she were an accredited Titian or Rembrandt, for which the full market price had been paid. Alice herself seemed to bask in his pride of possession.

But urgent matters now demanded purely feminine appraisal. Ginnie was hustled away to participate in them, with further details of the wedding costume sounding in her ears. Mark told them to get on with it. He would be somewhere around when they returned.

'Wait now – I'll bring it all to your place,' crowed Alice, thrusting her companion into the lift. 'I'll go back and pick it up. I want it all to be a surprise for you.' Ginnie reached her room, pondering the peculiarities of hotel life. The soothing tedium of the voyage to Capri, the 'leap' of old Tiberio, last night's dream: and this morning it was all this wedding chatter and taffeta ruchings in lime-green ... Alice was setting herself up for this single great event, of heraldic splendour. For some people, no doubt, the wedding was the thing; but how extraordinary that it should be the same for Alice, whose private life and being were otherwise so unimaginable. Ginnie thought of all the bonking that had gone on, and wondered how much Mark Brassey knew about it.

She must think about packing herself. She sat down on the bed for a moment, remembering the night they had both been in it. It seemed long ago, like faces bleached into anonymity by the strong light of a holiday snapshot. Would Alice send her the ones Mark and Marco had taken? At the thought of exchanging addresses and promising to meet again – all the last-minute labour of a holiday that was nearly done – a great enfeeblement came over her. It seemed impossible to imagine seeing Alice again. Mark might turn up, in his funny way, perhaps sitting next to her in the Tube, or spotted at the back of a Soho restaurant far inferior to his own one here, but the kind he would have to put up with in London life.

How would such a couple live together? – what would they do? Mark would go to his office. Would Alice run the house, arrange the flowers, look forward to a little addition to the family?

At the thought of Alice 'expecting', as her mother once used to say, Ginnie gave a sudden little hoot of laughter. It seemed too unreal, and yet why not for heavens' sake? Other girls did it – why not Alice? Why not Ginnie herself come to that, though presumably she would have to buck up about it, and so would Alice. Funnily enough, she could imagine Alice running the house and arranging the flowers more easily than she could see her leading the strenuous modern female life of jobs and equalities, car-boot sales and child-care centres. Alice did not seem to belong there, but somewhere older, more outlandish, more traditional even, and purely her own: in fact, in a curious way, somewhere more like Ginnie's own world.

An eruption at the door preceded Alice, no doubt loaded with wedding finery. But no – she only gave the impression of being so loaded: the personality of her coming was such that what she said would be seemed more real than what actually was. Any coming of hers was like that first appearance on the beach, when the actual manifestation of Alice must somehow have coincided with the buried fantasies in Ginnie's own mind?

But there was no time now for such speculation. The Australian girl flung her empty arms wide to illustrate the incompetence and treachery of which the most beguiling little shop in Sorrento had none the less proved capable.

'The bastards!' she wailed. 'And they promised faithfully to send it early this morning. I *wanted* you to see it all, Gin!' Her mouth puckered as if she was going to cry; and her burly arms returned on the rebound from their expansive and disgusted gesture, wrapping themselves round Ginnie's waist.

Physically prisoned in this fashion Ginnie stood it as best she could, uncomfortably conscious of the proximity of Alice's big emphatic mouth. Could this be the same woman to whose warm whiteness and darkness she had clung to in the bed, that morning nearly a fortnight back? As if growing conscious of her thought, Alice added to her discomfort by a squeeze: and her voice, suddenly plaintive, continued to lament the non-arrival of the wedding gear. Her eyes, searching Ginnie's, looked plaintive too. Uncertain apparently of what she found there, she put her big mouth close to the other's right ear and murmured huskily, 'So what about a cuddle, Gin?'

Ginnie's lack of desire for a cuddle was so complete that she marvelled that her big friend could remain unaware of it. How comic it must be, in marriage, to become pregnant as a result of total indifference to a cuddle, but no doubt it did happen. Still inside the jail of Alice's arms, she found her thoughts assuming fantastic shapes, like Proteus in his struggle for freedom. She beheld Alice, more than lifesize – but she was always more than lifesize – in her brilliant green wedding-dress. Lime-green Alice had said, and Ginnie was not sure quite what shade that was; but its tucks and gathers, or whatever they were, swirled in an emerald cascade round her hips and ankles as she dipped and swayed like a tree, curtsying with a wide smile to her Markie – a sturdy black figure standing well apart. Alice looked like a man in drag: but girls dressed up always did look like men in drag in Ginnie's experience – perhaps most women tended to look like men in whom some comic transformation had taken place?

As the vision faded she managed to detach herself, murmuring something about having to pack (there was no real need to yet of course) and advising Alice to go round to the shop at once, just in case something had gone wrong.

Privately she though the whole arrangement dotty. What could the woman be thinking of? Italian girls did not get married in green wedding-dresses. They wore white. No doubt there were reasons why Alice might prefer not to wear white, or might not feel suited to it, but why all this song and dance? Weren't the Italians, and Italian shops, wonderful, she found herself none the less saying. So clever, so quick ... but ...

Alice made no further reference to the cuddle. She looked grave for a moment, hugging her own arms in her dark purplish dress. Maroon, or rather 'marone', as she had called it, adding that it was her favourite colour. How few such chats they had had! But that was natural enough. Ginnie had barely met the girl before she had disappeared with Mark, bursting into view again on these few precipitate occasions.

Alice too now seemed aware of their fewness, and of the impending separation. She pursed her lips again as if about to cry; and for a sudden moment she seemed to Ginnie wholly real. Somewhere inside her a helpless graceless little creature was struggling and calling, longing to attract not the kind of attention people paid the outward phenomenon of the girl, but the kind that might be given to a kitten stuck under a manhole, or a tadpole struggling at the edge of the water it was trying to regain.

'Aw, Gin,' Alice pleaded, dispelling such notions, 'what time are you off then? and look, my sweet, I *reelly* don't like to ask, but would you do me a favour, a *reelly* big favour?'

Ginnie intimated, of course, that any favour within her current abilities could and would be done: and she found it a relief to promise this.

It was all this fabulous gear she had bought – for the whale of a wedding she was going to have. And Ginnie must, she really must, come to that! But of *course* she would. Alice knew she could rely on her.

And, as Ginnie had nothing but her holdall thing to carry – Alice glanced at this humble receptacle, lolling unzipped upon the floor – could she so *very* kindly bear to take back with her some of the stuff. It really would make all the difference – Alice herself had so much clobber to get home. Markie was going to try to change his air-ticket, but he mightn't be able to do that. And God she had such a mass of stuff! Would her Ginnie really not mind?

Her Ginnie was actually a bit relieved to find the great favour was no worse: though as soon as she had a chance to think about it she began to realise the tiresomeness of what she had let herself in for. One of her travel pleasures was to be able to take all she needed with her on the plane; so that she didn't have to wait at baggage reclaim, but could go straight through to the Underground. It was obvious to her that Alice's wedding gear, packed presumably in a box, would have to be checked in. Some travellers, of course, might get away with carrying it on with them, but Ginnie did not have that kind of nerve.

She remembered the joke about the thirty quid. Some kind of repayment was now being extracted – how deliberately was hard to say. And, thinking of the check-in annoyance, she had forgotten the further one of how and where the parcel was to be delivered.

But that, Alice assured her, was no problem. She knew Ginnie's flat was in Kensington – no distance from Earls Court, where Alice shared a pad on a casual basis with a couple of other Aussies. Just as soon as she was home she'd come round and pick the stuff up. Ginnie could do nothing else but agree; although she was by no means sure she wanted Alice to know exactly where it was she lived. And what further demands or advances might the girl not make when she showed up? Would Ginnie be drawn into her life, be sent on errands about her wedding, and perhaps be invited to it? Would she find herself among a train of other captives and servitors?

She did not at the moment feel equal to the prospect.

But at least the notion of the cuddle had become remote; even, it seemed, to Alice, who was now rambling on about one of her old boyfriends – God he was a real wag – who'd put up a notice saying 'Free Sheilas' outside the pad where Alice and her girlfriends lived. Ginnie laughed politely; and the other yawned and stretched herself, the sparse material of the 'marone' dress – in the bedroom sunlight it looked decidedly dyed – tightening across her bosom. Ginnie thought of the moment she had pulled that dress over her head and wondered neutrally if Alice had washed her bra yet.

Really that 'marone' dress itself seemed a curiously old-fashioned property. Surely the sort of girl Alice was might be expected to operate nowadays in stylish shorts and singlet? That crummy dress – Ginnie found herself thinking in the dated slang used by Alice herself, but didn't all slang tend to sound dated? – somehow went with the aubergine bikini itself. And of course, yes, with the green satin wedding attire, and all its ruches and tucks? All were somehow tawdry, improbable, and yet so much a part of Alice herself, as if vanished periods and lost displays had come again alive in her.

Alice was talking sense again. Ginnie would come out with them to dinner tonight, wouldn't she? Her last dinner, and Markie wanted her to come; and she was a real sport – a real sport to take all that clobber – and this sheila would never forget it, even when she was a happy married woman. And when she *was* a married woman her Gin must come and see them often ...

Now she must rush off and make sure that damned store had got the stuff ready. She'd stand over them. She'd stand in that quaint little place, and glare at the little old lady who ran it and her wrinkled-up son or whoever he was, until it was ready. So they'd see her at seven in the lobby?

When Alice had gone, Ginnie sat down on the bed, quite worn out. She would like a drink – the thought cheered her – and she would go out herself presently, and sit in her café and have a vermouth. How strange this intimacy that had come about, for intimacy she supposed it was. Yet it lacked the sense of desirable being, the sense that now urged her to go out and relax and have a drink. She felt in a way in love with Alice, at least at moments, but in another way she was quite indifferent to her; and the two states seemed to alternate without rhyme or reason.

Ginnie valued her contentment: indeed she relied upon it. But she knew its limitations, and was becoming more and more aware of them. It would risk complacency to feel she had had an adventure, and could now go back to normal life?

Well, all right, she would risk it. She would positively culti-vate complacency; she would be as smug as she could. In matters of the heart smugness is all? – or ought to be? And yet to have been taken over by Alice, to have become as it were one of her gang – that didn't thrill or gratify her but it gave her a solid feeling. It demarginalised her. Perhaps smugness was not all? She could, it seemed, be joined involuntarily and without trying to the human race, or at least to parts of it; and little as she had

69

previously considered the matter in this light she now found it to be something.

So they went out to dinner. Ginnie knew where they would be going, and of course she was right. They ate the *cervelli fritti*; they drank the *sangro de monte*; and in the morning Alice and Mark were there again to see her on the coach for Naples airport. Alice was carrying not one cardboard box but two, neatly wrapped and sellotaped. They were quite light and should not be too much trouble. It looked as if the little old lady had done a good job in packing up the wedding finery.

Both kissed her fondly as she boarded the bus. She felt she had known them all her life. But it was a relief when the bus started, and Alice began to wave. Before they disappeared Alice seized her fiancé in a humorous clinch, and raised a fist in salute as the bus heaved away.

Presently Ginnie had another pang. She had quite forgotten to say goodbye to her later, newer friends. It couldn't be helped. They had not exchanged addresses, and so that was that as far as they were concerned.

Ginnie, who had read many of them, published and unpublished, began to wonder on the plane how this would end if it were a novel. The trouble was that even on this unexpected trip she had only felt things for short periods, and now she had to admit that she felt nothing much. It did not even seem worth saying, like the lady in the French song, that she regretted nothing. There seemed nothing to regret. How would the story continue and what were its alternative endings? In any case she would have to see them again: at least she would have to see Alice.

Part Two

Interlude with an Overcoat

A S SOON AS he got off the train Tom was conscious of the cold. That was one thing he didn't expect. He had hardly been able to see out of the windows as the train rumbled the last bit over the causeway, sighed, and stopped.

And the train was hot. Stuffy perhaps rather than hot, but acceptable enough as he drowsed in his corner, peacefully conscious of the steady unfailing sound first of French and then of Italian conversation, and of the smell of real tobacco, instead of the sickly cardboard odour of English filter-tips. It was cheaper than flying it was said; and yet hardly cheap enough. If Pinky hadn't urged him, and even lent him thirty quid she no doubt needed herself, he couldn't have managed. Sedentary by nature, more than a trifle timid, Tom had none the less always longed to go to Venice; and the chance had come in the period between his thesis subject being accepted by the Graduate Board, and his having to get down to write it.

The thesis would of course not be about Venice. Its subject was competitive discourse in the field of modern poetics. Tom felt he would have no trouble having lots of ideas, although the topic had actually been suggested to him by his supervisor.

If only Pinky could, or would, have come with him. That at least was what he felt now, as he stood reluctantly on the platform, easing his rucksack on to his shabby blue-denimed shoulders. He even felt a strong desire to get back on the train, and the refuge of its stuffy warmth. But as if it might have suspected this, the train was already sliding very quietly back again, the way it had come. Tom was left alone on the platform.

At the time in fact he had really been rather glad Pinky had encouraged him, but didn't want to come herself. His small experience of being with other people on holiday had left him

71

fairly convinced that it was better to be on one's own. Even if the other person was one's fiancée? That must make a difference certainly; but although Tom adored the idea of having a fiancée, and that fiancée being Pinky, it was still as a practical matter better to be on one's own. Dealing with Pinky conversationally on a Venetian trip would be hard going in itself, he suspected. She would want to know things, and then would as abruptly lose interest in them; she would have sudden contradictory impulses when he was trying to pursue a sight-seeing programme, and would pull him impulsively into a discotheque, or a bar filled with deafening rock. And of course there were other considerations too. What, if anything, would she vouchsafe in the way of bed?

Plodding slowly up the platform, and quite uncertain what he would do when he came to the end of it, Tom pondered that question. Bothering about it would certainly have spoilt his concentration on Venice; but then would there have been anything to bother about, really? Pinky solved all such questions herself, and in her own masterful way. Masterful was certainly what Pinky was: right from the moment when she had given him a kiss like a smart tap on the nose, and shouted in his ear, 'Shall we get engaged?' They were in a disco at the time as it happened. Tom was so startled that he could only mumble, quite inaudibly with all the row going on; but Pinky had seemed quite unconcerned, looking cheerfully round them and humming something quite different from the music.

Tom had been enchanted by the unexpectedness of this. Pinky hadn't seemed to be that sort of girl at all. He had only been out with her a few times, having met her with a fellow student, whose girl was a friend of Pinky's. Tom had liked being liked. It was unusual with him where girls were concerned, even though he knew he was quite a personable young man. Somehow most girls seemed to grasp at once that he wasn't quite with it; but something about Pinky made him feel that even this could, in certain contexts, be a positive asset.

She was the older, of course. She told him once that she was twenty-eight, but he privately thought she might be more than that. Tom, who was twenty-two, didn't mind in the least. It seemed, on the contrary, quite a compliment that she should take this remarkable amount of interest in him, should actually want to marry him.

For Pinky had seemed to him at first the complete contemporary girl. Tom would have been less surprised and a good deal less enchanted if instead of saying, 'Shall we get engaged?' she had said, 'Shall we have a fuck?' Not that any of them had ever made such a suggestion to Tom, but he understood that was the sort of thing the girls were liable to say nowadays. Perhaps it was a matter of bravura rather than an actual invitation? Tom wouldn't have known, although he suspected that your really contemporary girl was a great deal more circumspect. In any case he wouldn't have liked it.

So he was both amazed and gratified when Pinky had suggested to him this bewitching alternative proposal. He had found her a Victorian ring at a pawnbroker's in the Strand: and she seemed to like it very much.

Pinky was distinctly a girl to ponder over; that was for sure. It gave him quite a pang of homesickness to remember the 'for sure' phrase: one she often used. He wished as he trudged up the platform that he was not alone, though in a funny way he felt he had come for her, like a knight performing a service for a lady. 'And you know you've always wanted to,' she had told him, getting the notes out of her purse and closing his fingers on them. Tom felt he loved her extremely at that moment, and he also longed for the time when he would be lying between those ample and muscular legs. Not that Pinky had ever indicated a readiness to receive him there, except tacitly in terms of the blest package deal of their now official future. Tom's attempts to embrace her had indeed so far fallen short even of an honest grapple: partly through his own diffidence, no doubt, but partly because Pinky, without seeming to try, had a way of disappearing from him at such moments, as if she were a reed or a laurel. She was addicted, however, to giving him sudden kisses on top of the head. No difficult feat for her, being such a tall girl.

A friend of Tom's who had met his Pinky assumed with natural envy that their relations were more conventionally intimate. A facetious fellow, he had quoted to Tom some rhyme about 'Oh what a form! Oh what a face! And she has orgasms all over the place' ... his own version, as he complacently pointed out, of the little Victorian jingle about the gipsy girl who did the fandango all over the place. Tom laughed of course, but he had secretly been very affronted.

His musings were abbreviated by the end of the long platform. Abruptly there presented itself before him a wide stretch of water, greener than he had expected, and looking far, far colder. The Grand Canal had the appearance of having its nose in the air, suggesting even through the icy greyness of the weather an annihilating feel of its own significance. History and literature undulated above it confidently, but with deference, personified in a purely imaginary gondola and gondolier. In fact of course there were none to be seen: only various fat putt-putting little craft whose steersmen, hunched in equally fat drab garments, seemed resigned to getting nowhere for a long while.

A larger vessel, like a river steamer, was at the quayside, seeming about to depart; and Tom hastened to get on board, awkward under his rucksack, as rails and ropes were shot home or released, and a disembodied voice raucously uttered the words 'San Marco'.

*

The next few days were chiefly to be remembered by Tom as a nightmare of cold. Shivering he hastened over innumerable hump-backed bridges, whose crumbling brickwork, gelid in the still air, seemed to have been arrested during what should have been an age-long dissolution into rich and powdery warmth. The watery thoroughfares beneath these bridges had diminished into an ooze of dark sludge, scarcely able to float the hanks of grime-coated seaweed above it. Winter seemed to have paralysed even the daily visitations of the distant sea.

Tom's breath hung in the air of churches as he gazed vainly at obscure martyrdoms or annunciations, almost as grimy as the seaweed, but alleged in the guide to be by the hand of Tintoretto, or even that of Titian. Tom soon ceased to care. The cold depleted him as it did in the water under the bridges. He was cold in bed, cold and damp too, the first night, when he had crept between the dank sheets, vainly eating the deformed remains of a milk chocolate bar Pinky had bought him at the station, oh so long

74

ago. The sweetness of the chocolate seemed to promise warmth, but failed to honour the promise, an analogy Tom felt, as he crouched in an evermore foetal position, of what the artwork and the stones of Venice were also doing.

At first, after arriving in the great square – the drawing-room of Europe someone had called it, but now it looked more like a disused warehouse stacked with shapeless and discarded plastic furniture – he had tried to find out if there was a youth hostel, a YMCA, or anything of that sort. He had so little money that he dreaded having to go to even the most modest of hotels; he could only have stayed at one for a night or two. The tourist office was shut. A man standing outside whom Tom addressed in a few faltering words of what he hoped was more or less Italian, leaned negligently towards Tom as if to assure himself – not that he much cared – that what he had been listening to was a form of human speech. He shrugged excessively, and then remarked to the air in a disagreeable and gratingly accurate English. 'Everything is closed. Hippies are not welcome. You had better go home.'

Tom resented being called a hippy, but he had to admit he probably looked like one, in his faded blue jeans and jacket, the patina of grime on which was as positive as any he would see in the next few days on Venetian stones and bridges and church pictures. Tom had worn that once quasi-obligatory uniform ever since he had become a student; and several years later, as an unemployed graduate, he still clung to it, not in any spirit of defiant and liberated youth, but really out of a sort of timidity. He felt it made him less visible, as if it were a version for his own milieu of a bank clerk's sober attire.

But here it made him just another hippy. And a solitary one it seemed. Why had he hit on the idea of coming to Venice at this time of year – the off-season? It would be so much cheaper and quieter – he knew from postcards and friends how crowded the place became in summer; and of course he had not even imagined the idea of winter in Venice – let alone the dead of winter. The dead of winter – that phrase was never so meaningful as it had become here.

Footsteps clip-clopped in the distance on the endless stones; a voice or two hung somewhere above him in the frozen air and died away. Poor Tom felt less like a visitor to Venice than a waif in Dickens, a crossing-sweeper in Victorian London. If only some Lady Dedlock of the lagoons would bear down on him, in her silks and furs, and give him the price of a square meal. For he had begun to feel hungry now as well as cold. He had been going to wear his old anorak, but Pinky had told him much better not: he'd be walking about all the time, and it would only get in the way; and it was never cold in Venice, not cold like it was in London. Everyone knew that.

Did they? Well, Tom now knew they were wrong. And no Lady Dedlock appeared. Tom padded on and on, if only to try to keep some warmth in his body. He found himself at last in a passage so narrow that two pedestrians would have had a struggle to get past each other; and that happened to Tom and another young man about his own age. Tom was too discouraged by now even to try his few Italian words, ready and prepared as they were. 'Somewhere to stay, please?' he asked. 'Please, do you know anywhere?'

The youth did not pause in the act of brushing past him, but pointed an arm and finger wordlessly up the wall to where a single printed word was visible on a small placard, streaked and embrowned as everything seemed to be in Venice. 'Locanda', it said. The youth was already gone, vanished in the darkness of the alley; and Tom had a vision of him pointing in silent sufferance to that mysterious and rather beautiful word, as uncouth young tourists, cumbered in gaudy gear that would hardly fit between the walls, accosted him summer by summer in their native speech. 'Locanda.' A bit lightheaded with hunger and cold, Tom thought of a place full of guitars and pizzas, with a dark girl to give him a welcoming smile. With some difficulty he found a doorway and a bell, which he rang.

An old woman came eventually, in black, her features not unlike those of the model in Giorgione's picture, which he was to see next day in the *Accademia*. Tom's heart sank as he saw himself trying to explain what he wanted. But to his amazement the ancient lady not only seemed to grasp the point at once, but replied to his halting request in English words with a distinct American whine or twang. Yes, he could rent a room by the month, payable in advance. No service. Having said this she

76

looked at him steadily without expression, her neat white head shaking slightly.

Tom, dismayed, explained that he wanted a room for a few nights only, a week, ten days at the most. Her head shook no more emphatically but she began to close the door. Desperate, Tom bleated out his 'Please', his pleasant features assuming without difficulty an air of supplication. The black door paused. 'OK,' said the old lady incongruously. 'Ten days – 40,000 lira.' She held out her hand; and Tom, whose mental arithmetic was of the most primitive kind, counted out precious notes. No doubt cheaper than a hotel, but still it was insane. He knew it. He'd have practically nothing to live on, but what could he do? His spirit felt broken. Some burrow, some haven to curl up in – that was all he required.

And that was all he got. The room she took him to was almost as narrow as the passage outside, and felt if possible even colder. His hands by now shaking like the old lady's head, Tom got his rucksack off and found the lavatory, whose existence she had indicated with a sibylline gesture. Even before he attempted to pull anything it made groans and gurgles, as if that salt sludge water were reluctantly on tap, to make a last appearance before sinking again into urban swamp.

Tom had no heart to go out again. On the frigid coverlet he assembled the last fragments of the food that had accompanied him across Europe. A squashed banana or two. Remnants of buttery bread and already sweaty cheese. Half an apple, well bitten and already brown. Their familiarity was odious, and his hunger gave him no appetite. Later in bed he had eaten Pinky's chocolate, and thought about Pinky. It made him no warmer.

*

Next day ground on, and the one following. He saw everything, his teeth chattering, but it did him no good. The weather seemed if anything colder. He ate in scruffy little cafeterias, going right back to the big car park at the rear of the island to find the most down-at-heel. Only later did he realise that these had much the same prices as trattorias, and ordinary small restaurants. His money was not lasting at all well. Once he found a mass of

77

discarded leaflets, all over the pavement but still comparatively dry. He gathered them up remembering something he had read about tramps on the embankment wrapping themselves in old newspapers. In his room by the passage – it was called, he saw the first morning, the *Calle d'Uomo Magro*, Thin Man Alley – he managed to arrange these inside his jeans, under his skimpy jersey, and even next to his skin, under the thin singlet (except on special occasions Tom was apt to economise on laundry by wearing no shirt.) As he did so he saw that some of them were advertising a giant winter clothing sale in the *Merceria*. Others appeared to be setting forth the programme of some revolutionary party. They rustled faintly as he walked, and tickled him round the middle and across the shoulder-blades. That was at least a new sensation, even if it made him no warmer.

His inside was just as forlorn. Crossing St Mark's Square at the rapid pace which now came naturally to him, he snuffed up the aroma of hot wines and punch, being served inside the big cafés; and in the warm interior of eating-places he saw men winding the pungently oily pasta round their forks. But even hot chestnuts, consumed in the open, were a fancy price he soon discovered, at least to him. They were sold near the *Accademia*, which of necessity became a sort of haven, after he had walked everywhere, and looked into all the guidebook churches.

Even the *Accademia* art gallery was barely warm, and it was expensive to get into, but once inside he could stay as long as he liked. Wandering round and round there as the day advanced Tom found himself endlessly presented at the temple, like the self-possessed little girl in the first gallery; or bound on the clock-sharp wheels of Tintoretto's St Catherines; evicted by negligent underlings from the feast in the house of Levi, where even Veronese's dog and parrot seemed to be getting a square meal. His favourite picture became the reception of the English ambassadors, in Carpaccio's story of St Ursula. A well-dressed cocky man with a snug black hat leant against a railing and watched the proceedings with humorous disdain. His furry gloves, ornamented with gold bobbles, which he allowed casually to dangle over the railing's top, were the warmest-looking Tom had ever seen. Tom, needless to say, had no gloves.

On the fifth morning he suddenly gave up. It was not far from his own room, by the square where the statue of the resolute condottiere urges his warhorse forward against the foes of the Venetian state. Gazing resentfully up, as he had often done before, at the hero's obliviousness to all his own petty urgencies of cold and hunger, Tom recalled the story of Henry James, whose hero feels more inspired in his own dealings as he eyes the indomitable bearing of the great Colleoni. He wished he could feel the same. Instead he was struck by a steady and ever increasing blast of icy air, which seemed like a ghost to traverse the square, quite quietly, on its way south from an even more arctic world. Tom's sub-garment of leaflets, forming a more insecure integument round him than the horseman's workman-like armour, seemed to quiver in the wind like spider-webs. Looking up at the light mocking blue of the northern sky he saw Alps protruding over the flat horizon.

It was the last straw. Something certainly broke. With a mental curse at Colleoni – an ungrateful one too, because the statue had possibly helped him to make up his mind, even to a negative course of action – Tom scurried rat-like over the square and into the stone thicket of passageways, where that terrible wind might not yet be penetrating. He would give up. He would catch the next train home. If he did that now, he would have enough before he left to go to a restaurant, eat some real food again, sit over cups of coffee, perhaps even a brandy. He had a sudden surge of exhilaration. When he got back Pinky would be there to welcome him and she would understand. A fleeting reflection indicated to him that Pinky had not in fact ever given proof in any context of such understanding. Sympathy was not her line, but Tom liked that. It made her more real, made him feel she wanted him, and wasn't just trying to make an impression. When she heard how cold it had been she would be sympathetic. Perhaps she would even let him creep close to her warm person; and at the thought of that Tom ran faster.

A man at the edge of the square, wearing an overcoat but still looking cold, watched him go; and then turned to stroll in the same direction.

*

79

Tom picked up his rucksack. He had not seen the old woman since he paid her, but now she materialised from somewhere beyond the lavatory, which was just as well, because he could hardly have left without letting her know. She nodded her white head, quite unperturbed. She had the money. Something in her old black eyes even suggested a hint of admiration that he had held out so long.

Tom had no idea about train times, having preferred to feel free. To enquire one day would be simple enough. And, in spite of his vision of restaurants, simple prudence now suggested it would be better to cling to the sort of place he knew, if he could find a superior example of one, rather than venturing into a place where you sat down at a white table cloth, and were hovered over by a waiter. Tom felt shy of them, although he now knew from the menus marked outside that they all seemed in much the same price range. But he also knew it was too early for somewhere like that: well before mid-day. First, at any rate, he would expend some of his meagre hoard of currency on provisions for the journey home. He found a secluded grocer without difficulty, and purchased bread, salami, and fruit, and a kind of industrial slab of dark chocolate, so uninvitingly packaged compared to the English product that it looked as if its true purpose might have been to scour a sink or scare away cockroaches. It did seem dry, solid and nourishing however. Butter and cheese he avoided, having a distasteful memory of the horrible bits and pieces he had compelled himself to finish up on that first evening. He wondered about a bottle of wine, and decided in its favour. Rather grudgingly they drew the cork for him. Venetians were grudging, he had already decided: in his experience here the sunny good nature of Italians was a complete myth. He paid in silence. In the military-type breast pocket of his jeans there were not many big notes left.

As Tom peered and paid in the dark spaces of the shop he had more than a look of his own mother, a parson's widow, who would be visiting the shops that morning at home in Tutbury. Of course she was proud of her son, the university graduate, although she wished he would come home more often. A man who had just come in and remained standing in the doorway, seemed briefly to contemplate Tom almost as if in awareness of this fleeting family resemblance. He turned and left without buying anything.

Tom wandered on down the stone street, towards a small and pleasant square with a newspaper kiosk. Wherever he went he had the sensation, familiar to all visitors to Venice, that he had been here before, or somewhere very like it. Now the prospect of going home even made him, for a moment or two, less conscious of the cold. At the edge of the square he spotted just the kind of lunch counter that would suit him. It was nearly empty still, and choosing a stool as far away from the door as possible he ordered a ham omelette, peas and chips, with a side order of sandwiches. They looked so good, sitting in a fresh snowy pile on the clean counter. The man behind the bar, with nothing to do, was quite civil for once. For the first time in days Tom began to feel in moderate spirits.

He was well into the omelette when he became conscious of being no longer alone in his snug corner. He paid no attention until a clipped voice spoke beside him,

'English?'

Tom, who had quite enough at home of being a Brit, or a citizen of the UK, supposed an Italian must be speaking, in spite of the accent. He looked up. His companion *was* English – no doubt about that. A melancholy middle-aged face, rather reddish from the cold. A hat, soft and brown, but simple in an excellent manner which suggested Bond or Jermyn Street. Tom was not being looked at, which relieved him. His companion was gazing reflectively at the bottles behind the bar.

'Think I'll have a *grappa*. Just the thing for this weather. Care for one?'

In a flash Tom realised he was being picked up. He could not but be excited by the knowledge. It had never happened to him before; but then he had never been in a context where such things did happen. There were plenty of gays about of course, and Tom knew a student who had been approached by one of the staff – unavailingly, as the student already had a boyfriend, to whom he was almost aggressively faithful. But the approach direct, or pretty well direct, he had never experienced.

To be desirable is always something; and now the idea gave him a bit of a thrill. Tom had not realised he was lonely; and indeed in the abstract he would have hated the idea of being accosted in English on this long-wished-for Venetian trip. Now it came as a relief. Indeed he felt a second of regret that it also came too late, now that he was practically on his way home, before he adjusted himself to the query, and produced with becoming modesty a reply that the offer was very kind. He had no idea what *grappa* was, incidentally.

He soon found out. The colourless, slightly oily looking liquid, with a dry pungent fragrance, was set before him in a small thick glass by the man behind the bar. 'Cheers,' said the man beside him, and drank swiftly and almost unnoticeably. Tom followed suit and set the glass down gasping, having drunk only a small portion of its contents. It was enough to make a great warmth surge out of nowhere and spread blissfully through him. Tom instantly took another sip and smiled through watering eyes at his companion.

'Strong stuff,' he commented rather foolishly.

The other smiled back; a surprisingly sweet, deprecating smile.

'What's it made of?' asked Tom.

'Grapeseeds.'

They contemplated this interesting fact together in silence; and on Tom's side with a feeling of camaraderie growing more marked as he got down another mouthful of *grappa*. 'Don't let yours get cold,' said the man, indicating Tom's plate of omelette and chips, and as Tom set mechanically to work again on the food, his keen appetite somewhat eclipsed by this wonderful new drinking experience, the man seemed to lose interest to him, and turned back, nursing his *grappa*, to his contemplation of the bar. Tom cleaned his plate, and could not but feel as he did so that the silence was becoming awkward, at least to himself.

'Thank you very much indeed,' he said. 'Do you live in Venice?'

The man did not reply directly. He turned on Tom the same charming rather weary smile, as if courtesy demanded of him an effort he would privately much rather not make. Tom waited for a few seconds; and then as there was still no reply he gabbled confidingly, as it seemed to him, and conscious that his face was growing ever redder through the beneficent effects of the drink, that he was just on his way home.

'Because it's so cold,' he said. 'I never realised it would be so cold.'

His new friend thought about that. 'A vile town,' he said suddenly, with quite unexpected violence. 'A vile town. The vilest town in the world. The vilest town in the world without any exception. Without any exception at all.'

He paused and stared at Tom, who with an abrupt sense of let-down realised he had been accosted by a madman, an eccentric, a bore, who for the price of a drink was going to hold Tom with his glittering eye for a large part of the afternoon, if he wasn't careful.

'Well, thanks awfully, perhaps I'd better be ...' he began, starting to slide off his stool, and then remembering he had not yet paid for his meal.

At that moment a big white plate was set down with a flourish by the barman. It contained a mound of pasta, compact and gelatinous, glistening with greenish olive oil, and mottled with fragments of herb and red pepper, and pale dappled open shells with something dark and succulent within them, as if Venus, newly blown ashore, had left behind her all sorts of little savoury intimacies.

The man reached unhurriedly along the bar for salt and pepper and a bottle from which he shook a brown liquid. A carafe of white wine was put before him. Dipping a fork into the ambrosial mess he began deliberately to eat. Pausing a moment he appeared to become aware that Tom was still standing beside him.

'You pay at the door,' he observed, with his mouth a little full, and then set to again.

Tom was dismissed. To say he was disappointed would be an understatement: he was in the depths of chagrin. Reduced to shamelessness by cold and hunger he had been desperately hoping to be offered another glass of *grappa*. Moreover he suddenly realised the ambiguity in this last instruction. Did the man imply that he would be paying for the *grappa* offered him, along with his meal? He gave a wistful look at the bottle behind the bar, and at the diminishing mound of sea-borne spaghetti, which for

83

some reason made him think of Pinky. With a wave of longing he imagined the two of them revelling in it there together, sitting not side by side but in a little alcove opposite one another, so that he could see the beautiful stuff going into Pinky's mouth, and perhaps get a kiss full of it.

The barman, a big fair man like many Venetians, was gazing at him now with his green eyes full of a placid speculation? Dare he order himself another glass of *grappa*, and continue to sit there, hoping the man would take some further notice of him? There was the money to consider, and in any case it would hardly do. He took the check for his meal off the bar, and awkwardly recovered his rucksack.

'Well, thanks very much,' he murmured, too young to be able to keep the disappointment out of his voice.

The spick and span lady by the entrance rang her till and gave him some change. The bill, as usual, was larger than he had hoped, and he was still fussed about the value of money, working back laboriously to pence and pounds. As he took the coins and turned to go, feeling it better not to look back, the man's voice spoke at his elbow.

Tom started. Looking in some way more distinguished than when he was sitting down, his friend from the bar was beside him, wiping his lips with a table napkin.

'I say, you're not going till the night train, I expect? If you're free, drop in for a cup of tea at half-past four. I'm parked at the Phoenix Hotel, just a ways from here, over the little bridge by the theatre. What's the name by the way?'

Tom, who belonged to the generation that only uses first names, got out 'Tom'.

'Tom what? Jones?'

His lips parted in that austere but attractive smile. Seeming to lose interest in Tom's surname he thrust the white cloth – it must be a large handkerchief, not a napkin – into his left sleeve, and stroked his chin, as if already contemplating some further scheme in which Tom would have no place at all. Tom was not unobservant; and he recalled an army friend of his father's who had the same trick of putting away his handkerchief in his sleeve. Army officer? Probably retired, possibly gay? Looking back at the bar he noticed the barman already removing the empty plate of spaghetti. Another glass of *grappa* had replaced it. Tom tore his eyes away from it. He had a faint hope that the chap (something in the way he spoke and moved made him seem like 'a chap', a term not normally part of Tom's vocabulary) might have been going to offer to pay the bill; in which case he would have been too late, and Tom might have recovered some of the initiative by saying so. This present order, for that was what it seemed like, left him gaping. Nor was he left to recover his powers of speech.

'Name's Grey. Major Grey. Room 224. Just come straight up.'

He turned back towards the bar. The spick and span lady at the check-out gazed at Tom as impassively as the barman had done, but without the least curiosity. She seemed resigned to living among males – foreigners or madmen – who had long since ceased to interest her in the smallest degree.

*

Having devoured all the sandwiches as well as his omelette, Tom now felt a little bloated. He had not spent much on food in the last five days – he couldn't have afforded to. But in addition to physical distension there was now a mental one. So much had had to be swallowed so suddenly, and not only the *grappa*. That still gave him a warm feeling, though it was beginning to turn a bit sour and headachey. He had a strong desire to sit down quietly somewhere and work things out. He knew if he did he would probably nod off for a few minutes, despite the cold.

Churches were shut in the afternoon. He had made that discovery what now seemed long ago. He had eaten so early that it was not much after twelve now. Should he now go on to the station, a longish walk unless he went down the Grand Canal on the *vaporetto*? He felt reluctant to do so; in fact he felt reluctant to do anything. His rucksack, though not heavy, was a nuisance. Some places, he knew, would be open again by three, or four; but that was already getting on for the time when this Major Grey – could there really be a person called Major Grey? – had suggested tea at his hotel.

Fantasies, a little muzzy with *grappa*, flitted before Tom's eyes. Major Grey wanted to adopt him? Or he would suggest Tom stay in Venice at his expense for an indefinite period? He would shyly reveal an immense knowledge and love for the place, and would take Tom into palaces and baptisteries where they would see fabulous works of art not normally accessible to the public. In spite of the cold they would even go to islands in a gondola – Major Grey would know a man, grizzled, heavily mustachioed, bluffly deferential, who would take them to some picturesque boathouse right off the beaten track. (Tom had some acquaintance with the works of Baron Corvo.) They would dine together in splendour at Harry's Bar, drink the punch whose fumes had wafted from the warm interior of the Quadri as Tom had padded to and from over St Mark's Square. And always there would be glasses of *grappa*, small, solid, reeking with pungency ...

Tom halted at this point. He took his rucksack off his shoulders and sat down on it, his back against a little niche in the wall. The stones, which would have been impossibly cold to sit on, laid icy fingers on his spine, dispelling the last warmth of the *grappa*. He remembered the sudden ferocity with which Major Grey had denounced Venice, the vilest town in the world without exception. It was hardly likely he would be a connoisseur of its hidden beauties. He also remembered realising that he had been picked up.

What did the Major want of him? The answer of course was obvious, as Tom knew very well. And what were his own reactions to it? As his head cleared, and he began to wonder whether he really would, should, or could, present himself at half-past four at the Phoenix Hotel, he realised that he was devoured above all by the liveliest curiosity. He positively longed to know what it would be like. The idea of physical relations with the Major was somehow so fantastic that he did not even try to envisage them, or believe in them even theoretically; and yet something there made an appeal to him, an appeal of closeness or comradeliness, an appeal that somehow took on the texture of good cloth, scented with tobacco and aftershave; and he rubbing his cheek against it. Tom smiled to himself, but he was an affectionate person; and his wish for affection was not necessarily confined to girls like Pinky: indeed Pinky had given him no great proof that that was what she herself liked, or was after. Girls didn't somehow, at least not in his experience.

What it boiled down to was that Tom would rather enjoy the proximity of this mysterious man who evidently wanted to know him. Proximity? Well ... and yet? ...

No, he was intensely curious – that was the point. He had been extremely lonely: he almost burst into tears when he thought of those dreary icy days plodding about, and the cold dank nights in the Locanda. The thought of staying at a real hotel, in almost any capacity, was immensely luring by contrast.

Aids? Like everyone else Tom knew all about that. But he also felt he could take care of himself. Prepared possibly to co-operate, but unimpelled by passion, he was sure he could evade without seeming to, as Pinky was in the habit of doing, come to think of it, and make the most of whatever fascinating situation he might find himself in.

In all this Tom no doubt showed his innocence. His schooldays at the local Grammar had been humdrum and studious. A homelover who had got on well with his ironically parsonical father, now dead, as well as with his mother, he knew about the ways of the world without having much experienced them.

And so four o'clock found him making his way towards the Fenice theatre, with whose whereabouts he was already familiar from earlier, unenthralled wanderings about. Now at last he felt positively exhilarated. Something was going to come of this surely? After he had got over the pleasurable daze induced by that unfamiliar drink he had found himself close to the back of the big Palazzo Rezzonico, whose discreet museum was, unexpectedly at that time of year, just about to re-open. Tom spent an hour or so among 18th-century pictures of the town in its louchest period – was that beginning to be appropriate perhaps? – and he was able to sit for a bit in the chapel and contemplate Tiepolo's ceiling painting of a wedding in the Rezzonico family. It reminded him agreeably that he was himself an engaged man.

His morale high in spite of the rather large entrance charge – that seemed less important now – he crossed the Rialto Bridge and made his way to Santa Maria Formosa, to visit again the picture that had most comforted him during the bleakest period: since his lunch-time encounter it seemed really long ago. There she was, Palma Vecchio's magisterial St Barbara, patron saint of miners and artillerists, flanked by the muzzle of her upturned cannon. Tom now felt quite possessive of her noble presence; and it struck him with some amusement that he was beginning to do what everyone did about Venice, or about pictures and art generally. He was beginning, in a somewhat portly way, to feel all a part of it: whereas at the beginning he had wandered, a forlorn and excluded applicant, from church to church, and façade and gallery, finding it all so exclusive in its distance, so far from himself.

That took up the time nicely; and now he was back again on the other side of the Grand Canal, and going to make his first social call in Venice. He supposed Henry James, and Robert Browning, and all the others had done that mostly by gondola. Well, in spite of his visit to St Barbara – his own personal saint as she now seemed to him – those grand folk of the past still seemed as far off as ever.

And here was the Fenice Theatre – they had all come there in their time presumably – with Goldoni's statue beside it, looking quite affable. Tom disliked the theatre, though he was never quite brave enough to say so, or even to think so, openly; and it struck him as he nosed his way round the tiny square, and into the recess where a hotel lay discreetly positioned, that he had taken above all to Major Grey's lack of drama. Despite his sudden outburst about the vileness of Venice, even in some degree because of it, the Major had exuded a surprising degree of naturalness, on that brief acquaintance. Tom liked the way he had ordered and consumed his own meal with unflinching self-concentration, in spite of the kindly impulse that had led him to offer a glass to the English student he had found beside him. He had seemed devoid of intentness, or intention.

As he hovered for a moment at the unnoticeable front of the hotel he found himself thinking that it was he himself really, who had been the more pushy of the two. But here he was, after all; though the Major might well be appalled, or merely vexed, to find a comfortably somnolent afternoon disturbed by this young imbecile. Still, he had asked for it. Tom entered.

He was at once conscious of the warmth. What bliss! At the reception desk a youth who seemed even younger than Tom himself directed him to the lift. It was the old kind, like a glass cage, with wheels and workings highly visible outside it, as if the martyred ladies of the school of Venice had deposited their pictorial apparatus there. It struck Tom that the youth below had appeared conscious of his – Tom's – destination, and had been asked to send him up. He began to feel quite important, especially as the young fellow had not seemed surprised by or contemptuous of him. Already he began to feel as at home in the hotel as in Venetian art. The encounter at the bar had made all the difference.

Yet both excitement and apprehension remained; and he felt the palms of his hands, as cold in this wintry town as its marble monuments, sweating as he knocked on the door. There was silence within. Tom knocked again.

The hotel remained very silent. Or was there some faint talk behind a door further down the corridor? That there should be no one here was one thing he had not expected. Was the man asleep? Reluctant to knock again he stood irresolutely and listened. Minutes seemed to pass.

A throat was cleared in the silence. A brown hat appeared in the dark well of the staircase, rising unhurriedly to Tom's level. 'Ah, here you are,' said Major Grey. He was carrying white paper bags and parcels, which he put down outside his door as he looked for the key in his pocket.

'Just been out to do a bit of shopping.'

The naturalness of it all delighted Tom. Iago – himself a Venetian, come to think of it – had planned each of his moves with care. Although he must well have understood the art of assessing and timing involved in a pick-up – and Tom bravely reminded himself that this still was one – that monster of the theatre seemed far away as the Major opened the door, and led him into a pleasantly done up bedroom in tones of dark pink and brown. The brass bed head, imitating an antique, winked warmly, and the sheets looked almost unnaturally clean, at least by Tom's unexacting standards.

Even more now he felt lapped in warmth. The penetrating chill of Venice's stagnant and drowning corpse seemed finally banished. Compared to the Locanda there was nothing Venetian about the room at all. It might have been in a hotel or home in some cheerful and bustling inland town – like Oxford or Birmingham, thought Tom, – the latter being not so far from his own home.

'Not like Venice is it?' remarked the Major with satisfaction, his comment chiming uncannily with Tom's own inner response. This already seemed to constitute a bond. Tom had helped the Major pick up the parcels outside his door; and now the latter began to open them and set out their contents on a small table.

'A few things for tea,' he said. 'One needs one's tea in this town. Can't stand those cafés, can you? Cream cakes. Coffee dolled up with a lot of brown scum on it … ugh. Sickening. Just like the canals.' He broke off and glanced doubtfully at the table by the bed where a litre-sized bottle winked back at the brass. 'You can have whisky if you'd prefer it, of course.'

Tom hastened to reassure him that tea would be the thing. Something about the Major's last offer, the parcels and the preparations, made him feel as if he were taking part in an advertisement for the English Way of Life. But how marvellous that it should be so! For never had he been more sincere than in wanting tea, now it was offered. It seemed exactly what was needed not only to dispel the last chills of Venice but to correct the after-effects of the *grappa*.

The Major disappeared for a moment to fill the electric kettle in his bathroom. He came back and plugged it in, and with it a small horizontal electric fire, which he set precisely on the boards by the edge of the carpet. Watching his reddish hands capably at work, Tom had a sudden feel of panic. The anonymous figure ordering *grappa* in the bar had not seemed particularly English, although it was the first word he had spoken; but the Major now not only seemed typecast, having unmistakably declared and defined himself, but also seemed to exist more and more each minute as a physical being, a creature of digestion, aches and pains, possibly bad breath – other things … Not exactly unreflectingly but unimaginatively, Tom had entered his lair; and would have to abide by the consequences.

These at the moment seemed the reverse of alarming. They ate brown toast, thickly buttered, with a pot of Tiptree strawberry jam; and the Major kept refilling the kettle to make more tea. 'Earl Grey,' he remarked, with a quizzical smile, as Tom imbibed his fourth cup with a blissful thirstiness, – 'Not one of the family, so far as I know.'

Filling the hotel room with its fragrance, the tea had also made Tom perspire, and become embarrassingly conscious that he too smelt, though less agreeably. Bathroom facilities at his London digs were primitive: those of the Locanda still more so; and Tom in any case was inclined to belong to the school of thought holding that since one needs a shower no more after two weeks than two days, why bother?

Now, however, he regretted that. He could only hope the Major's nose was not aware of him; and that he remained unaware, also, of the odd but perceptible rustling sound of the leaflets under his jeans and inside his shirt. So far they had vainly tried to keep him warm, but they were now succeeding in doing so all too well.

But the Major appeared to take no heed of such matters. He asked a couple of civil but perfunctory questions about Tom's occupation; and Tom replied to them politely from the depths of a well-being induced by toast and tea. What was going to happen now? Had he been a girl he thought dreamily, and girls never smelt bad, like boys, he would not resist a sudden movement and a rough embrace: he would turn up his mouth quite happily to be kissed. And after that? But the point rather was that although the room and the tea had in some way made him aware of the Major as a physical being, the Major just didn't seem the sort of person who could or would do such things. Was that perhaps what Pinky felt, when Tom felt inclined to try seizing hold of her? He was not the kind of person who could do it: he did not, in some way, fit into that real world.

The Major, at any rate, seemed quite indifferent into what world he fitted, if any. He had gone back to abusing Venice. Tom in his mind's eye could not help seeing an old lady, a friend of his mother and father, who used regularly to come to tea, the sort of tea which they had just finished eating, though there would have been cakes too, and little sandwiches. When tea was finished the old lady began invariably to attack one of her local targets: the doctor's surgery, the town planners, a delinquent grocer. The Major seemed equally to enjoy a daily rite of execration. Tom was delighted to oblige and co-operate, however passively.

He belonged to a generation that did not enquire into backgrounds, or even speculate about them. 'Placing' acquaintance, in their shifting world, was an unknown pleasure. And so Tom hardly bothered to ask himself where the Major came from; what he had done; even whether or not he was a real major, although the name had certainly struck him, when first uttered, as somehow too English to be true. Full of tea and toast, warm for the first time since he left the train, he was content to listen and to agree. He was also young enough to feel that life was the thing, and that it must hold all sorts of superior joys – sexual or merely social – to which others had access but not himself. Now he felt on the verge of some such excitement. Whatever it was, indeed, he could hardly wait for it to begin.

And yet it showed no signs of doing so. His first and potentially thrilling sample of social life in Venice showed, on the contrary, every sign of ending amicably in the aftermath of tea and toast, not unlike a tea-party at his parents' home. Tom felt suddenly reckless.

'Do you know any gondoliers?' he interjected into one of the Major's rambles about the loathsomeness of the place, its people, and its exaggerated reputation.

As he said this he leant forward towards the other, with his eyes deliberately sparkling and his lips parted. Tom knew how to flirt; although until now he had remained unconscious of the fact.

The Major's discourse ceased abruptly. First he looked Tom carefully in the eye. Then he cleared his throat and allowed an expression of extreme distaste to change the appearance of his reddish features. (He had no moustache.)

'Gondoliers? No,' he said shortly – as if quite horribly put out.

He blew his nose. Tom felt he had spoilt everything, with no way to make amends. And yet he still felt, with the transparent cunning or insight of the young, that something momentous was about to happen, even though it might not take the obvious form. So what could it be? He gazed yearningly at the Major, striving to project that yearning, entirely in terms of apology and good will. Just let me know what you want. In every fibre of his body Tom knew what he himself wanted: not to be chucked out into the cold dark Venetian night. He even looked forlornly at the bed, with its dark pink coverlet and very white sheets: warm, spacious and inviting.

The other appeared at a loss. He blew his nose again and gave Tom a disquietingly sidelong look. The young man realised how much the older man generally depended on the straightforwardness of his expressions. This look now was neither one thing nor the other. Tom was reminded of the adjective now current with the BBC back home. How many times, with his little transistor softly gabbling the morning news in his London digs, had he heard that to some body or other – a union, a party, or just to 'ordinary families' – something or other was 'unacceptable'. The word seemed to suit Major Grey. Venice, as he had made more than clear, was in the highest degree unacceptable to him. Acceptable, on the other hand, were his tea and *grappa* and marine macaroni; and apparently too the society of Tom, at least up to that moment. And now, with sinking heart, Tom felt himself joined with the rest of Venice to the melancholy panorama of unacceptability.

And there was nothing he could do about it. In the silence the Major began to gather up the tea-things. 'Pop in the loo if you want, before you go,' he suggested, not unkindly. The reference to the amount of tea he had drunk further confused poor Tom, who went drooping into the little bathroom, and self-consciously closed the door. As he unzipped himself he remembered reading somewhere that a standard ploy on the part of those who picked up young men was to offer them a bath. Tom could certainly have done with one. And was Major Grey even now going to retrieve the situation by erupting through the door, which Tom had naturally left unlocked? That seemed hardly likely. Nor would Tom have cared for the idea, as he knew quite well. What he wanted was someone who wanted his company, who offered him the things the Major had done, boring as the Major certainly could be about Venice.

In the loo he vividly imagined the other's face, and realised for the first time, now he was not embarrassed by actually looking at them, the unhappiness of the eyes. The young usually have no curiosity about the old; but now, forgetting for a moment what seemed his own failure, he wondered about the Major's. Where had the man come from; what was he doing here? He covered the awkwardness of coming back into the bedroom by saying, in what he hoped was a respectfully friendly way, that it seemed such a nice hotel. The Major agreed. Tom would like to have asked if he were staying there for long, but felt it unbecoming to seem curious.

'Back to Milan tomorrow, thank God,' announced the other, as if unbending.

'Ah, I don't know it,' said Tom humbly, wondering what the Major would do there; what he was doing in Venice for that matter?

The other did not enlighten him, and Tom, like a condemned man, prepared to be ejected into the cold Venetian fog. It was quite dark outside now, and before him was only the bleak prospect of trudging down to the station to await his train.

The Major was looking him up and down reflectively. 'You're not properly dressed for this weather, young fellow,' he remarked, as if suddenly aware of the fact; and going over to the wall cupboard he swung it open and with a click of hangers detached a large dark garment, which he brought out into the middle of the room.

It was an overcoat. The very sight of it made Tom feel warmer, for the thought of what awaited him outside had already begun to chill his blood. The Major laid it on the bed, and looked appraisingly at it, and then at Tom.

'Should fit OK,' he said. 'Slip it on.'

Tom needed, as he thought to himself, no second invitation. This was better than a sexual advance. And it was almost as if, when the noble garment had drawn itself round his jean-clad shoulders, and settled all dense and voluminous nearly to his ankles, he was being made love to by an entity as enigmatic as the Major, and as voluptuous as what he hoped of Pinky. Enrobed and enfolded Tom felt he could never be cold again. Automatically his hands went to the buttons and did them up. Now he positively confronted the Major, as if he had become a being to be reckoned with in his own right, a new and even formidable personality. He stood metamorphosed in the middle of the room, and smiled boldly at his benefactor.

94

'Take it off a moment,' said the Major. 'I think it should do you nicely.'

Tom was quite sure it would. Now he could hardly wait to plunge out into the dark world before the other should change his mind. He removed the coat reluctantly, letting his hands stroke its smooth dense nap, very dark grey in colour, almost silky in its texture. Silky too, but with a different sensation, had been the pockets, great bottomless pouches of promised warmth, which his hands had explored for all too short a time.

The Major laid it down again and patted it like a tailor. Tom saw with apprehension that he too loved the overcoat, or seemed to. Perhaps it had received, and even satisfied, whatever impulses of loneliness and affection Tom detected, or thought he had, in this mysterious man's eye. Why then was he giving it up? Realising for the first time the magnificence of the gift, and the impulse of generosity it signified, Tom felt a spontaneous impulse to hug the Major, to lay his head as if in ecstasy on that discreetly striped shirtfront, on the brown worn waistcoat tweed.

Instead he managed to say, 'It really is *very* kind of you, sir. Are you sure you can spare it?'

At which the other only nodded shortly, pointing at his own, and much lighter, brown raglan ulster lying on a bedroom chair, together with the brown hat.

That 'sir' came quite naturally, although Tom would normally have felt uncomfortably self-conscious about using this form of address, as he had once used it as an adolescent to masters at the grammar school. But somehow now it had a fine egalitarian ring, as if two equals were sealing their bargain of friendship.

The Major was still playing, as it were, with the great coat. Was he, wondered Tom, with a pang of jealousy, restoring his own sense of possession and proprietorship, after allowing Tom, like the intimate friend of a vain husband, to steal a glance at wifely charms reserved for the conjugal partner?

Next moment this horrible fear became a certainty. 'Want it taken back to London actually,' explained the Major. 'Belongs to a friend of mine. You could do me a good turn by delivering it to him for me. Keep you warm in the meanwhile.'

Tom strove manfully not to let his expression show how disappointed he was. The fact was he had fallen in love with the overcoat, as anybody might have done, he told himself, and his disappointment at being denied full possession of it could not but be correspondingly bitter, however unreasonable. He felt he was being allowed only to march in procession with his St Barbara, not to marry her and go to bed with her. His shoulders, thin and ill-covered again now, were bound to droop a little.

If he was aware of all this the Major gave no sign of it. He seemed to have lost interest in Tom, now that the great coat had been handed over. His voice was cheery enough but brusque as he wished the young man goodnight. 'I won't see you down,' he said. 'Got things to do before leaving.' He gestured towards an orderly heap of papers and files on the dressing table. 'Have a good trip home.'

He held the overcoat open for Tom to put on, and something in this gesture touched Tom, reminding him of the past – was it his father holding some garment of childhood in the same way? He hardly knew whether his disappointment was the almost equally childish one that he could not keep the coat, or disappointment at losing the Major himself so soon – perhaps a bit of both. Something about the coat, as about the man who had given it, seemed full of what he had, even if unconsciously, come to Venice to find; something to shove him uncompromisingly into life, the sort of life that seemed all around him in advertisements, and books, and on the media, a life of stark occurrence and real emotion.

Just why life in this sense should seem at the moment attached to the coat, and to its donor, Tom would not have found it possible to say; nor, in any case, did he ask himself the question.

The main thing was that the wonderful coat was all around his person again, flooding him with warmth and new assurance, as the *grappa* had done in its own more mephistophelian way at the lunch counter. And as he slipped from the Major's grasp and shrugged himself fully into the coat, the base thought occurred to Tom that his host had evidently forgotten to tell him where it should be delivered. Might there be a possibility of *keeping* it, after all, and without dishonour, if he were left with no idea of the Major's address, or the address of the person it should go to?

But almost as if he intuited Tom's unworthy idea, the Major was, in fact, giving him a last instruction; telling him the address the coat should go to was in its breast pocket. 'Won't be out of your way,' he said, knowing from their previous talk that Tom was a student in London. 'Nearer Earls Court than Gloucester Road, I should think. The phone number's on the card. Give him a ring if you like, but I understand he's usually in. Just go round in a day or two after you get back.'

He smoothed the coat over Tom's shoulders: the closest he had come, Tom realised, to a physical caress, and it seemed lavished entirely on the garment and not on him. And yet the gesture seemed to make him, for the first time since Tom's unfortunate query, quite talkative again. 'Wonder where the old fellow had it made for him,' he said. 'Left it with me when he came on a visit once. Got too hot for it, I suppose. An heirloom it may have been – quite possibly a family heirloom.'

*

Once again Tom was walking through stone passages. But how different they looked and felt. He felt master of Venice now, able to appreciate, with his own easy inner superiority, her aesthetic charms. Before, he had seen, not felt, how magical they were. Now, like Ruskin, or Casanova come to that, he himself brought all the appropriate state of mind. The idea of Casanova made him chuckle audibly and idiotically for a moment. Had he met a girl in a Venetian mask, or one who gave him the glad eye, he might well have stopped and been gallant, encouraged by the magic garment he wore. But as on other and more desolate evenings when he had tramped the stone corridors there was no one about. No doubt the cold saw to that.

He crossed the Campo Morosini and passed San Vitale. (From his map Tom knew all the place names now.) At the Iron Bridge he stopped and gazed down the Canal at the great shadowy form of the Salute church, its reflection wavering in the watery lights. He eyed Longhena's masterpiece with tolerant proprietorship, his regard more than equal to all its airy buttresses and curlicues. But of course: he was going the wrong way; and once again he chided himself in an audible chuckle. What did it matter to the master of Venice that he had left the little theatre square in a daze, and turned in the wrong direction for the station?

And why should he go to the station? Tom stopped more decisively, and looked at the Mickey Mouse watch that Pinky had once given him. He could read it quite easily in the lights from the water and all round him – it said between six and half past. Quite early. Why should he not go back to the Locanda, reclaim the five-day balance of his 40,000 lira? The old girl would have to let him have his room back. With the coat over him he would be as warm in bed as he was now, walking about the streets.

The thought of saving that money delighted Tom. And avarice, by a parallel suggestion, couldn't help reminding him that the coat was only on loan, that he was bound on return to restore it to its owner. With a faint hope – and how unworthy again! – that the Major might in fact have forgotten to leave the card in the pocket, he put his hand under the majestic collar – not fur, but feeling almost as if it might be – and entered the right-hand breast pocket.

No, alas, there was the card. And Tom manfully overcame his disappointment at the thought of not having to struggle shamefully with his conscience, as he would have done if there had been no address: he might have felt that he could do no more, and therefore have kept the coat. He would certainly not have gone back to the Major. That, for some reason, would have seemed out of the question.

Anyway, the card was there; and he felt quite glad, indeed relieved. *Hotel Phoenix, Venice* said the printed heading; and then 'For The Hon. Giles Parker', in a bold decisive hand, the sort he would have expected the Major to have. There followed an address in SW8. Tom put the card back, and his hand into the equally capacious left-hand breast pocket.

It touched a wad of crisp paper. He drew it out, somehow knowing exultantly already what it was. Notes! How many he did not look to see, but quite a lot of them. He pushed them back and looked around him as furtively as a thief. So the Major had turned up trumps. (Tom's father had been fond of that expression.) He could now not only stay his allotted time at the Locanda, but stay there in something like comfort. He began at once to walk back the way he had come.

Later that evening he sat in a real restaurant, eating steak and chips. A whole bottle of Chianti stood at his elbow, for Tom was not much of a wine buff, nor had he yet discovered that in Venice the Valpolicella, from a not distant part of city's former empire, is both better and cheaper. His landlady, as he now rather grandly thought of her, had been perfectly accommodating – probably she did not care whether someone who had paid the rent stayed in the room or not. She noticed the coat though, and her old black eyes looked maliciously amused for a moment, but also admiring. She thought she knew what he had been up to.

For the next few days Tom really enjoyed Venice.

Everywhere he went the coat went with him. He saw waiters in white aprons glance at it respectfully when he entered a restaurant. He always chose the small secluded ones, and found them and their clienteles surprisingly choice. And when he took off the coat, and folded it beside him, for he never allowed it to be hung up by the door, his tattered appearance did not give an unfavourable impression. Clearly he was a young Englishman in films, or a journalist perhaps, who chose to dress, as so many did, in student fashion; but whose magnificent outer garment mocked any suggestion of poverty. The overcoat had given him a *bella figura*; and when he found one *trattoria* he specially liked and went there two or three times he was recognised and greeted. His Italian improved too.

So the next few days passed all too quickly. He relaxed his city sight-seeing, and found that Thin Man Alley gave at its far end on to a wide *riva*, with the dark cypress plumes of the cemetery across the water. He investigated the English graves, which were numerous, and included one of an Archdeacon, whose family had 'Left him in Peace'. He would have liked to show that to Pinky, who always laughed, even if she didn't see a joke. He visited Torcello and the Lido, where the Alpine wind roved over sandbanks and mudflats, and the scoured sky looked huge after poky Venice. His coat was its own climate, proof against any blast that blew.

Safe inside it he did not think much about the Major; but on his last day in Venice an odd thing happened. He was walking along the *Merceria* and turned to look back at a display window which featured silk shirts and ties, tweed jackets and – yes – elegant overcoats. Tom was eyeing them complacently when he caught sight of Major Grey some way behind him, apparently walking with a woman in a dark cloak and hat. He only caught a glimpse before the couple vanished through a doorway. He wondered whether to greet the Major and to thank him; and he walked back a few steps before deciding the other would not in all probability want to see him, especially if he were with a woman companion. When had he come back from Milan, Tom wondered? The encounter made him feel in some way disillusioned about the Major; for Tom had a romantic view of him as a solitary man, friendless and self-sufficient, going austerely about his obscure and still perhaps military business. He had manifested himself to Tom only at the lunch-counter and the hotel, and that was enough. He should now have withdrawn himself from the world; but here he apparently still was, living among acquaintance and connection just like everyone else; perhaps even living with a woman. Tom felt disappointed. He could not quite have said why.

But the matter did not occupy him for long. It was his last day; and he had determined to give himself an especially good late lunch, before setting off in a leisurely way to the station. He had even considered spending a few more days in Venice, not at the Locanda but in a hotel: perhaps even – why not? – the Hotel Phoenix? The Major's bounty – conveyed, as it seemed, with delicacy in such a way that Tom could not have refused – would have made that possible. The notes in the overcoat amounted to considerably more than the sum he had brought with him to Venice; but he felt they were his due. He was doing the Major quite a favour, after all, in taking the coat back to his old friend. What an adventure to tell Pinky! He longed to see Pinky; and this as much as anything determined him to return at the end of the ten days he had planned originally.

He went into the trattoria he had marked down for his farewell lunch, removed his overcoat, and laid it beside him as usual. Tom was rather coy about his precious garment when he took it off, folding it to show only its dark and sober outside, for the sumptuous lining was in its own choice style startlingly flamboyant. It was composed of thick silk quilting, dark green in colour, and dimpled like the upholstery in an old first-class railway carriage. In one or two places the quilting had worn, and had been carefully darned by some unknown hand – a long time ago Tom liked to think. It must be this dense quilting which gave the garment its beatific, almost tropical warmth.

On this occasion, perhaps because Tom was eager to look at the menu, he left the green lining conspicuously uppermost, enriching the corner where he sat, like a damask hanging in the Doge's Palace. A tall sallow man had followed him into the restaurant and seemed to glance inquisitively at this phenomenon as he passed Tom's table. A natural enough curiosity, but it made Tom, who had noticed it, feel a trifle uneasy. Did the man have designs on his coat, or his wallet? – Tom had intercepted a very sharp glance indeed from his black eyes before he sat himself down among the hubbub some distance away.

Tom hastened to refold the overcoat, but in a minute he had forgotten all about the incident, concentrating on, and ordering, what he would eat. He had long decided to try some time what the Major had been putting away at their first encounter: that wonderful-looking pasta dish, dense with prawns and sea-shells, vivid with saffron and herbs. He had even contemplated ordering it on his first liberated evening, after he had become the keeper of the coat, but had decided – probably wisely – to stick in his hunger to what he had always liked best: the steak and chips. Tom was conservative in his tastes on the whole, and distrustful of fish. But now he gloated over the great whiskery mass as it approached his table, and set himself to it without inhibition, presently leaving only a few shards of blue-black shell, and a prawn's head or two. The young waiter looked his congratulations as he brought the *secondo*, a *fegato alla Veneziana*, and removed Tom's old plate with a flourish.

By the time he had finished his wine – he had drunk a white and a red – and paid the bill, the sallow man who had noticed the coat had probably left. Tom was in too happy a state even to remember the incident, but he put his coat on carefully and sauntered out into the frigid air. He had left his rucksack at the railway station when he had checked the trains. He felt wholly

101

at his ease; with a Venice now as much, and as demurely, his mistress as she had once been for Byron or for Wagner.

He had come, seen, and conquered. Moreover, as he remembered on the vaporetto, in his rucksack was still a bottle of wine and the salami he had bought, long ago it now seemed, at the grocer's, before he met Major Grey at that cafe-bar. The salami had no doubt remained fresh enough, under his cold bed in the *Locanda*. He could buy further provisions on the way, and fruit and more wine at Milan station. He even contemplated booking a couchette, but reason remounted her throne in time: even with Major Grey's mysterious bounty, the fee delicately bestowed for porterage of the overcoat, he had not *that* amount of money. A night and most of a day later he was back on the shore of the English channel.

*

Naturally enough, he was a bit less cheerful now; his holiday over, the writing of the thesis coming back uppermost in his mind. But there was Pinky to look forward to. She would want to hear all about his experiences. And he could a show her the coat! – The magical embodiment, like a talisman or a glass slipper, of all the excitements he had experienced.

In the customs hall at Dover, cigaretteless but with a modest bottle of whisky in his rucksack – Pinky sometimes liked a drop – Tom wandered to the Green exit in the somnambulistic manner of the returned traveller not yet adjusted to the mode of being of his native land. As he went through he happened to catch the eye of a young Sikh customs officer who was sitting in alert idleness on the other side, his thumbs folded and his eyes bright under his turban. 'Just one moment, sir,' he called out to Tom, who went up to him in all the suddenly conscious virtue of his non-possession, within the limits allowed, of any dutiable articles.

The officer may at once have noticed Tom's innocence, but he also noticed his coat. 'Now that is a very superior garment, if I may say so, sir,' he remarked smiling; and as Tom modestly acknowledged the fact, he patted the nap, the lappets and easy voluminous shoulders with admiration. 'Where are you getting it, sir?' he enquired. 'If in market abroad I will tell you at once there is nothing to pay, for the garment is most evidently not new. But I should like myself to stroll through such a market, I can tell you. Maybe you must have been finding real bargains?'

When he could get a word in, Tom explained that the coat was not his own, but had been lent him by a friend, to bring back to its real owner. When he heard this the young man continued to smile at Tom, from under his neat dark-blue turban; but he also began in a leisurely manner to rifle the rucksack, laying Tom's modest belongings on the counter. He showed some interest in the cockroach-defying Venetian chocolate, which Tom in his newfound prosperity had not attempted to eat; and then he put everything carefully back in the rucksack. Tom's ingenuous face and unaltered pulse-rate had evidently communicated themselves in some manner to the sensibilities which the men of the customs acquire. Briefly he maintained the jocularity he felt appropriate to Tom's age and appearance. But it was clear he had lost interest. Dismissing Tom with a friendly wave he turned back to contemplate other individuals in the passing stream.

The weather was muggy and mild; and for the first time the coat seemed to hang heavily on Tom's shoulders. He almost staggered into the train; and he removed it thankfully. Its job was completed; and in the tepid airs of England its opulent warmth seemed out of place. Tom was surprised now that he had ever been so anxious to keep it. He had indeed toyed with the notion of holding on to it for a few days, and enjoying the last sweets of possession before delivering it to Earls Court. But now its spell, like that of Venice itself, vanished in the workaday business of being home.

Home. Home meant seeing Pinky; but home unfortunately also meant his thesis, and going to see his supervisor, Dr Duckton, a wiry alert-looking man who usually wore a black leather jacket. Tom was somewhat in awe of him.

His decision to return the overcoat at once was confirmed by an absence of Pinky. He rang several times but she was not there. He rang the Hon. Giles Parker's number, and was surprised when a very Irish voice answered him. 'Wait now while I see,' it

103

said. And then, 'No, he's away out now, but you'll be getting him for sure at five o'clock. He'll be home if you call in then.'

At four Tom duly set out by Underground, his one desire now to be rid of that great and stifling incubus of coat. Pinky was still not available on the phone. Although he would call in on his own way home to be sure, he began to feel that she was certain to be out; perhaps for the evening, perhaps away for days, as she sometimes was. After all, when she had said goodbye to him at the station they had made no precise arrangement to meet on his return. Tom was disappointed; but, as he soon realised with surprise, not very much. Pinky in her own way could be exhausting; and by now he was feeling too worn out, and too lowered by the anti-climax of arrival, to wish for more than his digs and some supper, and bed.

He got out at Earls Court, and trailed back east through indistinguishable terraces. Two or three false starts and queries later he found the place and rang the bell. Voices could be heard inside; but nothing happened for several minutes, after which the door was flung violently open, and Tom found himself confronted by a tall and vague looking young man, who had the air of being in the last stages of intoxication. Swaying and muttering he thrust out his hands, possibly for support; and Tom, who had thankfully freed himself from the coat, now absorbed the shock of impact with its capacious bulk, and conveyed it into the young man's arms, with a few halting words of thanks and explanation.

He felt surprise, even in the brief moment, that Major Grey should have known such a person as this, and had him to stay. Behind him Tom caught a glimpse through the narrow hall-way of another room, with two men – could one of them have been the Irishman? – and a girl. Then an inner door was sharply closed. At the same moment the Hon. Giles Parker – if this indeed were he – collapsed sideways and outwards, recovered himself with a muffled braying sound that might have been one of apology, and shut the outer door with equal violence. Tom was left standing motionless on the landing. But he had known from that brief glimpse that the girl inside the room with those two men was Pinky.

Part Three

Naked Doctor

GINNIE was in the Tube when she saw Mark Brassey. He was just getting off and she was going on to her office not far from Russell Square, so there was nothing she could do about it. He disappeared in the crowd on the platform without appearing to have noticed her; but she was reminded by the glimpse of him that she had no idea of his address, or of Alice's either for that matter. Alice had come to call for her wedding parcels as soon as she got back, so she said; about ten days after Ginnie's own return. She'd rung up one evening when Ginnie was going through the proofs of one of her firm's authors – she did most of her work at home – and asked if she could come round right away.

It was not a very convenient moment, but Ginnie of course said yes. She was curious in any case to see Alice again, and to find out what she looked like – and what she herself felt about her – in the changed circumstances of being back home. Alice in fact was just the same, bounding into the little flat and embracing Ginnie warmly; treating her with the same coarse kindly proprietorship that had seemed to come naturally and instantly in Sorrento. Ginnie marvelled that she had once been in bed with this woman, but she was also relieved that there were no more flutterings of emotion and desire involved. At least there seemed not to be. She still felt amused by Alice; and she recognised in that amusement a kind of yearning too: she remembered a friend of hers saying of someone she had fallen in love with: 'He makes me laugh.'

Alice of course was full of laughs herself. Wasn't it a scream, she and Markie getting married? And Ginnie must come to the party – she'd ring again and give her the where and the wherefore; and Ginnie had been too wonderful to bring the stuff back,

105

and she couldn't wait to see it again and try it on. What a lark! But she hadn't opened the boxes to show Ginnie, though she mentioned the idea several times; and she hadn't had a drink, she was in too much of a rush; and that was the last Ginnie had seen of her.

It must have been about Christmas time, more than three months later, when she saw but failed to encounter Mark on the Tube; and then it made her realise that she had neither of their addresses. Alice's masterfulness had deprived her of will. After getting home she had obediently waited to be got in touch with; and the same paralysis had lasted until after Alice had picked up the boxes and breezed out. Afterwards she could have kicked herself. Although she was not quite sure whether or not she wanted to see Alice again, she would have liked at least to be able to get in touch with her.

Or did her failure to find out really mean that she had no wish to see either of them again – even at their wedding? Ginnie wondered this later on, but not until the further drama had begun to develop.

At first, as the weeks went by, she had put them out of her mind and got on with her own life, such as it was. Her mother had been ill, and had to be visited down at Chiswick. In fact she had a lodger in the little house down there, with whom she was on the best of terms, and who was able to look after her more effectively than her daughter could have done. Ginnie was well aware of that; but she felt none the less that she ought to get down as often as she could. From Gloucester Road it was a very simple journey.

In her own way Ginnie was really quite close to her mother. But she was often irritated, in spite of herself, by the airs and graces (Ginnie's own private term) the old lady had come increasingly to rely on in passing her days. Ginnie having been a late and only child her mother was in every sense much older. When she was married there had been the flat in Knightsbridge; and she was still inclined to make it clear to anyone who would listen, that Harrods, where she had shopped most days when her husband was alive, was her true environment.

Her daughter had preferred to come down in the world, as she was sure her mother privately considered the process. Certainly the young men who had been invited to the flat in the old days had never appealed to her, but nor had anyone else much. Ginnie found the intensity of love and friendship, as she saw them besieging and preoccupying other people, too much of a strain. She came early on to prefer a quiet life.

She felt guilty none the less sometimes about the money her mother had made over to her after her father died, and which enabled her to live in her small flat, and do a job which was congenial and more or less part-time. It was only natural she should not feel grateful – gratitude in any case is not a common emotion – yet it was equally natural she should remain attached to her mother, even fond of her sometimes. Besides, as time went on her mother had almost ceased to be critical of her daughter's lifestyle, or lack of it; and had come at least to seem to forget about the once absorbing question of a husband, and grandchildren. An affection all the more agreeable for being pointless had come to spring up between them, largely replacing the old preoccupations. Their chat and gossip, when they met now, was mostly one-sided, for her mother hardly wanted to hear what Ginnie had been doing, or whether she had met anyone. By which of course she had once meant anyone who might show signs of wanting to bear her daughter off, and give her a home of her own.

That phrase, which she had frequently heard from her mother in earlier days, had been a special source of irritation to Ginnie. A home of her own seemed so precisely what it would *not* be, if she were to be borne off – her mother so obviously did not think of Ginnie bearing anyone off herself. As it was, Ginnie felt she had a home that really was her own; and her flat suited her, though of course she hated or was bored with it sometimes.

Alice, and Mark Brassey, those wholly unexpected manifestations of her Sorrento holiday, had never really presented themselves in the light of new friends, or as becoming durable features of her existence. Once married they would disappear, she knew, even if they felt they should afterwards invite her at intervals. She could do without them going on being nice to her, and she would detach herself gradually.

The moment in the morning in bed with Alice, when she had finally slept, she continued to think about from time to time, until it ceased to give her a pang, and became quite a pleasant memory.

It was not so much that Ginnie had something hard about her as that a good many years of living on her own had helped to settle and confirm her in a naturally romantic and yet unsentimental view of human nature. What she had come to like was what she had heard a man at the office rather pompously refer to as the contextual bonding of the work situation. Towards present, and even past, colleagues she felt a friendliness which had no strings attached, no special obligations of caring or loyalty. You just worked and talked with them; and sometimes had a drink or meal or even an affair, although that particular aspect of bonding had never come Ginnie's way as it happened. It did cross her mind to wonder if Alice and Mark, in their different ways, had once held a similar view of whatever it was they did – 'bonking' apparently, in Alice's case.

Wondering about somebody, however briefly, tends to conjure them into existence. Spring was beginning now; and Ginnie had come back from one of her more moderately full days at the office, visiting the supermarket on her way home. She was looking forward, as she always did, to having her drink and making a small meal for herself. She seldom bothered to cook much, but she enjoyed her supper none the less, while listening to the 7.30 concert on Radio 3, and then to Kaleidoscope on 4. In fact she scarcely did listen, but she liked the radio on for those programmes. She also read a book. It was never one of the scripts she had to read or revise in the line of duty, but some old favourite she had read often before.

It was just while she was enjoying her tinned crab, with olive oil and lemon juice and a carton of cress, that the bell rang. Ginnie said under her breath a word she would not have uttered in public. The bell rang again; and then, after an impolitely short interval, a third time. She got up and stood still a minute to see if she could hear anything else. The door was in a corner of her living-room, and there was no answerphone for the higgledy-piggledy arrangement of two-room flats in what had once been a big house. She would have to go down to the outside door.

Mark Brassey looked just as she remembered, and as she had seen him on the Tube platform. Just the same, indeed, as when she first saw him by the bookcase in the hotel. What had been the name of the novel? *Ramazan the Rajah*? By Ruby somebody?

But Mark had an impatient look, which was not at all as she remembered him. He almost pushed his way in. As she led him upstairs Ginnie said it was nice to see him again. Would he like a drink?

He shook his head. His air of preoccupation increased. He looked at her carefully. She took nervous refuge in speech, saying she had seen him in the Underground but he had not seen her. He brushed that aside, implying that he had indeed seen her but had preferred to let it go.

'Have you seen Alice?' He spoke with an abrupt mixture of intimacy and authority that Ginnie found offensive.

'Not since she came to pick up her parcels.'

He ignored that. Reverting as best she could to a chilly demeanour, Ginnie asked him how he was. He ignored that too.

'Did Alice tell you anything?'

'When?' asked Ginnie, at once in a fluster. On her guard too. If Mark wanted to find out anything of what she knew about Alice, she was not going to tell him. Not that she felt she must be loyal to Alice. But if Mark was going to marry her he must find out about her for himself.

Mark appeared to take a different view. 'How much did you hear of what she was doing?' he persisted.

Ginnie felt she had heard a good deal. She recalled with an involuntary grimace Alice's evocation of all those cosmopolitan males on cruise ships, who spotted her on the beach and began to feel like a 'bonk'. After her own vision of the Pure White Woman of Sorrento that had been an upsetting moment. But she wasn't going to let Mark browbeat her now.

'I'd hardly met her myself at the time you did,' she pointed out. 'You were the one she must have talked to, surely?'

It was true that Mark had ample opportunity in those days to converse with the woman he had fallen in love with. Why shouldn't she remind him of the fact? It was his own fault if he were still in the dark about his fiancée.

Looking impatient, indeed exasperated, her visitor exclaimed, 'God! Don't you realise?' – and broke off as if he had thought better of it. He glared at her, and she did her best to glare back. She had the perturbing impression that they were locked into a misunderstanding which he, for some reason, was reluctant to dispel. But 'Realise what?' she none the less demanded, attempting to follow up her advantage, such as it was. He would not bully her into revealing what Alice had said when they were alone together.

But Mark seemed to give up at this point, as if finding beyond his powers of penetration the wall of density that either came naturally to her, or which she had perversely chosen to present. He shrugged his shoulders and turned towards the door, still seeming reluctant to disabuse her of an all but incredible out-of-touchness. Ginnie grew alarmed, especially when he muttered, as if for goodbye, that they might all find themselves in trouble. Was the man threatening her for alienating his intended's affections? Mark was a solicitor, after all, and might be expected to be litigious. Was lesbianism illegal in Italy, and had he somehow found out about the night she and Alice had spent together? Were the police out there going to prosecute Alice for undisclosed immoral earnings? Would she, Ginnie, have to appear as a witness?

All these things and more now seemed possible, at least to her flustered imagination. Staring at him in round-eyed dismay she suddenly remembered the query that might at least hark them back to their old relationship.

'And what about your wedding? When is to be then?'

'It's off,' he told her, as if relieved by a query which, however imbecile, could at least be answered with brutal honesty.

'Oh dear!' cried Ginnie, genuinely upset. 'I *am* sorry.'

'Yes,' Mark concluded on the way out, as if to give her a taste of the same treatment he must feel himself to have received. 'It's off. Alice chucked me.'

*

Ginnie suspected that what Mark had really wanted to know was if she had seen Alice, which of course she hadn't. And she must surely have made it clear, even if accidentally, that she was ignorant of anything that might have been going on. Mark must have thought she had been confided in; but women do not necessarily confide in other women, as Ginnie could have told him. Yet she remained discomposedly aware that he hadn't just come to tell her he and Alice were not getting married. What was he up to? Had Alice vanished, and did he think Ginnie knew where she was?

And yet she was shrewd enough to realise that whatever it was he was worried about must include all three of them. Why?

In spite of all this, and the real state of bother to which his visit had reduced her, Ginnie could not but remember her first peaceful encounters with him at the restaurant; and his placid pleasure in being curious, but not too curious. It had itself been a kind of confiding when he had implied that neither of them quite belonged in today's world: and his unspoken assumption that they both preferred things that way.

Ginnie was conscious of an odd sort of loyalty to those moments, so definitively cut off by the defection of Mark to Alice. Defection? Well, it was true the evening had ended in Alice, not Mark, carrying her off to bed. In a sense it was she who had betrayed him that night, after they had both seemed so sure, during their dining out, what it was they expected and wanted from their holidays.

If that were so he had certainly restored the balance next day. Just how he had met with and carried off Alice – or been carried off by her – was still mysterious to Ginnie; but there was no doubt that it had taken place. Ginnie found it difficult to recognise or imagine *folie à deux*, a mutual *coup de foudre*. There was no doubt it was Alice who had taken *her* captive, although at the time she had felt more like a customer who feels it would be uncivil to refuse the salesman's offer. And in any case there had been nothing – or almost nothing – romantic about that captivity. It was not what Ramazan must have planned for his Virginia, in the little old brown-paged novel.

Her own captivity had been sleepless, as Ginnie remembered only too well. Never before that night had wakefulness seemed so positive a state, but of course there had been compensations. Joy, of a sort, had come in the morning. How strange were people's motives and desires! But stranger still the stories that they told themselves, and then tried, perhaps unconsciously, to find a real-life equivalent.

111

Yet she felt sure she had never imagined anything like the woman of Sorrento. Or so she supposed. Had Alice simply been waiting in the depths of her mind, like a butterfly in the chrysalis? And now there seemed something like a fabulous flying creature about her – gaudy, agile and strong-winged. Ginnie suddenly longed very much to see her again.

The wish was granted very quickly. Only a few days after Mark had been trying, as it appeared, to discompose her into revealing anything she might know of Alice's motives and whereabouts, there came another ring at the bell. Only it was not in the evening this time, but between six and seven in the morning.

Ginnie could not have said she had a premonition, but she had certainly been thoroughly unsettled since Mark Brassey's visit. Even her mother had noticed something wrong, but she had long ceased to take an interest in Ginnie's moods, and what they might reveal of her current emotions. In former days, Ginnie had often been irritated by her mother's too conscious display of tact, always based on the assumption that her daughter's love life (as she would have spoken of it to her friends) was not going according to plan. She all too obviously knew that wise mothers did not ask questions or interfere.

Mrs Thornton had no doubt imbibed this hint from the agony aunt of a woman's magazine. She read them avidly while pretending to despise them; and Ginnie read them too, but without any pretence of contempt. She concealed the habit from her mother but not from the people at the office, who greatly respected her low-profile knowledge of the genre.

Going down in her housecoat, she supposed this must be an unusually early call by the postman. She kept the battered old door on the chain, though, and made the usual enquiry.

'Yes, what is it?'

An agitated young male voice from the outside said 'You don't know me, Miss Thornton, but I believe you know Pinky, Pinky my fiancée – and she asked me to come and see you. She's very much worried, and she hopes you'll help her.'

The voice gave a kind of gasp at the end of this speech, which sounded as if it had been prepared. Not with any sinister intent, but to try to convey a message as coherently as possible. The

112

voice itself was what Ginnie thought of as 'student impersonal': the lingua franca you heard all over London, which embodied in dilute form several local accents without being obviously any one of them.

Ginnie did not feel frightened by the voice, but she could make no sense of what it was talking about. She wondered vaguely if this could be a device for a break-in. There had been so many of them; Neighbourhood Watch was always in a tizzy about it. She often thought nowadays of something she had once read, and which had made a comical appeal to her, about the Mongol Empire at the height of its authority and power. It was the boast of the Lord Chief Justice, or whatever was his Mongol equivalent, that a virgin with a pot of gold on her head could walk from Baghdad to Pekin without being robbed or molested. In modern London, it had occurred to Ginnie, the girl would be lucky to make it to the bottom of Lexham Gardens.

Through the crack above the chain she could make out jeans, in the usual worn condition, and above them a pale and distracted young face. Jeans could mean anything, but the face reassured Ginnie. It seemed so clearly guileless. She opened the door.

She saw at once that the young man was in an even worse state of nerves than his voice had indicated. He cringed away as if Ginnie could do him actual bodily harm. After his prepared speech he seemed tongue-tied; and she had perforce to help him out.

'Who is it you want?' she asked. 'I don't know anyone of that name. Are you sure you've got the right address?'

'Pinky – Pinky my fiancée.' He seemed to cling to that word as if it gave him some crumb of solid ceremonial comfort and reassurance in an otherwise disintegrating world. Ginnie was naturally reminded of Mark and his fiancée, and felt as if she were becoming saddled with that quaintly obsolescent title: first from her oldfashioned fellow-guest at the hotel, and now with this apparently equally oldfashioned young man.

'You met her in Sorrento,' the young man went on 'You were on holiday together weren't you?'

Bit by bit of course the thing came out; and in the meantime Ginnie had made the young man tea, and offered him biscuits

113

which he was unable to eat. What was the matter with him? Why was he in such a state? He was in a state because of Pinky, his fiancée, who appeared to be the same girl as Alice. At the notion of Alice Ginnie began to feel distraught too, as well as excited. For it appeared – almost incredibly – that Alice, whose alias seemed to be Pinky, had some kind of close connection with this young man, whose name was Tom.

Unable to sit, or to remain still, he kept saying they must go as soon as Ginnie could manage. Pinky was in some sort of desperate trouble. He would tell her what he knew on the way. His fear and anxiety began to penetrate to Ginnie, who trotted about her tiny flat in a numbed condition, putting things – usually the wrong things – in her holdall. Tom had urged upon her the need to take what was required for staying a night, if need be.

At any rate she would be seeing Pinky-Alice, or Alice-Pinky again – that was for sure, as her own Alice would have put it. And yet what was going on was still incomprehensible to her. It appeared the young man Tom had known Alice for some time; and that she seemed to be, or so he said, his fiancée. Again and again that somehow faintly ludicrous title, or social state. Did Alice make a habit of going about getting engaged to people? Could it be why she had chucked Mark? No, that could hardly be. Alice-Pinky must be presumed to have been engaged to both of them – at some period, and for some reason.

And now she was in desperate trouble, 'hiding out', as Tom distractedly put it; although who she was hiding from – the police? some private enemy, or jealous ruffian? – remained wholly unclear. Nor was Tom even clear about where she was – somewhere on the coast he said.

It had all begun yesterday when she had left an urgent message for him to ring her. The switchboard at his college department – Tom had no phone at his digs – had accepted the call; but Tom had not got the message for some time. And by the time he rang her Pinky had been in a state. He had felt quite afraid of her, but he was also extremely alarmed and upset. It seemed possible to him that this 'trouble' of Pinky might have something to do with those odd people in the flat where he had delivered the overcoat.

Of course the first time he had seen Pinky after that he had

114

asked her whether she had been there, at that flat, adding that he could have made a mistake. It could just have been some girl with a resemblance to her. Pinky had looked quite blank, and had said – rather unnecessarily he thought – that this was some utter nonsense, that she had no idea what he was talking about.

'But you see, Miss Thornton, I really do think it was Pinky there,' he said earnestly, as he led Ginnie round the corner to the traffic meter where he had parked the car.

Ginnie was faintly amused by 'Miss Thornton', but she didn't tell him to call her Ginnie. She was too bemused by the general oddity of what Tom had been telling her. It seemed to make no sense, and yet there was something sinister about it – that could hardly be denied. Or at least fishy. Could it have any connection with Mark's visit, and his own odd behaviour?

Tom's Pinky had asked him all about Venice. But since then, although he had often rung her up and tried to fix meetings, she had always been busy, saying that she was just finding a new job, or going away for a few days. Tom said, rather pathetically, that she hardly seemed to behave like an engaged girl at all. She paid very little attention when he told her how much he loved her, and wanted to see her. Ginnie was touched by this, but increasingly puzzled. She found it hard to see how his Pinky, and her Alice, could really be the same person.

When he first got her message Tom had been delighted: it sounded as if she were needing him and calling for his help as an engaged girl might be expected to do. But when he had rung her at the number she gave he had been both alarmed at the sound of her voice, and staggered by the directions she at once gave him. What she required of him seemed no less drastic than it was brutally exact. He was to hire a car – she'd known he'd passed his test and had a licence – buy a map and petrol and a duvet or sleeping bag; get hold of Ginnie, and come down to Greatstone-on-Sea – the bungalow on the beach was called 'Silver Spray'. But above all he must get hold of Ginnie.

In a daze Tom had done all that she had told him to. She had given him Ginnie's address but not her phone number, and he had been too confused to think of looking it up in the book. By the time he had got everything ready the day before it was quite late. As it happened Ginnie had been out that evening; he had

115

called round twice and got no reply when he rang the bell; so in terror of finding her out again in the morning he had determined to come round at the earliest possible hour.

Listening to all this Ginnie felt flattered; more than flattered – chosen – like a Bride of Israel. For some reason Alice needed her – there seemed no doubt about that. Even more than a bride she felt for the first time like a mother, sought out in extremity by a normally captious and patronising offspring. What Tom felt she had no idea. Somehow he did not act quite like a lover going to the rescue of his mistress, though he may have seen himself in that light. But as they threaded an uncertain way together through the maze of South London streets she began to feel quite at home with him. He seemed a nice young man, and of course he was as bothered and bewildered as she was. Much more so in fact.

And yet their distracted chat in the hired Ford Fiesta, as they tried to get themselves out of London, revealed very little of either the knowledge or the ignorance they shared. Alice-Pinky had become an inescapable fact in both their lives. 'Alice may have been one of her names,' said Tom, glancing hopelessly at the traffic signs by the Elephant and Castle, 'but for me she was just Pinky. I should have found out more, I suppose, but it was so wonderful when we got engaged. I couldn't believe it,' he added despondently, as he strove with the mass of vehicles on both sides of them, while Ginnie peered in distraction at the map, and wondered how soon an accident would happen.

It was a nightmare drive. They had managed neatly to run into the morning rush hour on the South Orbital, and after what seemed hairbreadth escapes from thundering lorries they came rapidly to a standstill head to tail. Ginnie began to wish she had gone to the loo before she left – she had been too preoccupied to think of it. Hours later, as it seemed, while they were still crawling in the queue, Tom's worried voice wondered whether there would be time for him to jump out for a moment and disappear (if he could) down the bank.

Ginnie reflected, not for the first time, on the disadvantage of being a female in this situation. She spoke of this; and a concerned Tom turned for the first time to look at her. But first things first where he was concerned: gauging his moment he leapt out, and at least partly vanished. Ginnie removed her gaze from his concentrated back, and hoped they would not have to move until he was through. The man behind was just giving a first hoot as Tom regained the car.

Ginnie's own need, as they lost their way round a junction and had to crawl on and on for miles until they could exit and get back, was becoming more acute every minute; and she deeply regretted her early morning tea. She had bemusedly drunk so many cups while listening to Tom. She supposed that every drama in life contained these incongruous needs: needs which soon became major preoccupations. Ginnie wondered if the virgin with the pot of gold would have had trouble of the same kind on her long journey. Very likely. But the Mongolian Lord Chief Justice would no doubt have ignored that aspect of the matter, concerned only with the virgin's value as a public relations image.

At last Tom managed to stop illegally on the motorway, in a sort of giant cutting; and Ginnie scrambled self-consciously through a smashed up fence, where plastic bags and nameless refuse had been ground into the trampled weeds and brambles. She had a sense of furtive occupation, even of danger, as she crouched as if in a wind-tunnel, buffeted by the roar of speeding juggernauts. A mouse whisked from behind a bent lager tin, looked at her without fear or interest, and disappeared again.

After that the journey improved. From the map Tom had bought Ginnie was at least able to see their destination clearly; and at long last they came down from the weald of Kent on to a thinner but straighter road, which led them across a canal and on to a wide open expanse of field and marshland. Something in the feel of space made Ginnie's spirits rise, as if she were ten again and going on holiday. It was a kind of adventure after all. Perhaps it would all turn out to be fun of a kind from long ago – long before the encounter at Sorrento.

On they went, past bungalows and sheep, and churches standing up on small green hillocks. As they drove on the sky steadily increased, until each of these objects could be seen for miles. On both sides were wide reed-filled dykes, with the light above them hazy and silvery. Then suddenly what could only be the sea was in front of them, beside a dilapidated Victorian hotel and a line of terraced houses.

'The map says turn right,' said Ginnie.

In a few minutes or hours they might be strangers again, though both were too absorbed in their problems to think of that. Tom only gave a grunt.

'Should be anywhere along here now. Did she say exactly?'

'Not really, no. On the side of the road she said. Not the sea side.'

They drove on along a narrow ribbon of concrete, laid straight upon the grassy sand in what seemed an amateurish way. Every few yards the tyres gave a bump as they entered a new stretch. On either side plains and inclines of brownish and bluish shingle seemed to have spawned little houses, some rustic in style, some glass and cement, all with their windows turned compulsively towards the sea. The sea itself remained indeterminate; a presumed feature beyond bright wastes of sandy mud.

'The tide always seems out at this kind of seaside,' said Tom. 'But perhaps it varies.'

'I shouldn't think it ever comes in here,' said Ginnie. 'Not really.'

To themselves, even to each other, their voices had an unnatural and worried sound. They were bracing themselves to confront 'Silver Spray'. For both of them, though in different ways, Alice loomed as the ordeal.

The name and the bungalow did not seem to turn up, as if because both shrank from the fact that it would. They stopped every few yards to read names. Alice, or Pinky, had told Tom it was clearly marked.

The little houses began to fall away, and sky and space grew even larger. Ginnie began to wish they could drive on and on, into the wide open March day, between the sandflats and the miles of inland shingle, darkened here and there with low patches of scrub. But now fishing-boats were appearing, and a lighthouse marked in broad stripes of black and white. The road showed signs of petering out.

'We'd better go back,' said Tom.

They turned among tarry oddments, nearly getting stuck in the shingle. It was odd how they had missed 'Silver Spray' the first time, for there was the sign, done in white wire in the cinema script of the late thirties. They stopped, and Tom after a longish pause got out and looked at the sign more closely. The thin wire it was made of had rusted and was broken off in places.

'It doesn't show from the other side,' said Tom, bending his head to and fro, as if to give himself something to do before the bad moment.

It was one of the most nondescript of the bungalows, predominantly grey in colour, and very small. Sand and marram grass went up to the faded green front door, although someone in the past had put in a tamarisk and a euonymus bush or two, which straggled forlornly. It stood a little back on the landward side of the road, its blank front windows yearning like all the others towards the vast invisible sea, though the view was blocked to some extent by the seaward row of houses, raised up a little by the sand dunes. The one opposite 'Silver Spray' was called 'Sand Dunes'.

Ginnie and Tom avoided looking at each other. Each knew the other to be tense, in ways hardly as yet understood. Ginnie was having a persistent vision of Alice lying inside, dead in some way; the bungalow certainly looked just the place to be found dead in. Her present vision of it went with an accurate memory of the tall white girl in the purple bikini, swaying lazily down to the water for her lustral bath, with the motionless liner in the background.

There was a bell beside the door. Tom rang it. There was no sound of ringing in the house. Everything was very quiet, with the March wind, mild down here, soughing gently through the bushes, and the long marram grass.

Ginnie noticed a screw of paper tucked under the door so that it showed. Bending down she extracted it. 'Come round to the back,' it said simply.

They obeyed. The back door was open. Standing in the doorway was Alice.

Ginnie had a second's recall of a woman her parents had known when she was a child. Something frightful had happened to her which Ginnie's parents knew nothing about, until she turned up, looking much the same, a couple of years later. Ginnie thought of that woman now. Alice too looked much the

119

same. She was not dead, neither was she altered in any way; but she was certainly not the girl in the purple bikini. That was for sure. She showed no surprise at seeing them.

'Well, you poor things!' she said. 'Was it a hell of a drive? Come in, children. Welcome to my humble abode.'

For Ginnie she seemed to have no charm left. Like Tom she was wearing raggedy jeans, which on her were horribly unbecoming. A grubby teeshirt with some for the moment unreadable slogan looked out with her bust from the drooping jacket. All that remained was the overwhelming magic of her patronage; but for Tom at her side – Ginnie could feel it – that was enough.

They entered the little kitchen. A veteran refrigerator, streaked with rust, thrummed away, shaking on its top a plate with something half eaten. It gurgled and lurched into silence. Ginnie suddenly felt almost faint with hunger. She wondered if Tom did too.

With a competence that rather surprised Ginnie, Alice made them toast and a fried egg, turning whatever it was left on her own plate into a bucket and giving it a perfunctory rinse under the tap before putting Ginnie's share on it. Ginnie was rather touched by that. Tom got a plate of his own, a small one that looked cracked.

'This is the last tucker there is on the station,' announced their hostess, reverting to her Australian manner. 'After this yer on yer own.'

They both smiled at her uncertainly. There was nowhere much to sit, and Tom ate his breakfast awkwardly on the top of the refrigerator. Leaves from the neglected euonymus scratched the little window, which had a lace curtain half way up it on a rusty wire. Above it at the back of the bungalow there was nothing to be seen but sand and pebbles running into marsh tract and a chilly-looking salt lagoon. A sturdy church tower stood out from trees in the far distance.

'So here I am all on *my* own,' resumed Alice. 'And you two dear children have come to look after me. Don't think I'm not grateful.'

Later they were sent out to shop. Alice explained that the small supermarket was some way off. Picking tins off the shelves with Tom, and consulting with him as to their probable domestic requirements, Ginnie was seized with the sensation of complete unreality. What on earth was Alice up to? Why did she claim this desperate need of them, sending her distraught young messenger to knock up Ginnie in the dawn? Fortunately it had not been a day for the office, but she would have to do some telephoning soon. Another thing: Tom's status as lover and loved one seemed completely in abeyance. Alice, closer in age to Ginnie than she was to Tom, treated both of them with the same bossy maternal briskness, as if it were they, and not she, who needed help.

Ginnie could hardly know or admit to herself that she was in love with Alice, and that her original vision still beckoned her like a siren. Funnily enough, the word itself had come into her head back at the bungalow, looking out at the sea and at the back towards the saltmarsh. Alice seemed right for those parts, as she had done when she sauntered into the blue water at Sorrento. Ginnie remembered her own funny little room there, on its two levels, with the vertiginous outlook; and she remembered too that the hotel had been called 'the Siren and Victor Emmanuel', or something like that. Siren or dragon-fly, Alice certainly seemed to devour or to fascinate everyone she met.

Ginnie looked at Tom, who was staring bemusedly at the labels on groceries. Oddly enough he had just found a jar in the spice area called Major Grey's Mango Chutney. He added it to their trolley, involuntarily smiling to himself.

'What's amused you?' asked Ginnie. She felt at ease with Tom, precisely as she did with people at work. They had become colleagues. At the minute she had a script to read, and was annoyed with herself for failing to bring it. She felt she could even have shown it to Tom and asked his opinion.

Pointing at the pickle bottle he now explained to her about Major Grey. Although he did not go into the details of what had happened Ginnie was struck by what seemed a parallel with her own holiday experiences. But there was no leisure now to think of that: Alice at least had infected them both with her own underlying feel of urgency, of imminent crisis. Tom looked helpless at the check-out, and murmured some apologies about having spent all his money. Ginnie paid with her banker's card, remembering he was a student with recent heavy outgoings on car-hire etc. She made a clucking noise of sympathy, saying it was too bad of Alice – they must get her to repay Tom. At the last moment it occurred to her that they had bought nothing to drink. A bottle of the vermouth she liked could only improve an evening at 'Silver Spray'. They turned back, and decided also to buy two bottles of wine, a red and a white.

Back past the bungalows and dykes, along the mile of straight road to the sea, they spoke vaguely of Alice, but neither seemed to know what to say about her. Ginnie made some effort to ascertain his feelings, but Tom was still unable to say much. She thought that perhaps, like Mark Brassey, he fancied the feeling of being engaged. But Mark, who had reappeared so abruptly a week ago to interrogate her about Alice, remained totally mysterious to her. She thought of Alice at 'Silver Spray', in her horrid clothes, and wondered if Tom, like herself, felt a sort of increase of loyalty and tenderness towards a loved one who was looking far from her best. What an oldfashioned lot they all were was, for a moment, Ginnie's slightly sour reflection.

The March sun was already beginning to set when they got back to the bungalow. The great sky was luminous over its whole horizon, but the grey sea still seemed no nearer. Alice had told them to come to the back door, as before, and they carried their groceries laboriously through the grassy sand. As they turned the corner of the tacky little box Ginnie was startled to see Alice's face behind the curtain at the front window, turned not towards them but looking out down the road. She greeted them boisterously at the back; and Ginnie and Tom, who had had a long day, began separately to feel they had lived in the bungalow a long time.

They were certainly on top of each other. In front of the minute kitchen and divided by the dark passage to the front door, were only two rooms. Ginnie began to look round for the loo. Loos, or the lack of them, seemed to figure largely in their adventures since this morning. The nearness of the installation at Silver Spray was emphasised by a loud hissing, and she disappeared into it thankfully, while remaining conscious of the close proximity of the others.

She listened with interest to hear what Alice and Tom would

have to say to each other, but there was no intimacy in the remarks she overheard, nor any suggestion of a caress. Their relations seemed to exist in a vacancy, not unsuited to the time and place of their original meeting; with the idea of an 'engagement' to give hope for Tom, and, as Ginnie was beginning increasingly to suspect, to give some kind of unspecified convenience to Alice. No sex appeared to be involved. Everything now in human relations was supposed to be sex: but Ginnie was also beginning to wonder whether there wasn't much less of it about than people realised.

Nevertheless the meal that followed was far from not being a success. The vermouth helped, and they ate in the front room, where there was a reasonable sized table, and a fire which Tom had managed, after some efforts, to light. Alice produced her first show of warmth to him for this achievement, and Ginnie imagined the woodsmoke curling off the tiny roof into that huge pellucid sky, darkened now, but much lighter than inland, and lit by the recurring beam of the lighthouse and the red wink of more distant signals in France or on the sea. Alice fixed the folkweave curtains with a good deal of care, and remarked that Ginnie and Tom were just like a pair of holidaymakers. 'And that's what I want you to be,' she said. 'Look kids, I'll tell you all about it after supper. Promise. OK?'

She was as good as her word.

*

'But Alice, why on earth did you come down here?' asked Ginnie, as soon as she was able to say anything. Alice's explanation of what it was all about had left her at first without a word to say. Tom also stared at his Pinky, opened his mouth like a fish, and was silent.

Someone had to start somewhere. The most pointless part of the nightmare into which Alice had suddenly plunged them was the one that first occurred to Ginnie to ask about.

'Well, Gin, it's m'safe house, you see. No one knows I'm here – at least I hope they don't. I bought this funny little shanty to retire to' – she gave a great laugh, but her eyes, confronting theirs, were uneasy. 'I know it's a bit lacking in the mod. cons.,

123

but I like this place. All the sky, and that feel of the great bugger-all, you know. I guess it reminds me of Australia. And it's handy for getting abroad.'

For some reason Ginnie could not feel outraged exactly. Indeed she felt more inclined to laugh, even though the laughter might have become a *fou rire*, verging on hysteria. There was no doubt that Alice had gone too far. What she had done, and what she had told them, was, in a curious sense, too awful to be taken seriously. And in 'confessing' it to them she had not for a moment lost the initiative, the hold she still seemed to have over them both.

Tom was staring with fascination at the words done in dark green on her pinkish teeshirt. 'When you've quite done ogling m'bust, m'boy,' Alice told him, 'I'd like volunteers for washing up. Got to maintain the standards. Then I'll hit the hay. Never slept a wink last night, or the one before. Gin, you'd better sleep with me if you can bear it. You'll be quite safe – I'll take the camp bed. Tom, you can have the sofa in here. It'll be warm enough with that duvet you brought. We girls'll use the rest of the clobber. God, but it's a joy to see you both. I've been ever so lonesome I *promise*. I'm no end grateful to both of you dear things.'

Alice's teeshirt had indeed been the focal point of her explanation. 'Naked Doctor' were the words on it, in a flowing and rather tasteful script. 'That's the stuff you were carrying for me,' she told them. 'Oh, gosh I know I owe you an apology for that, chicks.' But look, it's not just for the money in it. This stuff's real good, *and* it doesn't do any harm. We know that – we've proved it. That's why I had these teeshirts made. We're so sure it's going to be a big hit, just as soon as we can get it legalised. It's less harm even than hash – more like coke. OK, you can say it's addictive, but ain't coke addictive? Coca-cola I mean – not the white stuff. The point about Naked Doctor is that it's the perfect drug; and, honest, we hope it's going to drive out the bad ones, once we get going. I don't say there's not a lot of money in it, but I wouldn't be in it – believe you me – not for a moment – if I didn't know it wasn't harmless. It's the real stuff for the future world.'

She paused and lit a cigarette. Ginnie didn't remember her smoking. So she and Tom had unwittingly carried back into the country several pounds, or kilos, or whatever, of a fabulous new drug.

Alice knocked back the last of her red wine. They had now finished both bottles. 'Gee, I know it's a mean trick,' she went on, quite humbly for her, but still with her usual air of patronage, 'but it's the certain way, you see. There's never any trouble when the carriers don't know. We've never had a failure yet.'

She paused again and brooded a bit, puffing the last of her cigarette. It had been then that Ginnie made her first comment, and asked about the little bungalow at Greatstone.

'Have you ever tried the stuff yourself?' enquired Tom, when Alice had given her lyric account of the joys of Romney Marsh. He was staring, as if still in disbelief, at the legend on her chest.

'God yes, got to try it, y'know. I wouldn't let you or Gin use it, even though it's quite harmless. I've never been into drugs myself – don't seem to need to – but the point is: it takes you off everything else – off the hard stuff. It's reelly wonderful. Like it was a solution, you know – the welfare state and the hippies rolled into one. That's why someone – not me I admit, I'm modest – dreamed up this name for it. Doctor, you see, what everyone needs today some time – and naked, sort of friendly. It'll be cheap too – undercut all the others. I tell you it's going to be a wow.'

For the moment there seemed to be no more to say. Ginnie felt unequal to further query. Neither she nor Tom seemed to have any need or nerve to reproach Alice. But they did not look at each other. Separately, in themselves, they had enough to do wondering how they could have been so stupid. That in itself was a banal occupation, but it could hardly be avoided. It did not occur to Ginnie for the moment to feel frightened for herself, but she was wondering about Alice: not about her explanation and her recent activities, but about the state she was in, and the reasons why she was here. She still felt drawn to Alice and now almost protective, but that romantic distant image – the White Queen of Sorrento – that was gone, and surely for good. So was any fondness for the memory of the early morning in bed together. Alice now seemed a miserable thing.

And yet Ginnie had to admit that there was still something noble even in her shameful frankness, in the very pretensions of her absurdity. She continued to dominate, to exercise control. And lying is her own form of sincerity, thought Ginnie, unconscious in the tension of the moment that she had inadvertently coined a *bon mot*.

Tom's thoughts were also incongruous and far away. He could not help seeing Major Grey in his mind's eye, and comparing that appearance and behaviour – so vividly remembered – with the taste of the chutney he had eaten at supper-time. He also thought of the great coat. Where was it now? He remembered how blissfully warm it had been in Venice: how heavy and stifling it had felt in Earls Court. In that silk taffeta lining, so cunningly wadded, must have lurked a great mass of this new wonder drug – the Naked Doctor. He remembered the Sikh customs man in the sleek dark blue turban, and how he admired the coat.

'A very select garment, sir' – was that what he had said? Well he had come very close to finding out just how select it was. Tom shuddered a bit, but then recalled his own perfect innocence at the time, which the customs man must have intuited too. Well well! – and that innocence was now a thing of the past. What did he feel now about his Pinky? – he could not take his eyes off what now seemed the appropriately pinkish shade of her teeshirt. She had turned out to be not his Pinky at all; and, no, he could not at the moment say he had any feelings about this new lady, one way or the other.

The wine being finished, and there seeming nothing else much to do or say, they embarked on a simple process of washing-up, hardly all able to fit into the kitchen. Ginnie washed and Tom dried: Alice did nothing much except saunter back and forth, carrying the odd plate. 'Think I'll take a shower,' she announced. 'There's no bath here, I fear, and bloody little hot water, so go easy with it, Gin.'

The builder's specification for Silver Spray, in what now seemed those cheerful holiday times of the 1930s, must have been very basic. Were happy holidaymakers expected to wash in the sea, Ginnie wondered, and if so how did they get to it? At some point lean-to extensions had been added either side of the back door, one of which housed a rickety shower, and Alice's presence in it was soon extremely apparent to her guests, particularly to Tom. Ginnie, noticing he looked pale and stricken, felt sorry for him. He must feel that his fiancée, and all his expectations of her, had somehow vanished away; and in her place was a now naked female drug-dealer, cursing the soap behind a cardboard partition a foot or so from his head.

And what about her own expectations as she lay uncomfortably in her night-dress – she had remembered to bring that with her – in the collapsed and lumpy bed? Was Alice, creaking and muttering as she turned over on her own makeshift couch in the corner, still asserting her patronage? Even in this act of penance and abnegation?

Though she felt she had no feelings of any sort now about Alice, Ginnie had naturally protested against her own use of the bed, such as it was, and invited her hostess to join her – striving with sincerity to make the offer seem one of mere practical convenience. Alice was friendly but firm. Seeming to acknowledge that her real self, as revealed in her recent disclosures, had put an end to any previous relationship, she saw her friends as good sports who had come to her aid; and for whom she would do her best impersonally and collectively, while retaining them under her patronage. Ginnie knew that Alice the drug-smuggler could only be awful, indeed horrible, in spite of anything she had told them about the new stuff. But perversely, as she lay sleepless, and thinking of that other sleepless occasion in Sorrento, she felt herself in some way rejected. And surely it was not for Alice to do the rejecting?

Each point of the sharp marram grass seemed to scratch the thin wall at her ear; but to this neighbourly crepitation, and the rustling of the sand outside, she drifted off at last. She woke suddenly to hear the noises again; and then, in the silence they made, a small sob. It seemed interrogatory, Ginnie thought, and she feigned sleep; but the next moment Alice was leaning over her, and saying in a small voice, 'Oh, Gin, I'm so miserable.'

As the other girl climbed on to the lumpy mattress beside her Ginnie noticed that she did not whisper, but spoke in a low murmur which carried much less far. A piece of Aussie know-how no doubt; and highly practical in a house like Silver Spray; but Ginnie's cynical thought did not stop her melting with sympathy, and a kind of joy, as tears touched her from the invisible face beside her own.

Alice was saying into her ear that she hadn't told the whole truth after supper; that the stuff *was* bad of course, one of the hard ones, and very valuable; that she longed to get out of the business; that she was in a real pickle now, and terrified of Markie, who she was sure had shopped her. But her Gin and Tom would go on helping her, wouldn't they? Just being here they gave her a kind of cover, like a real holiday couple. She herself hadn't been out for days, and she wasn't going to. And her Gin was oh, ever such a comfort.

Instinctively replying in the same low murmur as Alice, Ginnie felt she already knew all this. As if unconsciously, for it hadn't occurred to her to doubt the tale at the time – it seemed plausible enough the way things were today – she had not actually believed Alice: and she wondered now whether Tom had not done so either. But perhaps his feeling for his 'fiancée' – Ginnie remembered his distraught face when he had come to pick her up – had made him not even consider the question.

'What about Mark?' she murmured. 'He came to see me, you know.'

Alice gave a convulsive start that made the old bed protest. 'When was that, Gin?'

'About ten days ago. He said you'd "chucked" him, as he put it.'

'Yeah – well – it's like this you see. I liked Mark, he liked me – sort of instant attraction; but I got to admit I thought he was just the man for our set-up: solicitor, very respectable – I put it to him.' Ginnie wondered what sort of story she had told Mark – the one they had heard after supper, or yet another version? 'He seemed interested, but I think that was because of me. You know? Anyway, when I got back to London, and saw the boys, they wouldn't hear of it. Told me to drop him pronto.'

Ginnie, feeling a sort of shiver despite the warm proximity of Alice, naturally wondered who the boys might be. Rather falteringly she enquired.

'Well, never you mind about that,' said Alice, with something like a return to her old air of kindly proprietorship. 'A whole lot better you shouldn't know much about it, Gin.'

She was silent for a while. The world of dark outside seemed very close to them. Tense, quite unable to be close to her companion, Ginnie found herself searching for a topic, as if she were at a sticky dinner party. The one she found was a little unorthodox, but it worked. 'And do you still go bonking?' she enquired.

Alice shook with silent laughter, as if the question showed that her Gin had quite understood, and that all was well between them. 'Gin, you're a marvel,' she murmured. 'That was a gay time in Sorrento, wasn't it? I made quite a bit of money working at that hotel. But –' she broke off and seemed to ponder, laying her nose against Ginnie's flannelette shoulder. 'D'you know, I think the reason Markie and I hit it off was that neither of us wanted to do it. Sort of innocent – a bit like you. But, you know, I'm real frightened of Mark now. Don't know what he's going to do. He cut up rough, I can tell you. Never expected it somehow. He seemed such a calm sort of feller ...' she broke off again.

'And did you get that teeshirt made?' asked Ginnie, who was genuinely curious about this.

'Too right I did. Bit of a lark – sort of double bluff don't they call it? Kidding on the level? Funny thing – one of them did think up that logo – "Naked Doctor". It's good isn't it? Better not tell Tom.' She began to sound sleepy.

'Yes, what about Tom?'

'Oh, Tom's a nice boy.'

Silence came again. Alice's breathing against Ginnie's shoulder relaxed into a calm rhythm. She seemed to have fallen instantly asleep.

Tom, on his incredibly uncomfortable couch, supposed he must have slept briefly, at first; but he had been awake again long before the girls. There was a murmur then; but he failed to get a word until he heard his own name, followed by silence. What had they been talking about? He felt both wretched and exhilarated. Pinky's revelations had not so much shocked him, as they seemed of a part with the general confusion and excitement of life since the trip to Venice.

As for having been engaged to her, he now saw, blankly, that for him she had originally consisted entirely of his own longing to go to bed with her, and the promise that their engagement must necessarily fulfil this dream some time. His Pinky had been a product of his own lack of forcefulness. Now there was a real one, to go with the real world he seemed to have taken to living in.

From the sound of their murmurs the girls must now be in bed together. Tom's imagination neatly ejected Ginnie and put himself beside Pinky, or Alice as she seemed to have become. But nothing much came of this; and presently he too was asleep. Ginnie remained the wakeful one, until it had grown quite light outside.

*

They all felt constrained in the morning. In their small space the mechanical problems of washing and dressing could only have been solved by hearty camping-style badinage: none of them were up to producing it. Tom and Ginnie were practically speechless; even Alice was subdued. After a dismal breakfast, at which Ginnie was the only one to attempt a conversation, Alice seemed to arouse herself.

'Well, children, what are you going to do today?' she asked, with something of her old authority, but adding an appropriate seaside note, fondly impatient, quasi-maternal. The kids must really make up their minds, and not just hang around.

Tom and Ginnie looked at each other, which they were going to find themselves doing a good deal in the next few days. 'Well,' began Tom uncertainly, 'I really ought to get back to London as soon as I can. The work I'm supposed to be doing ...' His voice trailed away, and he looked at Ginnie again.

'Oh, but no!' Alice wailed, discarding the maternal role for that of a cruelly abandoned hostess. 'You *can't*. You can't *do* that, Tom dear! Not now! I need you, God I need you! Ginnie!' She seized her friend's hand impulsively. 'You're not to go – you're not to let him go!'

Ginnie said something about telephoning.

'But of *course*. The phone's right here. We may not have all the amenities in shantytown but we do have that. Now look, I tell you what. You ring up or whatever, and Tom too if he wants; and then why don't the pair of you do a bit of local sight-seeing? There's this weird little train, a real dinkum job, but it's *serious* –

130

no kidding – it gets you from A to B. Started as a millionaire's toy I believe, but now it's a real commuter standby – best way to get all along the marsh. I love it. There's one little engine all black, like a Canadian Pacific, and another looks like an old Rolls-Royce – probably was one once. Oh you must.'

She paused. She looks tired – drained – thought Ginnie. 'What about you?' they both said.

'Oh, I'm for home. I'm def. staying put for the present.' She folded her splendid arms and smiled at them, and then let her palms droop in a weary gesture of appeal. 'Now you will be dears, won't you?'

There seemed no alternative to being dears. After the phoning was done – neither Ginnie's office nor her mother seemed much concerned with her whereabouts and immediate plans – they set off in the car. Alice, having instructed them, did not come out to see them off; but when Tom went back in to get his wallet – there was no money in it now but there was his driving licence, and you never knew – she asked him whether there was anybody around outside. It seemed an odd question, but Tom had given up being surprised by the woman he had once thought of as his Pinky. No more of those swift kisses which had come like taps on the face and head. So completely did she ignore, or seem to have forgotten, their once presumed relationship, that Tom had necessarily to do the same.

He mentioned her query to Ginnie though. In fact the place had always seemed nearly deserted, awaiting the return of the summer bungalow dwellers. Now only one or two had signs of life, and smoke from their stovepipe chimneys. Silver Spray's neighbours were all clearly vacant. 'Sand Dunes' had curtains that were not only drawn, but pinned or tacked in place. The sea wind, perceptibly cooler this morning, blew fine sand over the pale concrete, where no cars seemed to have passed for some time. Only at one point down on the enormous sand-flats, were persons visible, trudging dimly along.

'She keeps saying we're holidaymakers,' said Tom, as they drove off. 'I don't get it.'

Ginnie didn't get it either. She noticed Tom's impersonal reference to their hostess, 'I think Alice is frightened,' she said, rather obviously. 'This Mark Brassey – you haven't met him, have you? – seems to have known about the smuggling business she involved us in.'

Ginnie saw no reason to tell Tom of Alice's engagement to Mark, or about the things Alice had told her in the night. Deception was beginning to come naturally to her, too.

'She's taken us both for a ride,' Tom said bitterly. 'I can't think why I said I'd get the car, and all that, and come down.'

Ginnie had no answer. She was beginning to find Tom a bit trying. That they had become yoke-fellows in this extraordinary business of deceit was itself an irritating factor. Tom was no doubt a 'nice boy', as Alice had said before she fell suddenly asleep, but his niceness did not preclude a very natural anxiety for his own interests. Nor had it stopped him falling wholly out of love with his fiancée, so far as she could see, when that love had found alteration.

Ginnie inaccurately recalled the Shakespeare sonnet about true love, and wondered if it applied to her own case. She hardly thought so. And yet something made her feel loyal to Alice, passionately loyal, although what the passion was she could hardly grasp. Romance was over – that she really *did* know, in spite of her melting in the night to that unseen tear-wet face. She could not abandon Alice, even though non-abandonment seemed to consist of this farcical business of pretending uncomfortably, and in company with young Tom, to be holiday-making.

Their presence was needed by Alice. It reassured her: there was no doubt about that. Ginnie thought of her mother on the phone that morning. Showing only the most perfunctory interest in what her daughter was doing, Mrs Thornton had wanted to talk about her lodger's latest boyfriend, who had come to supper two nights ago. Her mother had her own intents and purposes, as Alice undoubtedly had hers; but in both cases Ginnie's own role seemed to be that of a kind of home deposit – like Alice's 'safe house' – or Poste Restante. Never feel yourself undervalued, she thought wryly. I could give advice on that in the magazines.

Now they had turned away from the sea, and gone back to the straight road inland. A vestigial railway station previously unnoticed by them, long abandoned and derelict, heralded the still current activities of the RH & DLR. Tom parked the Fiesta – there was plenty of space – and they found a small empty booking-office.

'Romney, Hythe and Dymchurch Light Railway,' read Tom, in the flat voice of a holidaymaker, who asks for no more than that the time should pass. 'What do we do now?'

A smaller notice informed them the office would be manned ten minutes before the train's departure. In which direction it departed seemed a matter of indifference. They wandered out into a small siding of toy-sized lines under a corrugated iron roofing. Tom started to measure the diameter of the line with his handkerchief.

He was interrupted by a discreet but peremptory whistle. Whatever the time of the next departure, a train was certainly about to arrive. The miniature locomotive came on slowly on the line where Tom was standing. The driver, burly by contrast with his engine, was looking at them along its length. Tom stepped off the line and rejoined Ginnie.

'Green Goddess,' they read on a scroll below the boiler, as it passed them with authentic pants and wheezes and a waft of hot oily air, and slowed to a stop.

A surprising number of sober-looking persons, not evidently holidaymakers, climbed out of the small carriages; collected bikes or adjusted shopping-baskets and walked away. A solid figure was left sitting at the end of the train, in one of the little compartments that held one a side, two at a pinch; and now he slowly got himself out, and approached them along the cinder platform.

Ginnie gave a start. There was no doubt about it. Here was Mark Brassey.

He walked right past them in evident rumination. Ginnie, who stood slightly behind Tom, did not know what to do. But as she gazed after him, while the conductor entered his little office to sell tickets for the next voyage, he turned round abruptly and stared at her.

'What are you doing here?' he asked without ceremony.

Ginnie introduced Tom: there seemed nothing else to do. As if meeting a friend for a weekend visit, they walked with Mark slowly to the exit.

133

'So I've run her to earth,' announced Mark. 'I was hoping to do just that. Quite a coincidence. I'll take her back to London at once to see this man. If she co-operates, and she will, it will all come out all right.'

His voice was more pompous than she remembered. But perhaps he was less sure of himself? Ginnie determined, and at once, that he was not going to do anything to Alice. She stopped in her tracks.

'You haven't found her yet,' she said. 'And Tom and I won't let you find her, if you're going to give her away.' She felt her face growing hot. Tom looked embarrassed. Mark only looked surprised.

'I've managed to fix things to keep her out of trouble,' he said mildly. 'A good friend of mine is a specialist in that sort of thing. But she'll have to come up with me to London right away. As soon as possible.' Ignoring Tom, he favoured Ginnie with a long stare. 'Have you been in touch with her? How did you know she was here?'

'How did you?'

'She mentioned a holiday place on Romney Marsh. I had business in Folkestone, as it happens, and I thought I might come along to visit her. That little contraption' – he motioned at the train – 'is really very convenient.'

Ginnie felt quite at a loss, and Tom was no good to her. Turning on him now Mark enquired with a certain lack of civility how he came into all this. 'I'm a friend of Pinky, of Alice,' said Tom hurriedly, and looked at the ground as if he had already been found guilty in some way. It was clear that there was no point in trying to conceal Alice's whereabouts. Mark Brassey was the kind of man who would find it out anyway, from the local police station if need be. Looking more and more like delinquents, the pair had already lost the initiative. Mark eyed them steadily.

'If Alice comes with me,' he repeated, 'she'll be out of this mess quite quickly. If not, there's no telling what may happen. We'd better go along, don't you think?'

It was impossible to disagree with him. Ginnie saw that Mark was the one who could best take over the business, if he were well-intentioned. Alice had hinted he might go to the police about her, or the customs, or whoever it was. But now he seemed able and willing to help her out of the mess. Ginnie wondered why.

She wondered too, and with alarm for herself and Tom, how Alice would greet their reappearance in Mark's company. Could she think they had betrayed her in some way?

She need not have worried. As the little Ford stopped again outside Silver Spray, and the trio got out and walked round to the back, Alice was there at the door to greet them. She seemed to keep a perpetual watch from behind the lace curtain of the front window.

'Why Markie!' she exclaimed with rapture, embracing him. 'Where you bin, you wicked man? Since you vanished these sweet kids have come to keep me company.'

Mark looked both gratified and shamefaced at this reception. He produced a smile.

She dragged him over the threshold and turned to Ginnie and Tom, all her old masterly self.

'Now you dears run along for a bit while Markie and I have a good chat – what say?'

*

The upshot of the good chat must have been satisfactory, for Tom and Ginnie were soon summoned to be told that Alice and Mark were off – toot sweet as Alice put it – to London. She looked radiant. 'He still wants to marry me,' she confided in a whisper to Ginnie in the bedroom, throwing a few things into a bag while the other two conversed stiffly next door. 'Oh, Gin, I'm so relieved! It'll all be sorted out now, you'll see. I knew I could rely on old Markie.'

She peeled off the pink teeshirt. Ginnie wondered if Mark had noticed it, and if so what he had thought. Privately she was not at all sure that he would want, or indeed be able, to sort out the kind of trouble that Alice appeared to be in; but she kept any such thoughts to herself. 'Got a spare blouse, Gin darling?' the other enquired, standing hugging her atlantean shoulders. 'Gawd no, yours would never fit me.' 'What about the maroon dress?' Ginnie suggested with a flicker of malice.

135

'Christ knows where that got to. Be a sport, Gin, and let me try the one you've got on. It's dainty – Markie'll like that. You can wear a jersey or something down here.'

Presently they emerged, Alice bursting out of Ginnie's viyella blouse, which had a discreet paisley pattern. Mark didn't seem to notice whether it was dainty or not. The idea was to take the car and catch a fast train from Ashford.

'Now look after the place, you dears,' Alice exhorted them. Tom started to bleat in protest, but Alice cut him short. 'I'll be back just as soon as ever I can,' she told them. 'Now, you two, relax; and have a nice holiday. Do you good. And *be* good,' she added roguishly, giving Tom a light tap on the nose, the sort he had once been given in the form of a kiss. 'Don't get up to anything mother wouldn't like.' In a few minutes they were off, Alice driving, and Mark sitting beside her with his seat-belt very correctly done up.

Now the bungalow seemed quiet. For the first time Ginnie and Tom heard the whisper of the sea, which once taken in seemed to fill the whole of consciousness. Ginnie drew a deep breath. It was a relief to be rid of Alice for a while, but here she was, stuck with Tom. And their relationship now could only be a more awkward one.

Unexpectedly, Tom made it a moment later less so. 'Let's go down and see the sea, if we can,' he suggested; and they set off through the sandhills by one of the many gaps that ran between the bungalows on the seaward side. For once it seemed not impossibly far away. Wide arcs of ochreous foam came to meet them as they approached over dimpled tracts of firm, darker brown sand. Turning to look at the shore they had left they saw the bungalows peeping out of the pale sandhills, like ornaments set in brownish sugar. A mile or so further down was the shabby white Edwardian bulk of the hotel, and a line of tall lodging houses that would have looked at home in a London suburb.

They stood inhaling the salt air with conscientious greed. Then, and again unexpectedly, Tom burst into tears. Ginnie, with no experience of male grief in this form, stood by embarrassed. It seemed to her an unfair indulgence; and she could think of no response other than a hand on the shoulder and soothing words. She could not find any, and was reluctant for

136

some reason to give him a pat. None the less, as she stood uncomfortably by, he suddenly seized her. It was not a convincing or a well-constructed embrace; but Ginnie was glad he had broken the ice, so to speak, for it gave her a role and a cue. She did now try to murmur something as Tom's young beard scraped against her face, desisting as he found her mouth, but his lips on hers were dry and unconfident. As she gently eased him off she was aware that he had begun to withdraw anyhow.

He took her hand, which seemed appropriate. Linked like children – she remembered how often Alice had repeated and altered that facetious mode of address – they wandered quite contentedly along the edge of the foam in the direction of distant Dungeness. Beyond it loomed a presence which they knew to be the nuclear power station.

On and on they walked, as if walking was the answer to their problems, which in Tom's case it might well have been. Ginnie began to feel it was a long time since their skimpy breakfast. Dazed with the oddity of the whole affair she began to think of alternative titles, as she sometimes did in her reports on the scripts of would-be authors. 'The Adventures of Tom and Ginnie in their search for the Real World?' But, really, it was too absurd to be wandering about here like a couple of kids.

She found a civil pretext to withdraw her hand from Tom's grasp in order to bend and pick up the tiny shells, dark pink where a shining film of sand water swirled over them, but turning white as they dried in the hand. Tom had turned shy and silent. He seemed paralysed by his own feelings, or perhaps by the lack of them; and after his first attempts to involve her in them physically he withdrew from Ginnie into himself.

Once they had got going there seemed no reason to stop. Tom was used to farming country, near his parents' midland home, and he knew the impossibility of walking with any pleasure in such country. A parody of industrial landscape, with its stinking silage cylinders, old piles of tractor tyres and discarded plastic bags, it was criss-crossed with wire, divided into square weedless blocks of produce, brooded over, in still weather, by a miasma of chemicals. He greatly preferred an honest industrial scene, which today in any case would probably be broken down and abandoned.

But in this wide free acreage by the sea's edge they could walk as they wished. Miles of sand did not seem far, and the shingle and saltmarsh, when they turned inland, were just as free to wander across. Ginnie had had her shells, and Tom now took to investigating stones and driftwood. It was quite late when they found themselves plodding down the long corrugated ribbon of concrete back to Silver Spray. Alice had instructed them to leave the key under a flat pebble in the sandy grass, and now they let themselves in to what had become their new home.

Seaside life was hourly becoming more seductive to Ginnie. In this reassuringly derelict world it seemed unlikely that anyone could enter to cause them harm; although that, she knew, must be an illusion. But what wasn't illusory in the world she seemed to have entered, since she had seen Alice that evening down by the blue and green Italian water? Naked Doctor! Alice herself might be said to qualify, in some curious sense, for the words printed on her pink teeshirt. She had ministered to Ginnie in bed. But what was one to think of it all? Alice's confession in the night, that what they trafficked in was in fact the real stuff, had not surprised Ginnie at the time, after the shock of first being told how she, and Tom too, had been used to carry it. That world had made use of them while they seemed still outside it. Alice had made use of her. And yet ... She is still my naked doctor, Ginnie could not help feeling, even though it was in fact – or so Alice had told her – the name by which 'the boys' referred to some kinds of the true substance.

How confusing. And now they were both very hungry. Yet Ginnie could not face getting a meal, or mastering the spindly Calor gas stove, while Tom seemed to have lost all initiative. There was no wine either, but Ginnie did not mind that. What had accidentally become a long day of mild but unaccustomed exercise had left her indifferent to drink, even to her bottle of vermouth. Having slept, as it seemed, hardly at all the night before, she longed above all for bed and oblivion. Here Tom could be the obstacle. She might have been frightened on her own, she supposed, even in the unthreatening seaside vacancy of Silver Spray, but she could not help wishing that Tom had gone off with Mark and Alice – even that she had gone up to London with them herself.

But passivity had marked all her responses since this two-day nightmare idyll had begun. There seemed to be nothing she could have done about it. 'What could we have done about it?' Tom echoed her thought aloud, as they sat eating spam and bread and butter.

Baffled by those primitive gas rings, which were also in an uninvitingly greasy and neglected condition, she had made no attempt to cook; and she was aware that Tom covertly despised her lack of enterprise. This seemed highly unfair, and did nothing to increase their involuntary intimacy. Ginnie intuited that he was an only child like herself, but she was not prepared to feed him with questions about his home and background. Instead she asked him questions about Alice; but Tom had little more to offer, although once started, he seemed eager to talk about her.

'I suppose she sort of sent me to Venice,' he said, gazing at the pictureless cardboard wall of the bungalow in a way that would have looked portentous if he had not been so youthful. 'I even remember' – he laughed a little – 'that she said everyone knew it was always warm in Italy, and that there was no need for my anorak. She took it off me at Victoria.' Tom remembered with painful clarity how Pinky had given him a rather special good-bye kiss, as she put her arms around him to remove that skimpy green and purple garment.

'But you know,' he went on, warming to his theme, 'until I knew Pinky I always felt a bit outside the way things are now.'

'You mean like drugs and all that?' said Ginnie sharply.

Tom looked uncertain. 'Well, you know, my tutor used to talk about what he called the real world outside the university. I once said, "Well, isn't it real here?" He said I'd missed the point.'

'What point? I don't get it.'

'Well, no more do I really,' admitted Tom. 'I don't know, but take this Major Grey in Venice, whom I ran into.' He laughed unhappily. 'Well, I suppose I was supposed to run into him, really.'

Ginnie had already seen that. It was obvious that Alice had sent Tom out for that purpose. 'Well, what about it then?' she prompted. And let's stop saying 'well' all the time, she thought to herself. This is not 'Any Questions'.

'He seemed to be a bit of a fogey, but he wasn't – he couldn't have been, could he? – and when meeting him I did rather feel, this is life. And again, you know, in another sense admittedly, when I saw Pinky with those others in the Earls Court place. That seemed like the real world if you like. I mean, this drunken chap ...'

As Tom rambled on Ginnie was seized with a desire to laugh, but she was struck by what he said all the same, and in an odd way she even feel respectful. The effect of Alice on herself was comparable, she saw; but she had not presented the matter to herself at the time in quite the way Tom had. It was certainly extraordinary that Alice should have sent him off into the arms, as it were, of this Major Grey; and Ginnie even found herself wondering if he had found there any experiences like her own. She was certainly going to say nothing about those to Tom. But perhaps it had been the warm embrace of the drug-laden overcoat which had been real-life-enhancing for him, even though he had known nothing of its contents?

Tom had drifted on to another tack. 'You know thrillers about drugs and criminals and all that? At least we know now how untrue they all are. Being sinister and so on. Somehow, you know –' Tom sought confusedly for a comparison and remembered the shop in Tutbury High Street – 'it seems to be more like running an antique shop, if you know what I mean.'

'That doesn't mean they aren't sinister,' Ginnie reminded him. 'And just look how they made use of us.'

'Yes, but you see what I mean? Somehow one expects this kind of thing to be at the cutting edge of modern living,' said Tom quaintly. 'And then you find a Major Grey, or your own girl-friend ...' Tom swallowed painfully. 'It seems, well, so normal somehow, even kind of oldfashioned.'

Ginnie indeed saw what he meant. Perhaps drug-smugglers were exempt from the desire to be up to date, and in the spirit of the age, which seemed to afflict other people? Authors especially, she had noticed. Up-to-dateness, like slang, was something that tended to sound as quaint as the phrases Tom had used, when put on paper, or into dialogue. The modern era often struck her as no longer able to keep up with itself.

Tom had now got on to the quality of life. He supposed people

140

were always after a better one? Ginnie wondered if she had been as portentous at his age, and supposed she had. Her clichés were ten years older – more – but perhaps such things were ageless? 'The quality of life' always sounded to her like Merrie England: a phrase whose bandying about proclaimed that the opposite of it was going on. But she felt touched that Tom was now expanding a bit to her, and wondered if he had done the same with this Major Grey. She reminded him again how unscrupulously they had been made use of.

Tom had to agree to that, and by now they were both sleepy. But the bed problem still hung in the air, tired as they were. After she had yawned once or twice, Ginnie was disinclined to look Tom in the eye, fearing that she might meet there a hopeful or a calculating expression. Taking the initiative, she suggested they should put the camp bed which Alice had slept on, for some of last night, in the living-room. It would at least be more comfortable than the rickety sofa. Tom acquiesced in that; and Ginnie hardly cared whether he was relieved or disappointed: perhaps he hardly knew himself. She had no welfare illusions about compensating him for the loss of his Pinky, but if he came to her bed in the night, as Alice-Pinky had done, she supposed she would hardly be able or willing to keep him out. A lot of sex must be a question of good manners, she felt, if such things still existed; and it happened she had never been called upon to exercise them. Oh but she had! Vividly and suddenly she remembered the moment when Alice had pulled her dress over her head, and stood smiling peaceably before her in bra and knickers. And how grubby the bra had been!

What else could she, Ginnie, have done at that moment than what she had in fact done? And she supposed love had come afterwards – out of what? Perhaps it often did? Odd, or perhaps not so odd, that Tom had been talking of his 'real world', while she had earlier been amusing herself with the title of a book about it, and them.

So she reflected as she curled close up in the chilly trough of the bed – 'Silver Spray' did not seem to run to a hot-water-bottle – but now she was really tired, and in a few seconds she was asleep. Had Tom come in the night it was not likely that he could have aroused her. But he slept as deeply as she did, without any

141

moments of wakefulness in which to shed, or to simulate, further tears.

*

Both felt more cheerful next morning for having slept so well. With Tom's help Ginnie mastered the Calor gas taps, and they had eggs and bacon and toast. It really did begin to feel like the holiday Alice was always talking about; and after Ginnie had found Vim and made some efforts to clean up the stove, they decided to walk out again, and in the opposite direction. They had stopped saying anything about their situation, as if by tacit consent. The morning brought an illusion of freedom. They had been told to be on holiday; and, as Alice's guests, or prisoners, they had no choice but to behave as if they were.

Littlestone-on-Sea, the next settlement along the shore, was perfectly adapted to the feel of heady irresponsibility in the brilliant marine morning. No more bungalows – here was class, 1930s style, as if pickled in its period by the salt air, which had cracked and shrunk even the superior window casements. A fine sand had drifted into porches where later in the season the deck-chairs would be stacked. None had been put out yet, but all the houses had an occupied look, unlike 'Silver Spray''s companions. The solid houses along the sea-wall, some of them made of mellow brick, and in genuine Georgian style, gave an impression of well-bred affluence. Even the spacious and discreetly shabby road, merging at its edges into sandy turf, had an air of independence from attention by any local council. It led to a derelict water-tower in Tudor style, faded to an authentic hue of smoky orange. Beyond it were no more road or houses. A wide perspective of turf and sand-hills seemed sculpted for a purpose, unlike the tousled hillocks of bungalow town. On smooth patches of darker green there appeared tiny flags, blowing at the top of chequered poles.

'A golf-course!' exclaimed Tom.

He sounded quite excited, as if ancient and happy memories were stirring in him. They were, as it soon turned out. With a return of spirits which showed, thought Ginnie, that he really is a rather sweet character, he explained to her that his father had loved golf, and had taken him round a course in childhood and taught him the rudiments.

'I wonder if I could still play now,' he wondered. He'd rather like to try, thought Ginnie. Like the lady in *The Mikado*. 'Why don't you have a go?' she said.

Tom looked doubtful; but when they came to the clubhouse, and stood at first shyly outside an open door where a man was repairing what Ginnie thought of as one of the implements, the process turned out to be quite easy. The man inside was softly whistling a Scots air, and he broke off as they appeared and asked what he could do for them. No one else at all was about.

'Could I play?' faltered Tom.

The professional in his little shop looked less than enthusiastic when he saw Tom's ragged jeans, but perhaps the sight of Ginnie reassured him (does he think I'm his mother, she wondered) together with the young fellow's diffident politeness.

'I'll charge you a green fee at our special off-season rate, sir,' he promised. 'You being a student, I expect. And you can hire a few clubs – no problem. Does the lady like to play?'

Ginnie said no with suitable humility, and announced she would pay Tom's green fee, which seemed rather a lot in spite of what the man had said. After a protest Tom gave in, too absorbed in the prospect of his game to pay much attention to her generosity. Ginnie reclasped her bag.

'You could walk round with me if you'd like,' said Tom, already absorbed in preparations for his game, but Ginnie was now looking forward to a morning on her own in this new place. They arranged to meet at the clubhouse at one o'clock. 'I don't quite know how long it will take me to get round,' said Tom importantly, making tentative swings with his borrowed driver. Ginnie was amused by his new preoccupation, but also a little lowered in her own spirits. Yesterday, by the edge of the sea, he had seemed to need her, and indeed tried to make a sort of love to her. She hadn't responded much, and she suspected he was glad later on that she hadn't. Now he was probably quite relieved that she was not going to walk round the course with him.

But her spirits lifted again when she was on her own. She strolled back down the road and over to the sea-wall. This was a concrete strip, wave-shaped, and just wide enough for two to walk along the top. Littlestone was anxious not to make things easy for tourists and holidaymakers – that was clear. The road past the expensive houses was practically non-existent. A notice announced sea-wall damage, but with no promise that anything would be done about it.

Ginnie sauntered on past the houses, wondering who lived in them. A big dog on one of the lawns looked up for a moment and wagged his tail before dropping his nose again on his front paws.

She began to indulge in a small day-dream, in which she would be living in one of the houses. She could wander every day along the beach, beside the links, or along to the lighthouse, and inland over the saltmarsh. Should she have a husband? She couldn't decide. There would be obvious practical advantages in having a nice one; but however nice he was he might not care to wander about with her. Alternatively he might be very loving and always wanting to come with her; and that would have its drawbacks too.

Ginnie strolled on, scheming busily, but, as she soon came to realise, unsatisfactorily. Like the poet Wordsworth's, her morning joy had turned, rapidly and unforeseeably, to dejection. Even under this wide and always wonderful sky she felt the holiday was over as soon as it had begun, and the problems confronting her more pressing than ever.

Wondering about Alice got her nowhere. It was hardly surprising that she had preferred to dream about a husband in a house here beside the sea. The burden of involvement with Alice was fraying her nerves; even here and now, in the fine open morning, she could have begun to scream. And what about Greatstone and Littlestone? They seemed now to have nothing more to offer. Their almost mystic connection with whatever it was she felt about Alice seemed to have disappeared. Down here was Alice's place; and Ginnie remembered reading somewhere, or perhaps hearing it on one of those picturesque locality programmes on the wireless, that the natives used to say the world was divided into Europe, Asia, America, Africa, Australia, and Romney Marsh. That seemed appropriate. And yet just because it was Alice's place, like the bathing strand at Sorrento, there was of course no future in it, as there was no future in Alice herself.

But she could not bear to go on thinking about Alice. If only the woman had not come back to her, in this or in any other form.

With nowhere else to go, as it now seemed to her, she gravitated back towards the golfcourse and its clubhouse. As she went droopingly through the sandy grass on the edge of it, she made out the figure of Tom, slowly traversing the far distance. He must have been nearly a mile off, but across the sunlit level he stood out quite clearly. She saw him stop, and remain motionless for an instant. Some kind of rhythmic convulsion appeared to pass through him, and then he was once again in motion – a purposeful dark dot on the far off river of turf, marbled with pale bunkers. He looked solitary but not at all forlorn: he had discovered an occupation. His actions were more intelligible than anything she could manage at the moment. Was he thinking of his Pinky as Ginnie had been thinking of Alice? – was he regretting her, longing for her? Ginnie had a clear impression that at least for the moment he had got over all that.

The far-off figure stopped again, seemed to consider, and drew something long from another dot on the ground. Ginnie was reminded of her dawn fisherman at Sorrento, standing in meditation in the stern of his tub-like boat, while orange float bubbles appeared behind him. The creature had a purpose, as a poet said somewhere – was it Keats? – whereas she, like Wordsworth in his Ode, had simply gone from thoughtless pleasure in a walk and a place, and in her day-dreams about it, to the settled gloom that sat behind some horseman's back.

Was it gloom, or care, that sat there? She had both, she felt, at the moment. And how literary she was being about it! Ramazan would not have cared for that in his Virginia. She remembered a rather sprightly girl at school whose mother had told her: on no account start talking when a man is kissing you. And certainly not about books. It was shyness made one do it, Ginnie supposed. It must put them off their stroke, like in golf!

She wondered whether, in this tough and worldly day and age, with everyone knowing about orgasms and condoms, there was anyone who still had such feeble little thoughts as hers. Was she unique, or did everyone else secretly have these puny wonderings and misgivings? Ginnie rather thought she would prefer to be on her own here; but she doubted she was, even though other people seemed so modern. And yet what about Tom? – young and up-to-date in appearance as he was.

While she stood gazing with envy at his absorbed and distant speck, there started up from behind it a miniature tunnel of sun-bright smoke, bubbling busily across the marsh. It must be the RH & DLR, Ginnie now remembered, pursuing its useful existence down in this odd corner. She walked slowly on to the clubhouse. It would be an hour at least, she supposed, before Tom was back; and there seemed nowhere else for her to go in Littlestone. The long trail of smoke from the little invisible locomotive was dying away towards the distant hills. That was oldfashioned if you like, thought Ginnie, gazing wistfully after the last of the white steam as it vanished.

In front of the nondescript but somehow reassuring-looking clubhouse, with its white dormer and clock failing to tell the time, there was a putting green. A man in tweeds strolled to and fro on it, gently knocking about two or three balls. Ginnie recognised putting greens from childhood holidays at the seaside. She remembered her father – usually a bit sombre and absent but anxious to please – showing her how to hold the little club. As she skirted the green she saw the tweed-clad man address his ball towards a distant hole on the far side of the velvety surface. Instinctively she stopped and stood still. The pin or whatever you called it from the little hole was already taken out and laid well aside, and now the man spent a long time in motionless concentration. Ginnie was reminded of the two-minute silence there used to be on Armistice morning.

Both of them stood still, and she heard the larks singing high up in the pale cloudless sky. Then the man stroked his ball with firm deliberation. It began to roll, apparently on a course that would take it well away from the hole. But then it began obediently to curve, to slide over farther and farther until it was going straight for the hole, but more and more slowly. Would it make it? It did. There was a little wobble and a clunk and the white ball disappeared. The man straightened up.

'Good shot!'

The words were jerked out of Ginnie before she knew it, and she blushed. The man looked towards her as if surprised at being addressed, but smiled. It was a thoroughly nice smile. He had a

146

well-worn reddish face and neat grey-flecked hair, and might have been any age in the forties. As Ginnie moved on, trying to smile back without looking ingratiating, he came slowly across to her.

'Do you play this game?'

'Oh no,' said Ginnie, 'but I remember putting once as a child. That was brilliant.'

'Luck.'

His voice was solemn, but quizzical. His eyes examined her without seeming to, in a friendly fashion.

'Couldn't do it on the course. Certainly not at the end of seventeen holes, all square, or with your opponent one up.'

Ginnie supposed not. She had taken an instant liking to this man. Always fertile in experimental fantasies she had already begun to think he might be her partner in the house by the seaside.

'Do you live in Littlestone?' she enquired.

'No.'

His silence became tranquillising. He slowly picked up the golf-balls with which he had been putting, and before she knew how it had happened Ginnie found herself walking beside him back to the clubhouse.

Comfortable wooden seats, like park benches, were ranged in front of it, beside the flagstaff, and her new friend sank down on one of them. As she stood awkwardly before him he very lightly patted the seat beside him, and Ginnie found herself perched.

'So you're here on a holiday?' he said. 'You asked me if I lived here. No. But I wouldn't half mind doing so.'

He uttered the old vulgarism with precision, and a twitch of his pepper-and-salt eyebrows.

'It is a sort of special place, isn't it? We've only been here a day or two.'

'Who's we? You and your husband?'

'Oh no.' Ginnie was suddenly overcome with confusion at the difficulty of explaining about herself and Tom and Alice. 'I came with a friend, and we're staying with another friend,' she got out with what accuracy she could, and knowing it sounded lame, but the man was only paying her an absent-mindedly benevolent attention.

147

'Places like this are all that's left now,' he remarked. 'There are flowers here, later on, growing in the rough, you know, and the sandhills. Trefoil, Houndstongue, Ladies' Bedstraw.' His relaxed gaze caught Ginnie's for a moment. 'Fellow I met in the clubhouse told me of a little thing he's found. Only place it grows now in England, he says. The Striated Corn Catchfly. Something like that.'

He was silent again, and seemed to muse. 'I should so much like to see all those flowers,' said Ginnie – genuinely, though of necessity putting an artificial wistfulness into her voice.

'Too early in the year. July's the time, I'd say. Before the people's holidays. Children, and all that' – his face assumed a look of acute distaste – 'though I hope it wouldn't get too bad here.'

He mused again for a little. 'But there's no country left in this country. "Areas of outstanding natural beauty." I *ask* you. What's that supposed to mean? Places tramped bare by proles. Preservation's a lot of rubbish. An honest country, such as England used to be, would let it all go. But our so-called rulers would find that "unacceptable" no doubt. Their favourite word. I suppose ordinary families – that's another of their favourites – wouldn't like it.'

Oh dear. Ginnie felt so let down. This man was just another bore after all. Her interest in him, and by extension in the magic locality itself, fell away. Such sentiments, so leadenly familiar today, quite lowered her spirits again, even though she didn't necessarily disagree with them. Her new hero, with whom she might have lived happily in a sea house, had speedily proved himself unsuited for the purpose. It was sad, and disillusioning; and yet she still felt she liked him.

And at least it turned out that he didn't need to talk. They fell pensively silent, gazing out over the course. Ginnie, whose nervousness usually compelled her into some sort of speech when silence fell in any company, was happy to preserve this one. Her new friend's remarks about modern England might be as predictably tedious as those of any other bore, but at least he did not ask to be agreed with.

But then, unexpectedly, he started up again. 'God but I hate this country now,' he commented as if to himself, but in tones of true venom. 'Place is insane. All this cant about criminals' rights when it's not safe to walk the streets. Not only is it not the burglar's fault, but they say being burgled forces you to realise that crime is all our fault. Seems cockeyed to me.'

Ginnie sighed. Again it wasn't so much that she didn't agree, at least partly, as that her sense of the appropriate was hurt. She felt about such talk as she used to, when a teenager, if people made dirty jokes or boasted about sex. He should have some regard for my feelings, she thought, as well as for what's wrong with society.

And then again, wasn't he a bit out of date – about crime and so on? But perhaps everyone was out of date – she and Tom certainly were? None the less, she abruptly remembered, the pair of them had been involved in a criminal enterprise, which was actually still going on. She stole a glance at the man beside her, hoping he would not intuit in some way that she was herself one of the criminals he was denouncing. There was so much crime now, surely, that no one was sentimental about it, as he seemed to think? But perhaps he would vote for hanging or flogging her?

Still, she felt she must say something. 'Well ...' she began (like 'Any Questions' again – were things as bad that?) and she was just bracing herself to continue when the figure of Tom appeared, topping the little eminence of marram-grasses, with a bunker behind it, which hid the 18th green from the homecoming golfer. He looked despondent, and was here well before his time. That must be because he was no longer 'playing'. He dragged one club disconsolately behind him: the rest in the makeshift bag the 'Pro' had lent him, were slung awkwardly over his shoulder. Slowly he approached the clubhouse, so downcast that he appeared not to notice Ginnie on the bench, nor her companion.

Ginnie felt bothered. Should she introduce Tom to her new acquaintance? The seeming relationship between them might serve to confirm all the latter's most oldfashioned prejudices. But she need not have worried. Tom saw her at last and approached – then stopped. He looked amazed. The two males confronted each other like incongruous champions in some outlandish tournament, for the man beside Ginnie still held his putter negligently between his knees. He seemed surprised too, Ginnie thought; but if so he contained his astonishment very much better than Tom.

'Is this your friend?' he asked in a placid voice.

Tom was upon them before she could reply. He stared at her companion, swallowed, looked wildly at her. Ginnie could not understand what was the matter with him. Had his golf game been such a fiasco?

'This young man and I have met before,' said her companion. 'I've come down to see Pinky,' he added to Tom, as if it were the most natural thing in the world.

There was a pause which he seemed tranquilly prepared to prolong. 'How did your game go?' enquired Ginnie, in what sounded to herself a high and unnatural voice.

Tom took it up, however, with a sort of relief, telling her he seemed to have hurt his shoulder, and that he was so out of practice too – had to give it up. She commiserated. Her new friend said nothing at all.

Ginnie pulled herself together. 'Well,' she remarked, trying unsuccessfully to catch Tom's eye – the young man was standing there looking quite stupefied – 'I suppose we'd better be getting back.'

'Where to?' said the man beside her, in a now interested way. It sounded so natural as he said it that Ginnie could only reply that it would be back to their friend's cottage.

'Ah, Pinky's place?' said Major Grey, for somehow it was by now clear to Ginnie that this must be who the man was. How Tom conveyed it to her she didn't know, but he – or perhaps the man himself – did it somehow.

'I'll come back with you,' said Major Grey. 'I've got a message for her.'

'She's not there,' cried Tom wildly. 'She's in London.'

The Major – Ginnie already thought of him as the Major, for Tom's account had stressed the title, and its associations – appeared to muse again for a space. This capacity was what had charmed Ginnie, she now realised. A musing man about the house, or smoking his pipe in the front garden, by the sea wall. But she must stop all this nonsense: things were getting serious.

'Doesn't matter a bit,' the Major delivered at last. 'Not a bit. I'll run you two back, and leave a message for her. That's the best thing. I'd like to see Pinky's place.'

They were as clay in his hands, unable even to exercise any joint consultation. A BMW sat in the carpark, and they were back at 'Silver Spray' in minutes, almost it seemed in seconds. Major Grey's grizzled eyebrows rose as he got out of the car, but he made no comment. Ginnie, in her place as surrogate hostess, made some feeble gabble about being afraid they had nothing to offer him. He paid no attention, in the friendly style that seemed natural to him.

'Funny girl, isn't she?' he remarked as they stood cheek by jowl in the tiny kitchen; and then he ushered them out and back to the car.

'You're coming out to lunch with me,' he told them. 'Fancy Pinky kidnapping you like this. And keeping you half starved, I'll be bound.'

They were off down the straight road again and presently turned right across the marsh, heading towards the line of the downs. Ginnie sat down beside him, wearing her seat-belt and feeling both like a school-girl and the willing captive of Ramazan the Rajah: roles by no means incompatible, she reflected. She watched the Major's hairy hand by her leg, expertly changing gear.

'Used to keep a little plane in these parts,' he observed once, glancing at the windsock on a miniature and apparently deserted airfield, which seemed a natural part of the flat landscape. 'Lots of old wartime stuff around here. Before your time of course. Before mine too, if the truth be told.'

In Hythe he turned off the High Street, drove past a canal and a rustic cinema, and stopped outside a small restaurant. They ate tagliatelle and escalopes, and drank chianti out of a straw-covered bottle. Ginnie remembered the days when it had been fun to take one away and turn it into a lamp.

It was nice to have a proper meal; but the arrival of the Major, who had still not formally introduced himself, seemed to have deprived them both of the last vestiges of independence. Alice had begun the process: it now seemed complete. I am more callow than Tom, thought Ginnie as she finished her zabaglione, feeling like a cat as she licked the spoon. And yet she couldn't help making a forlorn attempt to flirt with the Major. She wanted at least to assure him that he and she were sexual equals, and Tom a mere youthful outsider.

Unfortunately he took no notice. And it was positively painful to remember the happy moments when they had sat peacefully side by side on the bench. He had not ignored her then: he had seemed in his own quiet way to welcome her presence. Now she felt she was 'showing off'; and though he took her up and responded, so that except for Tom they would have had a lively time, Ginnie did not feel happy at all. In spite of all the cheerfulness, the real and full implications of their predicament seemed about to close and to harden round them.

Tom said nothing but only ate and drank, with his eyes on the table. The Major ignored him. Ginnie tried once or twice to draw Tom in, by referring to Venice, but she noticed the Major said nothing about that, and neither did Tom. The absence of reference, and something in the Major's eye as he looked at Tom, seemed like a warning in itself. Nor was Pinky, or Alice, mentioned again. The Major chatted: she responded. But why has he asked us, she wondered?

There seemed no obvious answer. Over coffee she looked at him with deliberate intentness as she talked, willing him to disclose what he wanted. Was it her? Most unlikely: he seemed quite unaware even of her degree of concentration on him. She rather admired him for not noticing it, as she supposed men always took that in, if nothing else. What must it feel like to be Major Grey? How did he regard his present career as a drug smuggler? Did it seem natural to him, a part of himself? Had he been more real, so to speak, on the putting green, than acting up to her now in the restaurant?

The plump proprietor with a black moustache stood them each a *strega*, and the Major took out his wallet in a leisurely way while Tom and Ginnie – she felt back to childhood again – murmured embarrassed thanks for their meal. 'And now,' he said, consulting his watch, 'I shall have to be going. Quite a lot of things to do. I'll leave you young people in town. You'll want to shop I expect, and all that, and you can get the funny little train back home. Jolly little affair.'

And so they were dismissed, without the chance of finding

out what – if anything – was happening. They were instructed to tell Alice – he still called her Pinky – he would ring her next morning about arrangements, at ten o'clock.

'But suppose she isn't back?' said Tom.

There was a kind of hopefulness in his voice which might have surprised Ginnie if she hadn't been concentrating so hard on Major Grey. 'She'll be back,' said the latter, in his calm way. 'Or if she isn't, it doesn't matter. I'll ring now and again till she comes. You've given me the number.' he reminded Ginnie, as she offered to write it down for him. 'And now I must be on my way.'

In a dream Ginnie walked beside Tom, back through the streets of Hythe. He too seemed deeply preoccupied, and hardly answered when she, pulling herself together, said they should stop on the way to the station to buy some bread and milk. It was already quite late, well past three o'clock. Their lunch had been a prolonged affair, and it had been kind of their host no doubt; but neither of them had really enjoyed it. Ginnie was still too staggered to have really taken in that her friend of the putting green was the Venice drug operator who had fitted out Tom with his overcoat. The need to get bread and milk – and toilet paper too, she remembered – was the only thing that she seemed able to hang on to.

Tom, meanwhile, had been jolted in another direction. Major Grey had ignored him just as his Pinky had done. From the way he had been treated he might hardly have met the Major in Venice at all. Tom felt absurdly wounded, and less by the Major's cold-shouldering him than by the defection to the Major of Ginnie. They had chatted away to each other and taken no notice of Tom, as if he were a small boy. It was an almost unbearable reminder of his present status, now that he had lost Pinky. Brooding about her, Tom felt almost indifferent to the Major and his drugs: even though his own Pinky must also be the Major's Pinky, for she had sent him straight into the Major's arms. No doubt she had been in them herself.

It *was* unendurable. She had attached herself to him in such a natural way. They were engaged: he would have been having her – all splendid nearly six foot of her – before long. All that was over. And she had *been* there! – at the bloody bungalow – in bed in the next room, in the shower practically at his elbow!

No wonder he had burst into tears, there by the sea's edge, when she had left. He had wanted to go to the sea as if to her; as if a barge would come and bear him off to her, like King Arthur to the queens. The tears had come as swiftly and unavoidably as a fit of vomiting; and he had concealed his shame by throwing his arms around Ginnie, pretending – and now he saw not very convincingly – to have suddenly fallen a bit for her.

Well, why not try again? She and Grey had disregarded him, just as Pinky had. Tom made a face to himself. What a rotter he was being; and it didn't seem to worry him, at least not in the midst of all these other worries. Sometimes I'm like this, sometimes like that, he thought. There was a friend of his doing a graduate course in German who had always been going on about some Austrian novelist, of astounding intellectual subtlety. Apparently he wrote about men without qualities, no fixed personality, who might do anything any time. The friend had decided he was a bit like it himself, and suggested Tom was too.

Yes: why not? Tom wished he could remember the fellow's name – he could only recall that it had reminded him of breakfast food. Muesli? Something like that. But why not have a go at Ginnie? After all, without Alice (as he now firmly thought of her) they would have the bed to themselves. It would be absurd not to try. He was now positively hoping that Alice would not come home that night; and, knowing Pinky's old habits, it seemed unlikely. Perhaps, with Ginnie, it would be as cosy as it might have been after he and Pinky had got married?

Ginnie would be in a difficult position to resist him; and Tom honestly felt she mightn't bother very hard to try. Forlorn, and desperate for a crumb of comfort, he began to look forward to the night, as he might do to supper and a drink.

The unsuspecting object of these desires and designs walked on beside him, immersed in her own thoughts. They passed like two sleep-walkers through the streets of Hythe in the general direction of the little station; and, when they got there, found they had missed the 3.30 train. The next was at five. Ginnie took Tom back again to do the shopping.

Tom had noticed as they left the restaurant that it was called

154

the San Marco, and had thought bitterly of Venice. But neither of them had noticed, and nor had Major Grey, a car parked outside the restaurant some distance behind his BMW. The driver had been sitting in it for some time. When they came out he had yawned and opened a newspaper, reaching behind it into his pocket for cigarettes before remembering he was trying to give up smoking. Then he had got ready to drive off.

*

After a small supper they sat over Nescafé. Tom was planning to open his campaign by telling Ginnie, in a neutral sort of way, that the camp-bed was almost as uncomfortable as the sofa. The palms of his hands began to sweat, and he took furtive glances at her when she was doing something else. But Ginnie was taking very little notice of him. She was worrying about Alice, wondering about Major Grey, and thinking that she really must somehow get back to London tomorrow.

How often, had poor Tom but known it, has a seduction been spoilt, not by any positive intention to refuse on the part of the lady to be seduced, but by her total preoccupation with quite different matters. In any case, Tom's plans were doomed to disappointment. Alice reappeared at about ten o'clock.

She came breezing in, more full of bounce than Ginnie could remember even in the old Sorrento days. Ginnie offered her food. After their big lunch they had not been very hungry, and she had put out more than they had eaten. They had felt rather low too, both being disinclined to discuss Major Grey, and their outing. But now they told Alice about him, and about the lunch, and gave her his message. She did not seem particularly surprised, or even interested. She was too full of her time with Mark Brassey.

Insolent in her radiance she swept away any idea of food and produced a bottle of whisky. They all had a glass, and Alice chided them for sitting there looking so glum. Then she told them to drink to her re-engagement.

Markie, it seemed, had turned up trumps. The lawyer colleague had quite understood the position Alice was in, and he had reassured her. Whatever happened over that business it would not be her funeral. Of course it had been very wicked of Markie to get her involved at all – involved with the law that was. But now she had a foot in both camps, *and* she always had Markie to fall back on. She thought it would be for keeps this time.

Her eyes were actually sparkling as she looked from one to the other: Ginnie had not known that the old phrase could actually describe the process. Ginnie knew Alice didn't care what Tom or she felt about it all. Her first story about Naked Doctor had been so obviously intended just to cushion the blow, that Ginnie didn't think even Tom had been deceived. She hadn't asked him: too full of the whole situation as they had been, the details had seemed not worth discussing. She was grimly amused at the idea of Alice 'falling back' on her old admirer, but she accepted the idea that they were together again.

So, necessarily, did Tom. 'No hard feelings now, my sweet,' Alice told him, giving him a swift peck on the cheek. 'And be a good sport. It wouldn't have done, y'know. I need a mature feller like Markie, to keep me in order and sort out me problems.'

Tom naturally had no reply to this, other than trying to look like a good sport; and it is to be feared that neither of the girls greatly cared at the moment that he in fact looked so woebegone. Ginnie didn't know he had been hoping to seduce her; and Alice seemed entirely absorbed in her new future. Ginnie saw that with something like envy. There was a solidity about her and Mark, in relation to each other, which seemed quite different from anything else in Alice's unreal and kaleidoscopic existence. Ginnie did not flatter herself that her own relations with Alice, whatever they could be said to be, were anything other than equally unreal.

The phone rang. Alice froze at once, and looked from one to the other of her guests. She also looked quickly towards the only cupboard in the place, a gimcrack affair which Ginnie had once tried to open, thinking it might contain clothes-hangers, and found to be locked.

'Shall I get that?' asked Tom with sullen helpfulness, as Alice made no move.

'Yes, do,' she said, and licked her lips.

Tom picked up the receiver, said hullo, and immediately handed it to Alice. 'It's Major Grey,' he said.

An extraordinary look of relief transfigured Alice's tense face. She seized the telephone and poured out her usual torrent. Whatever replies there were seemed to occasion her amazement, joy, surprise and ecstasy; and there was nothing unusual about that too. Ginnie picked up the dishes to wash up, and Tom slouched after her. Now that he was not going to be able to go to bed with her she seemed to him immensely desirable, and he had some forlorn idea of giving her a squeeze. But the sight of her at the sink, with her back to him and obviously thinking of something quite different, had a discouraging effect. Cheerlessly he picked up a plate and began to dry it.

The phone pinged as Alice put it down next door. She burst in on them, uttering one of her great whoops, seized Ginnie round the waist, turned her to face Tom, and tried to set them in motion together like a couple of puppet dancers. Both their faces expressed fatigue at this surfeit of high spirits. She pulled them back into the sitting-room and poured more whisky into all their glasses. 'Oh, such a sweet man,' she chanted. 'He'll ring up again in the morning. Just wanted to see I was here OK.' She sat down at last and grinned at them. 'Well, you two little blessed virgins – what sort of time you been having?'

The two days came over Ginnie at that moment like two months, and very exhausting ones. Violent, and to herself wholly unexpected, irritation flared in her. 'I don't see why you should say that,' she cried out. 'Just because you go bonking and all that, and smuggle drugs!' The sound of her voice warned her that this was not the kind of thing that could be shouted successfully: and her outburst ended on a sob that was more like a snort. Tom looked hang-dog, as if he wanted to be well out of it all. Alice put her arms round Ginnie, positively crooning with pleasure. 'Oh, Gin, but you're wonderful. Why, you're my little extra virgin, just like that super dinkum olive oil.'

*

Later on, when they were in the sagging bed, Alice apologised. 'I felt so over the moon, Gin, and the sight of you just completed the picture, made my day, y'know.' Then she poured out to Ginnie the full riches of her present prospects. This lawyer guy, Markie's friend, had been so reassuring. She'd probably done nothing, at least nothing they could prove bad. She only had to tell Markie she loved him and wanted to marry him and he was all over her. But – and it was a very big but – whatever should she do now, Gin? Because Bobby Grey wanted her to go off with *him* – 'and he's really loaded, that man'.

'As a result of all the smuggling?'

'Now don't go all like that on me, Gin. He's no saint of course, but I'm very very fond of Bobby. Known him a long time too. If he picks me up tomorrow with the stuff – that's what the phone call was all about – he may take us off in a little plane, so he said. That's just to France of course. He's that kind of guy. After that we might go to South America – all sorts of places. He likes to travel. And I like the good life. Never had all that much of it.'

Alice snuggled down, stretching out her long legs comfortably. It was true that the lumpy old bed did feel more like home now. There was the usual sound of the dry tough marram grass tickling the flimsy shell of the bungalow. A dim beam of light, swooping and fading with hypnotic reassurance, regularly crossed the ceiling. There was the faint chug of a fishing vessel, way out to sea, and the only other sound was Tom's regular breathing from next door. The young man had found refuge in deep sleep from what he probably considered the heartless neglect of the two women.

A long silence followed. Ginnie thought of that first night in Sorrento, after Mark had taken her out to dinner. But now she was less wakeful – indeed she was just going off – heaven! – and thinking of *cervelli fritti*, and ... Alice, she could hear as she sank down into sleep, was fast asleep herself.

Then Alice began quietly to weep. Ginnie was awake at once, listening to what seemed a heart-breaking sound. To herself, she realised, it brought a great warm spreading pleasure. She held Alice to her and shushed her gently, stroking her hair, her cheeks and nose. The feel of those features, invisible in the gloom, reminded her of that first white image at Sorrento. The coarse wiry hair seemed to grow docile under her hand.

158

'There there my darling, what is it?' she soothed, and the trite words sounded touching, at least to herself.

Alice snuffled, and blew her nose feebly on the sheet. 'Oh Gin, if only you and I could go away together. I sometimes feel I could be happy with you. Be a girl again.'

Ginnie doubted if Alice had ever been a girl, in the sentimental sense she now used the term. She said nothing and continued her stroking. She felt almost like crying herself. The falsity of the thing seemed more moving than simple truth: not that truth in such a case could ever be simple. But she also was aware of a new and unexpected kind of depression. A person like Alice lived in a real – or was it an unreal? – world, which could not be reached, which made any true intimacy impossible. Alice lived in response to some mysterious will within her which she, Ginnie, could never bring into her own experience.

Sea wind sighed round the bungalow, and the faint pulsation of light came and went on the ceiling. 'Why are you called Pinky, Alice darling?' Ginnie hoped that this might at least clear up something of the identity of the girl beside her. 'It's me name, Gin,' murmured the girl after a peaceful dozy silence. 'My grand-dad was from the Ukraine or some place. His name was Pinkorenko, and my dad changed it to Pinky – better in Australia in those days. He was in the building business in Sydney. Always going bust. John Pinky and son – except that it was daughter.'

'What was your mum like?'

'Never knew her really. An auntie brought me up. Can't say I cared for her greatly, but she wasn't a bad old thing.'

Alice's murmur ended in the beginnings of a snore. Ginnie's attempt to know had got nowhere, but it didn't seem to matter. She lay on her back, gazing at the dim pulsation of light above her.

'Gin darling?'

'Yes. You go to sleep.'

'Y'know, I'd love to marry Markie in that dress.'

'Does it exist? I mean, did it?'

'Course. But what you took was just trimmings. Round the stuff. I never bought the dress itself. Too dear for one thing.'

'I always thought of you as a maroon girl, but that green you described would suit you. We'll find you another dress.'

'Y'know, I think I'll go off with Bobby tomorrow. Isn't that the best thing really, Gin?'

Ginnie could think of no reply. But Alice was asleep in any case. Ginnie put her lips gently to the invisible cheek. A faint unconscious murmur came, ending in a snore, a sound so docile Ginnie seemed to sink into it.

Then she was awake again. 'You know, Gin, this'll surprise you,' Alice was whispering.

'Yes, Alice?'

Alice sounded less sleepy now than overcome with an embarrassment unexpected by herself.

'You know all that I told you, about bonking and so forth?'

'Well, yes?'

'Never did any of it. I made it all up, Gin,' said Alice sheepishly. Ginnie could feel her blushing. 'I kind of took to you. And I wanted to show off to you. Make you think I was one hell of a girl. Not true.'

'Not true?'

'If you want the truth I've never done it either. Not the real thing I mean. Never fancied the idea somehow.'

This was too much for Ginnie. She was seized by a fit of invisible and inaudible giggles, and went on until the bed shook and she was gasping.

'Oh, Alice. What a one you are!'

There was no reply. Alice was either asleep or her confession had temporarily silenced her. What a new thing for the bold girl to feel actually sheepish! Ginnie moved closer and began to cuddle her big friend reassuringly. Alice gave a long sobbing sigh, quietly, like Ginnie's giggle, so as not to wake Tom, and allowed herself to be comforted.

'I do love you, Alice,' Ginnie said presently.

'Oh I'm so glad, Gin.' But Alice's voice was already drowsy again; and with her head heavy on Ginnie's shoulder she was nearly asleep.

'Just before you go off, what about Major Grey tomorrow? Or Mark?'

'Well, a girl's got to do it some time. You'll have to too. I could

160

fancy Bobby, though he won't want to marry me. Markie would, though. I think I'll take Bobby.'

Ginnie reflected that she would rather take Bobby too. She thought of their peaceful moments sitting together outside the clubhouse. Living with a man might be nice if it were like that.

Had Alice told her something true at last? Perhaps she had, but with her you could never be quite sure. Alice might be having her on again, except that this time there was no reason for it. Something in the shamefaced sound of her voice touched Ginnie deeply, although at the same time she wanted to start giggling again. Of course Alice might yet turn out to be a positive Messalina of lubricity, as well as guile; and yet Ginnie didn't now really think so. If only the smuggling business could turn out to be as untrue as all the bonking!

Alice was snoring more positively, her nose practically in Ginnie's ear. It was nice though. She managed to ease her position a trifle, and was instantly asleep herself.

She woke from a deep pit of unconsciousness to hear the small voice again close to her ear. 'May we get up, Gin,' pleaded Alice meekly. 'I'd love to see the sea with you – don't know why – just for a few minutes. Before the things I've got to do today. God, ain't life a battlefield?'

They lay quiet a moment longer while Ginnie tried to wake herself up, and then together got cautiously out of bed. Alice had a coat, and Ginnie put her mac on.

'Shan't need our shoes. Sand's so soft here. Gets everywhere. I like it.'

They padded over the concrete road which, as Alice had said, was soft with sand, and through the dunes to the beach. Heaving faintly in the shimmer of distant lights, the sea was now not so far. Clasped together the two women stood at its edge, letting the cold spume swirl gently over their ankles. By the hills above Folkestone the sky was turning a lighter shade of grey. Alice cried quietly and happily, nuzzling Ginnie from time to time. It was not, so it seemed to Ginnie, all that romantic even at dawn, even when a fine feather of lemon yellow light appeared on the edge of the dark downs. And yet she suddenly remembered Ramazan the Rajah, and putting her arms around Alice she gave her what she thought of as a passionate kiss.

161

Then she began to cry too, just as happily.

'I'll always remember this moment, Gin,' sobbed Alice, thus rather spoiling the present sense of it. But what did that matter? Romance and the real world seemed to Ginnie pretty close together at that moment, if not much the same thing.

When they got back Ginnie must have fallen into a sleep as deep and tranquil as Tom's. She remembered Alice's warm flank against her, after the chill of their little outing, and then she was jerked suddenly awake by a shriek in her ear. It seemed like a scream of rage and despair.

'Ginnie you *shit*, get up! – get up! Where is it? What have you done? *Find it for me!*'

Stupid with sleep Ginnie sat up and flinched from an enraged stranger, flailing about in the slip she had worn in the night. Alice's face, distorted by whatever violence now possessed her, was thrust into her own. Her voice was ugly and hoarse with rage.

'*Where is it? Where's what was in me suitcase?*'

Alice went on screeching, pulling Ginnie to and fro by the front of her nightdress.

'What on earth are you talking about?' screamed Ginnie in her turn, really cross at last. 'Don't shout at me like that. How should I know where your suitcase is? I haven't seen it.'

Alice suddenly sagged and collapsed on the side of the bed, holding her face between her hands. 'Oh Gin, it only needed this,' she wailed desperately. 'My suitcase with all the stuff in it, don't you see? I had all the stuff you and Tom got home – near a million quid's worth I shouldn't wonder. It's gone. What's happened?'

By now there were accelerating sounds of Tom getting up in the living-room. He must be hearing every word.

Alice, it appeared, had crept into the living-room while Ginnie was still asleep, to get her suitcase out of the cupboard. Tom was fast asleep of course too. She'd unlocked the cupboard with the little key, or thought she had – the door came open anyway – and brought her case back into the bedroom. The stuff inside it was gone. The cheap case now lay open on the floor, its back practically off. There was certainly nothing in it.

A few underclothes and bits and pieces that might have been

in it lay around on the floor. Alice stirred them lackadaisically with her toe. Tom, with frightened face, looked round the door. He had the air of one who has decided once and for all to have nothing more to do with the female sex.

But when he heard what had happened, Tom, again the practical man, went to look at the cupboard. He reported that the flimsy little lock had been forced, and a screw of paper inserted to keep the door closed.

Alice interrogated them with terrible calm. Yes, they had come back to the bungalow with Major Grey, and taken the key from under the pebble in the usual way, to open the door. Tom had put it back before they drove off.

The Major must have returned when they were still in Hythe. Where was he now, presumably with the loot? Tom professed to wonder feebly whether he had just come to pick it up for Alice, for when they would be going away together. Alice ignored him.

But later on she had calmed down. Ginnie made a cup of tea. As she ran the water and filled the pot she wondered what Alice would do now. There seemed no end to the things she had lied about, or hadn't told Ginnie. Now she seemed cut off for good, formally abstracted into another world, where disaster ruled and she sat blank-eyed, like a tragedy queen. Ginnie thought numbly of the night they had spent together – the last, no doubt. Ginnie felt certain of that, but far from certain what she felt about it. But Alice would not be going off with the Major, to whatever joys together had been planned. She supposed Alice had thought it all up before she came down to the bungalow, with the stolen drugs (how had she stolen them?). She would have concerted matters with the Major, and had a few days to wait while he made the preparations. That was when she and Tom had been called in, to ease the strain.

When had the Major decided, if he had, to steal the drugs and go off with them on his own? Ginnie remembered the flirtatious but not happy lunch, Tom's sour embarrassed young face; the Major's hand on the gear lever as they drove like the wind along the straight road, with the high plumy reeds in the broad dyke beside it. When – at what point – had he decided to do it? Was it when they were actually chatting, and his reddish-looking distinguished features were puckered towards her in their friendly smile? Or had he always planned to ditch Alice, as and when he could? Perhaps it was he who had suggested she should steal the stuff?

And had they – 'the boys' – found out that she had stolen it?

Next door Alice was bearing up. Ginnie heard her talking quite rationally to Tom, asking about the trip to Hythe, and even which engine had pulled the little train they had come back on. Tom, she heard, could answer that one. 'I love those engines,' said Alice, in a calm valedictory way, just as Ginnie came back with the teapot and cups, and Tom, looking wretched, rolled his eyes up at her, but without any appeal or collusion.

They sat over the pot. Alice drank hers calmly, as if it were the last she would be drinking. Ginnie, and sometimes even Tom, started an occasional laborious remark. Ginnie reflected that this was what the radio and paper must mean when they said a bereaved person was being 'comforted' by someone or other. Alice showed no signs of being comforted.

And then the phone rang. She was up in a flash and pulled off the receiver. 'Bobby?' she cried, her face transfigured.

There was a click – the others could hear it – and a mono-tonous buzz. Alice continued to hold the receiver while her face crumpled up. She burst into tears.

Perhaps after that they did manage to comfort her. Tom sneaked out, and Ginnie sat with her arm around Alice, thinking about her confession, and pointing out that there was always Mark Brassey, who wanted to marry her. (Or did he? Was this yet another of the things Alice had lied about?) Alice sniffled and blew her nose like a little girl and tried to cheer up. When Tom looked in again she was telling Ginnie about what a wonderful time she would have had in foreign parts with Major Grey.

'And now he's left me, the bastard. *And* pinched all me stuff. But you're right, Gin. I'll be telling tales with Markie instead. And he'll stick by me.'

As time dragged on, and they tried to eat some breakfast, she seemed to become conscious of the miasma of despair she had made around her. 'Well, kids, can't be helped. Don't let's get cross-eyed with grief, every which way. Look, here's Markie's number, in case you need it. And we'd better all get back to town.'

God, think that I was going to be away on a plane today with Bobby Grey.'

Tom rather spoilt things – he was tiresome out of disappointment, or perhaps deliberately perverse – by asking what was Major Grey's real name. Somehow, he said, since the time he picked the overcoat up it had all seemed so unreal, including the name the man had given him. 'Whaddya mean?' said Alice crossly. 'He was a major in the army – Brit army I heard – and his name's Bobby Grey.' But Ginnie saw what Tom meant. It had startled her too to find that Alice Pinky's real name was Alice Pinky, and now that her own friend of the putting-green really was a Major Grey. How literal real life was. Clearly Tom and she were inveterate romancers, even about this thing they were involved in – even when they were so much involved in it.

So these people were real enough, even down to their names. And presumably quite commonplace too. Not like film villains. She probably didn't improve things, she realised a second too late, when she found herself asking how Alice had got hold of the stuff Tom had brought in the overcoat. But to her surprise Alice took that seriously. She had got it away from the Earls Court pad, she said. When the Hon. Gerry (that was the one to whom Tom had handed over the coat) was stinking drunk.

'But I'm not scared of them,' she said, looking suddenly scared. 'That was the point in coming here. Natch, they don't know about it.'

It appeared that Alice was wrong about that.

*

They were still sitting at the table, and Alice was telling them now about Dr Syn, after whom one of the little engines was named. 'He was a parson on the marsh, I heard – ages ago – seventeen something. Very respectable cove – maybe got transported to where I come from. Fact is, this business takes all sorts – you'd be surprised. Some even brighter at their books than you, Gin.'

She broke off abruptly. It was not the phone this time; though Ginnie and Tom had been aware, as they sat there, that Alice was still hoping against hope for another call, a real call from Major

Grey, who had said he would ring about now. Looking through the window, Ginnie saw that a car had just drawn up outside 'Silver Spray', parking next to Tom's little Ford. Three men had got out. Alice had jumped up, and was looking at them through the front curtain.

She had gone a little white, but not much. She unlocked and opened the unused front door and went out to meet them. With a distracted rush of loyalty and love Ginnie saw her as superb at that moment, like a Roman emperor going to his death at the hands of rebellious guardsmen.

Except that it wasn't really at all like that. Alice sailed down the path, if the sandy tract between the tamarisks could be called a path, and greeted the newcomers vociferously. 'Why hello, dears. So good of you to come down. I'm ever so grateful. Step in a moment, and meet these two nice kids who've been helping me out.'

Looking polite but bored, even a shade embarrassed, the trio came back with Alice to the front door. Ginnie and Tom backed away from the window as they did so. They were too full of the situation even to exchange glances. Automatically Ginnie tried to find for her face the expression of one who had been 'helping out'. But do they know we know, she wondered?

There seemed to be a pause at the door, with conversation and a lot of laughter. Then the door opened, and the little bungalow seemed full of them.

Alice had a flush on her face now, as she shrilly called on Ginnie to rustle up a cup of coffee for the guests. The one who seemed to be the leader besought her not to bother in a cultured hesitant voice, bending his rather prominent eyes benevolently upon her. Fascinated, she gazed back at him, and he looked away as if abashed, repeating that she mustn't go to any trouble. He was slight and rather bald, wearing what she recognised as a well-worn but well-made suit, such as her own father used to wear to his office. He could have been a fairly high-up civil servant.

'Good morning,' he said, shaking Ginnie's hand, 'I'm John Armistead. So sorry to disturb you; but we have to attend a meeting in London with Miss Pinky, and we thought it might be convenient to give her a lift up. Hope it won't disrupt your holiday too much.'

Absurdly, as she recognised, Ginnie none the less felt gratified that he had singled her out for this pleasant and courteous approach.

'Oh yes!' now chimed in Alice in a loud tone, waving an arm. 'This is Mr Armistead, and this is the Hon. Giles Parker, usually known as Gerry; and this is Mr O'Connor, always known as Pat.'

The weedy, elegant fellow, who wore a waistcoat and a watch-chain with a gold seal, was already engaging Tom in man-to-man discourse. Ginnie remembered Tom telling her how he had been weaving about drunk on the threshold when the overcoat had been returned to him. He was quite sober now. And in a piping enthusiastic voice he was talking golf with Tom; telling him what a nice little course Littlestone was, with some holes – the 16th and 17th particularly – quite the equal of the Royal St Mark's at Sandwich. Whistling faintly, Mr O'Connor moved about the living-room with a pleasant smile on his face.

Escaping into the tiny kitchen was a relief, Ginnie had to admit to herself, but really because it was the sort of social scene that would have overwhelmed her a bit under any circumstances. And yet its familiarity was disarming. Passive, even paralysed, as she had felt for what seemed now so long a time, she could not believe – how could belief enter into such a situation? – that they could do anything to Alice, still less to her and to Tom. This Mr Armistead seemed a rational and rather anxious man, not exactly overburdened but certainly preoccupied with the difficulties of organising a meeting, making sure that members were present – all that kind of thing.

And it must be a business, with quite an extensive membership. She wondered again about Major Grey. How did he fit into all this? Were they looking for him too, as it seemed they must have been looking for Alice? Were they expecting to find the guilty pair together? Would they search the bungalow for the goods whose disappearance had given such a shock to Alice?

And what did Alice feel about Major Grey? Earlier in bed she had mentioned to Ginnie that he could charm the pants off any woman. Her later confession, however, suggested no practical knowledge of this talent. Ginnie remembered them so well sit-

167

ting side by side, in the thyme-scented sunlight by the club-house, with larks singing. Her own fantasies about living with the Major in a house at Littlestone might have been a bit absurd, but he seemed to have taken pleasure in sitting there; and certainly without any suggestion that he was anxious to remove her pants. (What an odd metaphor, and not untypical of Alice's out-of-time idiom, with which she was now so familiar. That sort of approach, must, she supposed, be what it referred to.)

But Alice must know him well, and evidently have been all set to go off with him. For the money? Or rather as her proper partner in the theft of what amounted to money? What had first tempted Alice to steal the goods, whatever they were? Could it have been love of Major Grey? Somehow Ginnie didn't think so. It was Mark Brassey, she was sure, whom her friend had the real soft spot for. And that could still work, if Alice could get out of whatever trouble she was in here. Mark would be waiting, as it were, to help her on the other side.

As her hands mechanically got the instant coffee ready, and looked for the biscuits and the sugar bowl, the thoughts jostled feverishly in her head. Or rather, Ginnie recognised with the kind of clarity the emotions of the crisis called forth, they seemed to crawl, very laboriously and in a puzzled fashion, a long way behind whatever it was that was happening.

She would find out soon enough, she supposed. In the meantime she carried in the mugs of coffee and got a jug of milk to offer: at least they had that in abundance. Ages seemed to have passed since she had bought it yesterday in Hythe.

Tom was still deep in discussion with the Hon. Gerry, as Ginnie too now thought of him. The back of Tom's head, constantly and vigorously nodding, was an index, as Ginnie could see, of whatever stresses he must himself be undergoing. Like the two women he was on his own. Social life suddenly seemed very isolating. Ginnie handed the mugs and the biscuits, and all three of the newcomers thanked her, as if they were under a special obligation to do so: after causing trouble by arriving like this.

'And – oh yes – Miss Thornton, isn't it?' said Armistead, coming up to her. 'So we wanted to thank you – and, yes, well, for looking after Miss Pinky and everything. We understand you

and your young friend have been so helpful and sympathetic ...'
He looked at her in a regretful and responsible way, and looked
away again. Is he going to offer me a cheque, wondered Ginnie.
What precisely were the ethics of drug-smugglers towards their
unwitting carriers? A certain delicacy? Or did they regard a free
ride as a bonus for them – something allowed for in the account-
ing?

The Hon. Gerry was appealing to Armistead now about some
technicality of golfclub membership he had been explaining to
Tom. As he listened, Armistead had the look of patience which
goes with frequent glances at the time. But Ginnie did feel, even
if with a certain desperation, that if they could keep things on
this level they must all three be all right. Alice herself seemed to
endorse this hope, strolling about and chatting in turn to the
other three; not meeting Ginnie's eye but thanking her too, as she
drained her mug and devoured a biscuit with gusto.

As he finished his coffee Armistead put the cup down (he and
the Hon. Gerry had received at Ginnie's hands the honour of a
cup and saucer) and said they must really be off. Alice offered
them the hospitality of the loo. They declined but then the Hon.
Gerry changed his mind. While he was in there Alice gave them
her last instructions. 'Keep the home fires burning, Gin, while
I'm off, and keep young Tom in order, and have a nice day. So
glad he's come back to golf. He'll be improving like hell in a day
or two, you'll see. So you two go on and have a lovely holiday.'

She had no case in her hand, not even a plastic bag; and
instead of showing the three others out she was first through the
door.

Then it began to happen.

But Ginnie could never afterwards recall quite how it had
started. Tom, whose face during the last few minutes had gone
from white to dark red, shouted, *'Pinky, don't go!'*

He rushed at the door, violently pushing the back of the Hon.
Gerry, who happened to be going out second, and was in the
narrow doorway. This latter merely accelerated his progress,
leaving Tom disengaged. At the same time Pat O'Connor, the
last to leave, gave Tom a light, almost deferential tap on the
shoulder, and said, 'Now calm down, young fellow.'

Tom's cry had certainly sounded histrionic. But as if beside himself with fury, and hostility at the Irishman's gesture, he now turned and rushed at Pat with flailing fists. Pat stepped smartly back with a whistle of calculation, and then kicked Tom hard just below the right knee.

Tom screeched and fell over sideways, clutching his leg. Ginnie, shouting something in her turn, rushed at Pat, who, smiling apologetically, hit her in the face.

Incredulous, even in that second, at what seemed to be happening to her, Ginnie found herself flying backwards until she collided with the table and overbalanced on the floor knocking all the breath out of her.

Casting a considering look not at her but at the groaning and recumbent Tom, the Irishman slowly drew a screw of paper out of his breast pocket. He unfolded it and sniffed deeply. He appeared to consider a moment, with plenty of time in hand. There was the sound of the car outside, driving away. Then he seized Tom by the ankles and pulled him over to the wall. Tom screamed again.

Ginnie had managed to get up and reach the phone. She had got it off the hook when the Irishman, not touching her, flicked open a knife and sliced the cord. Ginnie, staggering, put her hand to her face, which felt enormous. Her ears and whole head were roaring, and her eyes hardly able to focus. The Irishman now looked at her for a moment, and took another pinch from the envelope, as if it were snuff. Then he caught her by the middle and rushed her through the passage into the bedroom, where the momentum he had given toppled her face down on the bed.

'I'll be going to make love to you now,' he suggested, as if it were a question of good manners. His voice was soft and amicable. Ginnie scrambled up as he came across to the bed, and tried to reach the door, with some idea of getting to Tom; but he pulled her back so that she lost her balance again. He moved as easily as a big fish, whose actions seemed to cause a disproportionate shock when in contact with its prey.

Ginnie screamed for help once and was about to utter another scream when she received a blow on the mouth that finished her, as the kick had Tom.

Pat pushed her flat on her front again, and then reversing her,

170

pulled up her skirt and the mac she had been wearing as a housecoat. He seized her briefs at the front, and gave them a sharp tug, as if to remove them in the horizontal rather than the vertical plane: but since the material stoutly resisted this unnatural mode of divestment, he tugged again and again, swearing now as softly as he had spoken before.

Terrified of receiving another blow, Ginnie would have pulled them down if he had let her, and she tried; but misinterpreting her efforts he hit her again, though not so hard, before recommencing his ineffectual siege. It was in sharp contrast to the effortless economy which had silenced her and dealt with Tom. Now he seemed to have lost his touch. He persevered none the less, and at last the elastic and cotton tore away. In a daze of pain from her head Ginnie opened her legs, with some idea of giving both of them the least trouble.

But with no further obstacle before him her attacker seemed to lose conviction. As if giddy he closed his eyes, and passed his hand over his forehead a number of times.

'Sure and it's the snow,' he murmured, as if in apology. 'I'll be up and right in a min-oot.'

He spoke a little like a medical man who has regretfully to postpone a promising course of treatment.

Zipping up his trousers, he walked out of the door; and Ginnie, lying paralysed on her back, found herself watching him go. She noticed that his last action, that of fastening his trousers, seemed to have regained the cat-like decisiveness of his previous doings; and she remembered the grateful moment in childhood when the white-gowned dentist folded his drill and swung it out of the way. No more of that this time. Even at this moment it astonished her that the memory should return: the terrified emptiness of her mind registered a flicker of gratitude for it.

She heard the Irishman moving about and presently he seemed to be outside, fiddling with Tom's car. Her instinct was to lie still and sham death, or at least unconsciousness. With Pat about there was nowhere to try to run to. Tom's instinct seemed to be to continue groaning, as if the noise, like a burglar alarm, would guarantee him against further violence.

Ginnie heard the car door slam, and the engine started. There was the sound of it reversing on to the concrete road. Their attacker seemed to be leaving.

The engine revved and faded, and there was silence except for the lunatic groaning of poor Tom, in his agony next door. Ginnie was drenched in sweat and her head rang and throbbed like bells. She continued to lie as she was, stretched out as an offering for the Irishman's return. Disinclination to move seemed a way of dealing with her situation, as Tom's groans were desperately seeking to deal with his. Her thoughts now ran about everywhere like ants, in a rational but distracted way. She heard the Irishman's voice muttering 'Sure, and it's the snow,' and something about a 'min-oot' – that must be a minute of course. Luckily he seemed to have been wrong about that.

Ginnie's middle parts felt cold and exposed, but she still did not move. Must be the shock. Post-operational. But there had been no operation? Cold; and the snow. She knew from books that used to be a term for cocaine, but was it still, in the modern world? Didn't they call it crack, or something?

Funny that all slang sounded out of date when spoken. Why was that? She had wondered before. She must get up. Was she lying wounded in the snow, like the retreat from Moscow? She felt wounded even if she wasn't. She remembered from *War and Peace* how the groans of the wounded on the battlefield seemed to those who are still hale and hearty to have a feigned sound about them. Here she was lying with Tom, like the wounded on a battlefield, and the world of fitness paid no attention.

She staggered up after a time, holding her head, and went through to Tom. Lying in the corner where the Irishman had dropped him he looked at her as if for help. His leg must be broken she thought; the pain must be terrible. She instinctively turned away to pull down her skirt, though Tom gave no sign of noticing the state she was in. She sat down and putting her hands to her head made a pathetic noise herself, almost in time with Tom's groans.

She must get an ambulance, the police. The police? – No! She realised she daren't do that. And Pat had cut the phone. And where was Alice?

Ginnie tried to utter some comforting words to Tom, and found she could scarcely speak for her swollen mouth though no teeth seemed loose, thank goodness. She must get help somehow. She got herself out of the house and on to the road, tottering like an old lady. One or two of the bungalows might be occupied, but she couldn't bear to try them. No neighbours, full of sympathy and curiosity. Her one idea was to get to the hotel, where she could find a telephone, tell an indifferent receptionist she had had an accident, get a taxi to take Tom to hospital. And she must ring Mark Brassey.

It was only half a mile to the seafront hotel, but she had to stop several times. Her head rang, and she could feel one eye all puffed up. She became increasingly conscious she had no knickers under her torn skirt. She buttoned up the raincoat around her as closely as she could.

Part Four

Home from Home

MARK BRASSEY leaned back and considered lighting a cigar. He was dining with Ginnie Thornton in a small restaurant near St Martin's Lane to which he had always been partial. Ginnie sat placidly opposite him in the little alcove, and herself considered lighting a cigarette. She had recently got into the habit, which was not really surprising. It gave her some pleasure now to defy the smoking ban in the office.

It already seemed a long time since that morning, when she had at last reached the hotel on the Littlestone seafront. Eventually the ambulance had come for Tom; and no one at the hospital had seemed in the least interested in how the accident had happened, or who they were, or anything about them. But they were friendly and efficient. They kept Tom in for the night to do an X-ray and let Ginnie go back in a taxi to the bungalow. She would have greatly preferred, that afternoon, to have caught a train from Ashford station instead, and been back in London in her own flat. But she felt she must return to Silver Spray. It was true that she felt she must pick up Tom's things, and her own, and see what she could do to close the place up properly. And it would be better for herself to go back, like getting in a car and driving again immediately after an accident. Besides, she had grown so fond of the place.

And there was always a chance that Alice would return. She hadn't, of course. Indeed Ginnie somehow knew she wouldn't. But as she sat nervously in the bungalow that night, drinking tea and bathing her eye and cheek in hot water, as the hospital had advised, there was the faint, faint hope that Alice might come breezing back in the old way. It was about as likely, as Ginnie was all too consciously aware, that the gang, or the boys, would decide to pay a nocturnal visit, to go over the place more thoroughly. In spite of what had been done to her and Tom, Ginnie didn't really believe they would, any more than she believed that Alice would return. She hardly even resented Pat O'Connor, as she would not have hated a wild animal for knocking her down and hurting her. It had been, she now saw, more like an accident caused by Tom's intervention than a policy with malice aforethought. Mr Armistead had not been a man of violence.

For the same reason she hoped that Alice must be safe and sound somewhere. All the same Ginnie cried into the hot water as she bathed her swollen eye, mouth and cheek. Alice would not exactly have cherished or ministered to her – Ginnie had no illusions about that – but her being there would have been comforting, and her warm presence in bed. Ginnie had been cold that night, and still could not find a hot-water-bottle. She even cautiously filled one of the empty wine bottles with hot water from the electric kettle, but the cork began to leak and she had to push it out of the bed. A nightmare had started while she was still cold and awake, in which she walked down to the sea's edge, as they had done the night before, and found Alice lying there, with the foam crawling over her, and sand in her mouth.

The image was so terrible that she had seriously thought of getting up and going down to the beach. But she was too frightened now to go out again. Instead she sat shivering in bed with everything on, even her macintosh. She was not only cold but afraid to undress. Indeed she would never have slept at all if she had not remembered the bottle of whisky Alice had brought down with her from London. She hated the taste of whisky, but she now jumped out of bed and got herself some as soon as she thought of it, although even a full glass in her hand did not allay the terrors. The lighthouse beam, the marram grass tickling the thin walls, and the far off seaside noises she had once – long ago as it seemed – loved at Silver Spray, now seized her with tremors and uncontrollable shudderings. But muzzy with whisky she had become unconscious at last.

As well as a fine day, morning had brought the relief of a hangover. By the bright sea light she had found her disintegrated knickers, lurking nearly under the bed. As she picked them up it seemed incredible that those things had really happened to her; that a clean pale hand covered in black hair had seized them by the front, and wrenched them until they had come apart. What would have happened if the Irishman had kept his nerve, and had not been affected by his pinch of 'snow'? Presumably, in that case, she would not have been in the state she still was. She owed her continuing virginity to the cocaine, or the crack, or smack, or whatever they called it. And how painful would it have been? Very specially agonising, or not much worse than other things that had hurt one?

She remembered her odd practical instinct to accommodate herself to what he was going to do – she had been in terror too of another blow on the face. She wondered if the sight of her down there had put him off. Could men be so easily discouraged? Or had she herself been more specifically rejected? Ginnie could not help grinning at that, even as she sat weakly on the side of the bed with the ruined pants in her hand, and a truly appalling headache: the result of whisky as well as of the damage to her face. She must first of all find some aspirin; but she doubted there would be any in the bungalow, any more than a hot-water-bottle.

Somehow she knew quite clearly that these things would be getting worse, not better, as the weeks went by; that they would be turning more and more into obsessive dread and recollection. Well, there was nothing she could do about that: she must just prepare herself. For the moment she was pleased to feel still calm and sensible about it; although as she moved about the bedroom she soon started shuddering again, and began to cry. But the headache was a great help, and there was a lot to do. She had to pick up Tom, and get him back to London if the hospital would allow it. And then she must get in touch with Mark Brassey.

The sun was shining as she left the bungalow, and the larks were singing high above the sandhills. She heard; but was too preoccupied to take the pleasure in them that had been a part of wandering about at Littlestone, while Tom was playing his golf, and she had met Major Grey. After locking the back door she had wondered whether to put the key in her handbag. Was it possible that Alice might still come back, or even Major Grey, although that seemed most unlikely? There was nothing for him to come back for, and he might be – probably was – far away. At any rate she had hidden the key under the stone, in its usual place. Then she had walked to the hotel and ordered a taxi.

Mark Brassey seemed not entirely surprised by what had happened. He sounded calm and reassuring. He had told her not to worry about Alice; to carry on as normal. She had indeed resumed her life, thankfully finding that her office and her friends and her mother were quite incurious about whatever she had been up to. Just staying away a few days, she said.

She had visited Tom several times at his digs, while his leg got better. It turned out not to have been broken, but the bone and the sinew were very badly bruised. Tom's response to their experience struck her as odd in some ways; and she wondered if her own behaviour seemed the same to him. Really, no doubt, he was just embarrassed. He even seemed to imply, although with great forbearance, that if it was not exactly all her fault, still she had been in some measure to blame. That may have been because she said nothing about what had taken place in the bedroom; and it seemed clear that Tom preferred to think he had been wounded in the course of protecting her, and attempting to frighten away the intruders. It struck her as curious, and indeed interesting, that males could invent and believe their own version of such events. Females who had been raped, or nearly raped, had no such resource to fall back on: it was not open to them to pretend to themselves that they had been attempting to seduce the attacker. Possibly it might be comforting to try?

She let Tom know that the little car he had hired had been reported stolen, and the hire firm informed that he was ill, following a minor accident – nothing to do with the theft. Mark Brassey had sorted all that out. Tom did not mention Alice, his Pinky; and Ginnie found that surprising, but she did not bring up the subject. In spite of her fairly frequent visits, which Tom at first seemed to find soothing, their instinct for mutual silence about what had taken place, whatever their separate motives, made them feel increasingly strangers to each other. Ginnie supposed that given time they might have started to reminisce together; but, as things were, Tom seemed sick of the whole business; and she could see why, though she herself could not feel quite the same as he did.

178

Indeed, not at all the same. For one thing, there was Alice. She did not exactly long for Alice, but she thought a lot about her. She had become a large object in Ginnie's life, a white elephant that had once been the White Woman, that romantic vision seen from afar. Ginnie supposed she was lucky in a way. Other romances might have landed her with an unsuitable husband, an unwanted child. Alice had just become something which her consciousness had daily to work its way around, to push patiently and gently aside as she shopped or visited Tom, or read her scripts and went to the office.

As soon as his leg was better Tom went to stay with his mother in Tutbury, and Ginnie felt guiltily relieved that she no longer had to make the trip to the end of Fulham to see him. She wondered what he would tell his mother about his accident. Fortunately for him he had no problem; anyone might have suffered a severe contusion on the knee, and she knew his mother would make much of him, and be delighted to wait on her son as a no longer very demanding invalid. Lacking any physical evidence of injury, except for her bruised face of course, Ginnie simply had to keep quiet about her own experiences. Her mother would have been thrilled, no doubt; but in the circumstances she was not prepared to donate a parental thrill and put up with all the ensuing fuss and curiosity.

She was amused, and rather touched, to see that Tom before he left was feeling secretly guilty about not asking her down to Tutbury, perhaps for one weekend. Apart from the uneasiness she now caused him, he would not wish his mother to draw any conclusions about such a visit by a woman considerably older than her son. And so Tom seemed to be going out of her life, if not quite so abruptly as he had entered it.

And then, nearly a month after it was all over, Alice had rung up. Mark must have given her Ginnie's number or else she had found it in the phone book. She sounded on top of the world, and was so, as she had once proclaimed. Always disliking the phone, as well as inhibited by it, Ginnie did nothing to stem the torrent of her friend's exuberance. How was her Gin? And they must really get together some time. She herself was off to Australia for a bit – going home really – but they'd keep in touch, and Ginnie had been so marvellous, and she'd never cease to be grateful.

'I must see you, Alice,' Ginnie managed at length to say. 'Where are you? Can you come here?'

'Well, not right now, Gin my sweet – I'm all tied up at the moment. I'll be in touch now. I do promise.'

'Yes, but Alice, what's been happening?'

'Nothing's been happening, Gin, nothing at all. All's going like a dream. No probs. None.'

'But Alice, there are lots of problems. What about those men who came? What about you? Are you really all right? Are you still in touch with them?'

In touch with them. Ginnie found herself putting it as delicately as she could, almost as if already acknowledging that Alice was disappearing from her into the world she had inhabited before, the world which would never come any closer.

There were too many questions she might ask. Had Alice known of Pat O'Connor's activities after she had driven off with the other two? Or did she know, and wasn't going to speak of it? All such queries seemed to have become meaningless: Alice was vanishing away.

'Look, Gin dear, Markie knows all about it. You just ask Markie. He'll put you in the show. He's been wonderful you know.'

No doubt he had. Ginnie had already asked herself if Mark had known what had happened to her and Tom. She herself had said nothing when ringing up, beyond reporting that Alice had gone off with the men, and that he must help if he could; help to find her and take care of her. Mark, imperturbable, had said he would do all that, and that she was not to worry. Ginnie's reticence about herself and Tom, and what had happened to them, was not so much a kind of modesty – though that came into it – as a real and overwhelming anxiety about Alice. She had of course suggested coming to see Mark, but he had demurred, saying that he was fearfully busy; that he had things in hand; that he knew Alice would be all right. Ginnie suspected he did not want to see her at that moment, and be burdened with the possible consequences of her own story.

And here indeed was Alice, on top of the world.

On the phone, Ginnie could think of nothing to say. Or rather, out of all the possible and palpitating things she might have asked, she found herself choosing to enquire how they had got up to London.

'Oh, I drove,' said Alice blithely. 'Gerry's always drunk and has lost his licence, and Armitage doesn't drive.'

So that was how it had been. And still Ginnie couldn't bring herself to say over the phone what had happened.

'Oh, and Gin?'

'Yes, Alice?'

'There's one other thing. I'd like you to have Silver Spray.'

Ginnie could scarcely believe her ears. Here *was* gratitude, and in its most tangible form. But also in an absurd, an impossible form. How could she?

'But Alice dear, how could I?'

'Now Ginnie, I mean it really. Don't go all like that. Just take the place – I know you sort of love it. It'll be your safe house now.'

'But the money, Alice? You know what prices are now. Even ...'

'Even for a shack like that,' said Alice with her old raucous laugh. 'D'yer know, Gin, I hardly paid a cent for it; and I don't need the money. Can't explain why at this moment of time. Just you have it. There's a dear. Markie's got all the details and he'll fix it all for you.'

'What about you and Mark? No chance? I mean, is it still on?'

'Oh no, that's all off, sweetie. He thought better of it at last. Can't say I blame him.'

'Won't you come and see me before you go?'

There was just a faint hint of impatience in Alice's voice now, in response to the urgency in Ginnie's, as she lamented, 'No time, Gin my darling – simply rushed off me feet. Now ta ta, and I'll be in touch, I promise.'

And that was all of Alice.

Ginnie put down the receiver. She felt so confused, as well as deeply touched, that she hardly knew if she was desolated as well. It also left her – perhaps deliberately on Alice's part – with a feeling of helplessness, as if a dog or baby – something smaller but more awkward than the white elephant – had been suddenly thrust into her arms at the last moment of a goodbye. Was it some form of compensation? Even a bribe? How much did Alice

181

know, or guess? How had she managed to explain matters to the gang? Had she laid the blame for the theft of the cargo, which Ginnie and Tom had carried, entirely to the account of Major Grey, who had apparently made off with it?

Ginnie had no way to deal with all of this. She must get in touch with Mark. It was enough for the present to know that Alice was alive and well, and in tearing spirits. But going away. Ginnie did feel that. But like the bungalow that had suddenly been thrust into her arms, just like a baby pet, she had felt she would have to deal with the matter later.

The thing she clung to was that Alice had needed her when she had been lurking down at Silver Spray. She had wanted her to come, quite urgently; lifted up those splendid arms in supplication. Or so Ginnie now liked to feel. It made it easier to think about Alice. And she went on thinking about Alice.

But so, at first, did Tom. Ginnie had been wrong about that. He had not said anything to her of course, but he naturally had not been able to get his Pinky out of his mind. He had endured Ginnie's visits to his digs as best he could, perfectly conscious of the fact that they soothed her, because she had supposed them welcome to him. He had not disabused her. She had offered to help him to the station, to get the train for Burton-on-Trent, from which he could get a bus or taxi to his mother's place. He had managed to avoid that. Instead he had got his friend Des to give a hand.

Des, who was the man with the passion for Musil the novelist, had nothing much to do. Like many graduates he was just waiting for something to turn up. After completing his M.Phil course, in which he had discovered the writer whose name Tom always just failed to remember, he had supposed further suggestions for passing his time would be put in his way by the university, or the state. But both seemed to have lost interest in him. Left on his own, he had seen a good deal of Tom, who was just starting on his doctorate, and he had taken to visiting him when his leg was bad.

Des had met Pinky and known about Venice, and had been slightly jealous of Tom on both counts. Tom had wondered whether to confide in him but had decided against it. Des had become inquisitive; and though Tom was fond of him he had

182

been rather glad to see the last of him at the station, standing on the platform in his ragged jeans, looking like a carbon copy of Tom himself.

Tom was trying to forget what had happened; and that was the chief reason for his caution with Des. The Musil expert would have been all too interested in the things that had happened to Tom, and in what his reactions had been. At ease at home with his mother, in that boring but reassuring limbo with which the young who return home are familiar, Tom found his attempts not to think about it becoming more and more successful. He knew he had played a most inglorious part in the whole business. He had heard Ginnie scream, and he knew that something very nasty must have gone on in the bedroom. He had screeched himself, from the appalling pain of that kick, which still made him sweat to think about it. He saw, too, that if he had not provoked the Irishman in that stupid way, probably no harm would have been done.

Then why had he shouted out, and gone for Pat O'Connor? It was inexplicable to him now, and seemed quite outside his nature. Was it just that he could not bear to see Pinky going away like that? But he was already indifferent to Pinky: he had been going to try to seduce Ginnie instead. Nor had he thought of leaping to Pinky's defence; it had not really occurred to him at that moment that she might be in any danger.

He had already begun to think of them both as witches, who were controlling things to suit themselves, and leaving him in the cold. Naked Doctor indeed! – naked witch-doctor more like – and yet never naked for him. Tom's reflections at this point became positively venomous: and even the recurrent sight of Ginnie's poor face – his own fault of course – left him unashamed. He felt quite proud of his lack of feeling. From now on he would be tougher and stronger, particularly in regard to the female sex. He obviously had it in him to be so.

But even then, in the train, he had remembered Ginnie's swollen face. He had in fact asked her tenderly, not just out of curiosity, what she had said to her friends and colleagues (she had never mentioned her mother). Ginnie had laughed, and told him she had run into an area railing on a foggy evening; and no one she knew had been in the least interested.

183

He saw her face, in the train, and felt a sudden pang. He also thought it would be nice, as things were, to have some of that Naked Doctor stuff. In default of it he had fumbled in his pocket and found a small cigar which Des, who smoked the brand whenever he could afford them, had given him on the platform.

*

The cigar that Mark Brassey was about to smoke was a much grander affair. He gazed at Ginnie across the table with something like affection. By the time he had asked her out to dinner – about a fortnight after Alice had rung up – her face was nearly back to normal. Just a very slight lopsidedness perhaps, an asymmetry which Ginnie, looking in the mirror, had decided was not entirely unattractive. And now here she was, after a good meal of the kind that she and Mark both seemed to go for (though no fried brains, alas) thinking about a cigarette in the manner to which she was now becoming increasingly accustomed. 'Nearly got raped? Calm your nerves with a cigarette.' Perhaps forward-looking tobacco companies, in this day and age, might like to try that as an advertisement.

Better for you, in any case, than Naked Doctor. In his relaxing way, which had not disturbed the leisurely progress of their eating pleasures, Mark had discoursed on the drug-running fraternity, and on the use of drugs, about which he seemed recently to have learnt a good deal. In spite of her recent experiences Ginnie heard him without a shudder. Perhaps she too was tougher than she had been; though, unlike Tom, she did not reflect consciously on the matter. Emboldened by food and wine, she asked all the questions she could think of, although it soon became clear that Mark himself did not necessarily know all the answers: or perhaps that he wasn't prepared to give them. He seemed to Ginnie to have got over Alice entirely; and yet to have acquired a new and somehow juicier lease of life, both from her and from the activities of the people she had presumably 'worked' with. Ginnie wondered how much Alice had originally told him in Sorrento. And 'had' worked with? It was unclear to her whether Alice was still in business. Or might she in fact be launching out into new fields?

184

In the way Mark was talking of her something hinted at that: something hinted, too, that he himself was not entirely out of contact, in a business sense, with what was going on. But he reassured her. She and Tom would not hear anything from the authorities, nor from the gang. The Irishman, he thought, had probably been instructed to stay behind to keep an eye on them for a few minutes, to disconnect the phone, perhaps even take the car. 'Just so that from their point of view you wouldn't do something silly,' said Mark. 'Lose your heads. Unlucky that went wrong. And I'm really sorry.'

Ginnie, who might well, she felt, have lost something else, did not pursue the point. 'But Alice did steal the stuff, didn't she?' she demanded, to put their discussion on a different footing. 'The stuff that Tom and I brought home? Surely the gang, or whatever you call them, didn't like that? That was why she was so frightened, wasn't it? And was going to run off with Major Grey, and sell the stuff and live happily ever after?'

Ginnie paused. But though it was only the second time it had taken place, the restaurant relation between them seemed so intimate and cosy that she found it easy to carry on. 'I think in her own way Alice *was* in love with you,' she said. 'If it hadn't been for Major Grey, and the million pounds, I think she really wanted to marry you, and – well – sort of settle down.'

She had a sudden vision of Alice in the emerald wedding dress which had never been bought, gliding demurely down the aisle on Mark's arm. She herself would follow, bearing a wreath. A bridesmaid? A matron of honour?

She gulped down a lump in her throat and smiled at him. 'I know she was really fond of you. But I suppose she couldn't get away, couldn't get out of it? And I suppose in another way of her own she didn't want to?'

Mark acknowledged her smile with a smile of his own, like a benevolent buddha. 'Well – thank you. I agree with you as it happens. I've regretted it myself. But on the point you raise: why, no; certainly the gang didn't like it. But the odd thing is, you see, that a group like that is just as helpless when dealing with a criminal in their ranks as society is today, though maybe for different reasons. In both cases it is usually easier "not to proceed with charges" – in other words do nothing about it.

About the only way the police can get the clever members of a drug ring – apart from people like yourself and Tom who were actually carrying the stuff, knowingly or inadvertently – is if they kill someone.'

Ginnie blanched a bit and looked anxious.

'Don't worry. They weren't going to kill Alice, or any rough stuff like that. She was too valuable to them for one thing. Still is, probably. In keeping a watch on Alice, by the way, they learned a more important fact: that this Major Grey was double-crossing them too, or was about to do so. I fancy someone – probably this Irishman O'Connor – must have followed him back to the bungalow – seen him take the stuff. That could have been a tricky situation.'

'Trials in the life of a drug smuggler,' said Ginnie smiling at him again. 'This Mr Armistead whom I met seemed a most reasonable man, but a bit harassed.'

'A very competent business director,' said Mark. 'Just like ICI. He would be deeply upset if he knew about Mr O'Connor's behaviour. But a business has to employ these types sometimes, who may be unstable and unpredictable.'

'He was certainly that,' said Ginnie. 'But Alice *was* frightened?'

'She certainly was. If you live in that sort of world you never quite know what to expect. I tried to persuade her at one time to be a witness, you know. Wouldn't do. She wouldn't bite at all. And I fancy she had the wind up a bit over this Major Grey caper. She'd planned to go abroad with him and the goods – OK – and he was going to pick her up down there on the Marsh. But it was all a pretty dicey business. Our Alice is more nervy than she looks. That was one reason she wanted you to come back and hold her hand.'

Ginnie felt the tears prickling her eyelids. But she had resolutely taken another mouthful of duck and orange and washed it down with the fine red burgundy Mark had ordered. It was no use feeling sentimental now about Alice. And she hated to think of herself and Tom trustfully journeying home with pounds of that horrible stuff in their belongings.

'Our friends aren't really big-time, you know,' Mark was saying, 'in spite of the money that's involved. Armistead may be good, but I suspect that like Alice herself the rest are a bit amateurish.'

'But Alice and her friends must have caused an awful lot of harm – must still be causing it,' she said, as toughly as she could. 'Can nothing be done about that?'

'Well, no, not really,' said Mark, putting down his fork and rubbing his nose judicially. 'As I say, they sometimes get caught in the act. Besides ...'

'They might have caught us,' Ginnie interrupted bitterly.

'They might,' said Mark, 'but ...' Again he paused, and smiled a little to himself.

Ginnie saw that he had something he was saving up, and that he was giving himself the pleasure of making her wait. Obligingly she prepared herself to be on tenterhooks.

'I agree: and apart from the drugs there was plenty of nasty stuff involved,' he went on, with a commiserating glance at Ginnie's face. Automatically she put up her napkin for a moment, to mask the side where it was still slightly tender. 'Still going on no doubt. I'm afraid you and Tom had a nasty time of it. And of course, as you say, the risk involved in not knowing what you were carrying. But there was a funny thing about that.'

He broke off again. While she waited patiently, Ginnie brooded over herself and the rape question. She noted that Mark's natural reaction, like Tom's, was not to ask questions about it. And she was grateful to both of them for that. The papers were always full of stories about girls who were obviously determined to let the world and their friends know the worst. It was true that she hadn't experienced the worst; but none the less she didn't want to talk about it. It was just one of the ways in which she, and an unknown number of other women, were different from the way women were supposed to be, and to behave, these days.

And of course by not wanting to hear all, and to 'comfort' her, Mark and Tom were behaving with what today was considered typically male chauvinist behaviour. She could only feel that she was grateful for it.

As it happened, Mark supplied the next moment another example of such behaviour. He refilled their glasses, giving himself slightly more than her. She felt that was only proper.

187

He smiled then, and said: 'Did you ever look at what you were carrying?'

'No, of course not. Those boxes with the wedding clothes, as she told me, were all taped up. I asked at the customs if I should open them, and they told me not to bother.'

Ginnie had indeed gone conscientiously through the Red Channel, although when they were saying goodbye Alice had told her there was nothing dutiable in made-up garments, some of them second-hand, and that she could go through the Green. When she had told the nice customs officer what was inside them he had laughed and said 'Your wedding?' She had told him it was a friend's; and the customs man had chuckled understandingly as he made a chalk mark. 'You next time perhaps,' he had said.

Mark listened to this with polite amusement, still full of what he had so obviously yet to tell her.

'Well, it must have looked like the real stuff,' he said at last. 'I wonder what they would have thought when they tested it? – you would have been in custody of course. A substance? yes, but what substance? Chalk, sugar maybe – I don't know. All I do know is that it wasn't the real thing.'

'Wasn't the real thing,' she exclaimed in real and gratifying astonishment.

'No. It was a bogus cargo. The point, as I indicated, is that the group had already rumbled Alice. They decided to test her. Quite simple. Her chief task, and value, was to find unwitting mules, like you and Tom. They let her go ahead, but gave her a dud lot, to see what she'd do when she arrived.'

'Does Alice know this?'

'She does now.'

So the ebullient creature of the telephone had long been told, by Mark or more probably by the gang, that she had stolen something quite useless.

'But Major Grey?'

'Grey wasn't in their plot. That was the point. I think they wanted to test him too. I think he's always been a bit gone on Alice – strange, isn't it, the way she affects people?' Ginnie bowed her head. 'But when it came to the point he couldn't resist the notion of clearing off himself with the loot. So he's somewhere – on the continent, I don't know – with a perfectly value-less cargo he may still think is worth a million pounds or so.'

Even Mark must have been gratified by the stupefaction he had brought about in his guest. Ginnie gaped at him.

'But how do you know all this?'

Mark assumed his most worldly look. 'Well, I've come to have my contacts – on both sides. I won't say more than that.'

'Did you know about all this that time when you came to see me?'

'No. I was just beginning to sniff things out. I wondered how much you knew. And whether there was anything I could get from you.'

That time, which now seemed a long time ago, it must have been clear to him that she had known nothing at all. And now she could think of nothing else to ask. She looked down at her plate.

'I was concerned when I heard they'd been down,' went on Mark. 'They've got some rum types. There's that apparently half-baked aristocrat called Parker, and your friend, O'Connor, the IRA man. He's in it to get money for his lot in Ireland, of course. They say Dublin's full of drugs. But where isn't? Ought to be legalised if you ask me. Might be some drawbacks, but it could be the finish for all this.'

Ginnie surreptitiously licked her fingers and wiped them on her napkin. They were a bit sticky from her Charlotte Russe.

'Yes. I felt very sorry about you, Ginnie. Very sorry indeed. And for young Tom too, of course. But it was worse for you.'

Mark looked at her really very nicely, and Ginnie was touched by her Christian name. The first time he has used it, she thought.

'I don't think Alice knew quite what had happened. But I heard. She had too much to think about for herself – too busy working her passage again with the boys. She told you they may be sending her to Australia?'

'Alice will be pleased to get back home for a bit,' Ginnie suggested.

'Get back?' Mark look puzzled. 'She's never been near the place.'

'What can you mean?'

189

'Her folks were refugees at the end of the war. From somewhere in eastern Europe. Settled in Bolton.'

But Ginnie was past being surprised. Alice was so far away now. Too far for anything else to matter.

'How do you know?' she asked none the less, in order to keep the ball rolling.

'Found out a bit about her. Had to.'

She would never be right about her Alice, as he evidently was. Again she felt the tears beginning to come; but she relaxed herself deliberately and took out her cigarettes. 'Is it all right to smoke?' she asked.

'Certainly,' said Mark. 'And I might have my cigar.'

*

Alice had been as good as her word. Mark had all the details on the bungalow, and its 'sale' to her was soon completed. So far from being frightened of the bungalow after what had happened there, Ginnie quite longed to get down there again, even though she was not sure she cared for the responsibilities of ownership. Mr O'Connor and his like were, as she well knew, all round her in London; and their unexpected arrival at Greatstone-on-Sea seemed to her to emphasise the distance and otherness of that still magical spot, rather than its all too normal vulnerability. Maybe that illusion went with another romance; that of her brief lover (as he still absurdly seemed) on the putting green by the links. How magic had been the moment when his ball had rolled steadily and quietly over the green velvet surface, and into the hole! No wonder she had a fantasy of living with that mysterious but accessible man. Living with him in one of the grander and bigger seaside houses: although she could only imagine the drawing-room, the bedroom, and bathroom: all drenched in sea light; all beautifully got up, and in immaculate order. But Ginnie had done nothing to make them so.

Really, she was too absurd! Did she seem more absurd to herself now than she did before all this happened?

Ginnie sometimes wondered about that, as she went to the office or sat in the flat tidying up a script, and it continued to amuse her. Major Grey existed as a person; there was no doubt of that. Possibly, and from what Tom had said, he had existed even more vividly for Tom in Venice than he had later for Ginnie herself. What was his role in the modern smuggling romance in which they all seem to have taken part?

Major Grey could hardly be real to her, either in her fancy or as he seemed to exist in fact. But was he any less real than the world the media were presenting all round her: full of crime and cant and guidelines and social justice, prisons and education, the death of the environment, the disappearance of the family? All the nuisances Major Grey had harped on in that joyful but also disillusioning moment when they had sat on the bench together.

What an awful fellow he must be. And where was he now? Still living mysteriously on the continent? Or in Tom's Venice? Still assuming he had the equivalent of a million pounds in his suitcase?

It was odd, Ginnie had sometimes ruefully to reflect, that the only real people she had met in all this had been Mark and Tom; and she felt not the faintest interest in either.

Well, no, that was not quite true. Tom was a nice boy, as Alice had once observed; and she wished him well. Mark had been very kind to her; and she looked forward to dinners with him, at properly spaced intervals. She was confident he would want them that way; and she looked forward to them all the more because she knew he would look forward to them himself, in his own highly personal style.

He would also have the pleasure, Ginnie thought with some amusement, of enquiring periodically, in his own polite un-stated fashion, if she were still a virgin. She fancied that if she were not, she would not tell him so.

So, yes, she did have an interest in Mark; like having a bit of capital in some stable concern. She saw now that he enjoyed fixing things – it was his metier – rather like the distinguished lord, also a solicitor, whose benign features sometimes appeared on television, when he had been arranging a libel case or a royal divorce.

Would Mark have married Alice? Again, it was an agreeable speculation. She rather thought not, in the end; though something very important had clearly happened to Mark right back in the old Sorrento time. He had fallen in love, in fact. And Alice

191

with him? Ginnie thought so too, although that was harder to determine. She was inclined to think that Alice had been genuinely enthralled by the idea of a wedding, and marriage to a man like Mark; but that was not quite the same as being in love. Or was it? Ginnie would not profess to know; and yet she felt that her own fancies on the subject had something in common with those of Alice. Had that brought them together?

Tom, no doubt, had adored his Pinky for the same sort of reasons. He had wanted to marry the wonderful girl, rather as Alice herself had dreamed of a wedding with Mark. As it happened, she had just had a letter from Tom, enclosing a picture of his new girlfriend. Rather indistinctly it showed a nice-looking child, her smiling face crinkled by the sun. Tom said they hoped to get engaged soon, and that his thesis was going quite well.

Ginnie thought of the night time, when she and Alice had walked barefoot over the sandy road from Silver Spray, and down to the ghostly sea. She remembered the trace of pale yellow over the dark hills to the east.

She felt she would never see Alice again; and yet she would not be at all surprised if Alice were to walk into the flat tomorrow. As Tom's friend had told him: it was a question now of this, now of that. Perhaps on the seafront, or on the links or the putting green, she would some time meet another Major Grey. They might have a drink together, in the clubhouse. Ginnie was vague about clubhouses, but supposed they might be the kind of places where a drink could be obtained in cosy surroundings. It would be agreeable to walk quietly home to Silver Spray afterwards, thinking about him.

The telephone rang. It was her mother. Could she possibly come to supper on Wednesday, when Mrs Thornton's lodger was bringing an old friend – well, not old actually, she had said – really quite young. Ginnie said she would.